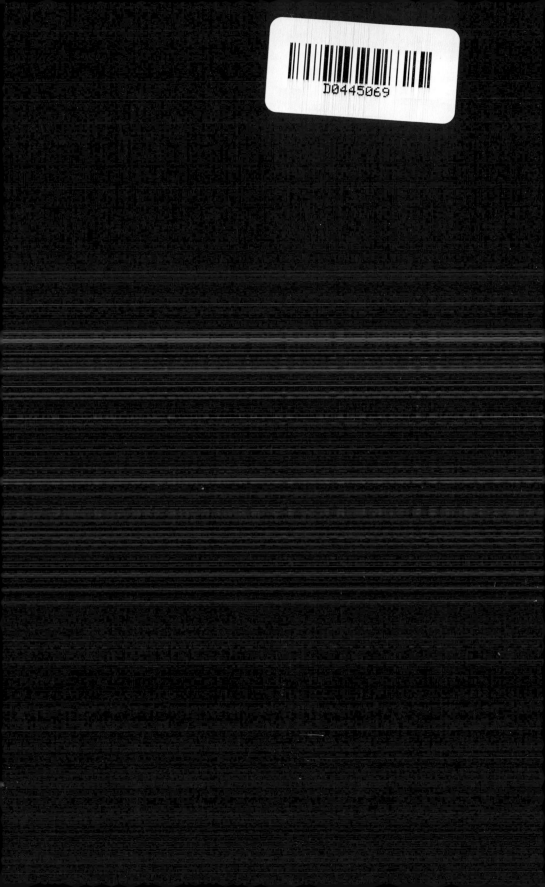
D0445069

PROJECT NAMAHANA

PROJECT NAMAHANA

JOHN TESCHNER

A TOM DOHERTY ASSOCIATES BOOK
NEW YORK

PROJECT NAMAHANA

Copyright © 2022 by John Teschner

A Forge Book
Published by Tom Doherty Associates
120 Broadway
New York, NY 10271

www.tor-forge.com

Forge® is a registered trademark of Macmillan Publishing Group, LLC.

The Library of Congress Cataloging-in-Publication Data is available upon request.

ISBN 978-1-250-82719-7 (hardcover)
ISBN 978-1-250-82720-3 (ebook)

Our books may be purchased in bulk for promotional, educational, or business use. Please contact your local bookseller or the Macmillan Corporate and Premium Sales Department at 1-800-221-7945, extension 5442, or by email at MacmillanSpecialMarkets@macmillan.com.

First Edition: 2022

Printed in the United States of America

0 9 8 7 6 5 4 3 2 1

To my grandparents:
Bette & Alan,
Jean & George,
Doug, who died younger than I am now,
and to all my ancestors.

Although many forms of reward are meted out for dutiful compliance, the most ingenious is this: the individual is moved up a niche in the hierarchy, thus both motivating the person and perpetuating the structure simultaneously.

—Stanley Milgram, *Obedience to Authority*

PROJECT
NAMAHANA

PROLOGUE

THE HAUL CANE road was a hundred years older than statehood. From the highway it was identical to the private roads that came before and after, its open gate lost in the guinea grass that overgrew the abandoned fields beyond. But it appeared on the old maps as an ancient trail, and it was still a public way, though neither the state nor county would claim it.

The road ran straight until it crossed Namahana Stream at a concrete spillway and began a twisting ascent into the hills, toward the center of the small island. When Jonah was a boy, his mother could drive it in her two-door Cortina. He remembered the hypnotic whip of green rows, black ash at burning season. He'd brought his own son many times to the sugar ditch high on the mountain. Now, the road was so washed out, he wasn't sure his four-wheel drive Tacoma would make it to the dam.

Makana was beside him in the passenger seat, the boy's two cousins sliding in the bed. They'd spent their lives in the backs of pickups, but that didn't mean they couldn't get flown onto a rock or under a wheel. At one deep hole, Jonah reached through his window and banged the door with a flat palm. The boys hopped out. The cab tilted forty-five degrees. Makana swayed into his father's shoulder and let his warm weight rest there until the truck came back to level.

At the dam, the water barely reached the sluice that diverted the stream into the irrigation ditch. "Plenty low the water," Jonah said to Makana. "Go see if can."

Makana scooted down the mossy concrete blocks, shoved his boogie board ahead and flopped on, raising his feet, crossing his ankles. He gave a few practiced strokes. "The water stay warm Dad."

"Then no scratch your feet."

The ditch ran beside the road a hundred feet before swinging into the tunnel. Jonah would never forget how it felt to turn the bend and float in darkness until a tiny oval of sunlight finally blinked into view, slowly revealing the low, jagged walls blasted through the dead volcano.

He stood on the edge of the ditch, watching the boys float one by one into the tunnel. The pale soles of his son's upturned feet faded quickly in the darkness. Dean and Kalani were right behind. Kalani did a slow 180 as he entered, flashing a grin and throwing a shaka with his thumb and pinky.

Jonah raised his hand and shouted, "I see you at the pool!"

Kalani nodded and floated backward into the tunnel mouth.

It was only eleven and already hot. The trade winds had died three weeks ago. Jonah had never seen the stream so low, or felt the water so high on the mountain be anything but biting cold.

He'd been on the West Side all week, helping his cousin finish a remodel, working through dinner the night before, then driving all the way home to Wainiha. He sank into the driver's seat and closed his eyes. There was a rope swing at the end of the tunnel; the boys were in no hurry. The whole point was to get away from the heat.

The first drops fell in his dream. He woke in the roaring half-light of a downpour, water rapping the windshield. It took a moment to make sense of his panic. The boys in the tunnel. He checked his phone. Almost noon. The adrenaline subsided. Plenty of time to reach the pool.

The rain fell straight past his open window. Then it ended. Pale, tattered clouds settled overhead. Dark mist tumbled from the upper valley. Thin white ribbons forked down Namahana's face.

Jonah left the car and started up the trail, climbing at a steep angle through a deep track. In the slick red mud, he grabbed handfuls of tall grass. His legs were stained to the knee. He left red prints on the stems as he passed.

The sun broke through as he topped the ridge. Hot vapor rose from wet leaves. The sky resumed its stern, tremendous blue. The path followed the ridge line a few feet then plunged into the next valley. In a forest of fire tree and strawberry guava, he passed a tumble of stones, an ahu marking an ancient boundary. For a moment, he saw the valley as it had been, unchoked by the invasive trees, the hillside staircased in curving terraces, green stalks of kalo mirrored in their sky-blue pools, pale smoke rising from a village, the sound of children's voices.

With each step, Jonah expected to see the boys emerge from the trees, wet shorts clinging to skinny thighs. Gradually, expectation was replaced by something else. It wasn't fear—the boys had been raised in the old style: there was nothing on the island they approached without humility—just an absence, or an ebbing. The world's comforting predictability steadily drained until he sensed every flicker and rustle of the forest with the hollow precision he felt in the final moments of a boar hunt or in the glassy hissing stillness of a wave about to close above him.

Then he reached the pool.

He saw the stream coming down the valley and pouring over a low fall. He saw the tunnel at the base of the ridge, a fan of standing ripples where it met the still water. He saw the knotted rope hanging from the old mango tree. He saw the dam, collecting spinning leaves and smooth black water through its iron grate. He saw the boys, floating by the concrete lip.

He waded in, the water cool after the rain. Silky ripples rocked the surface of the pool.

The boys bumped against the iron grate.

Dean and Kalani floated face down. Makana's eyes were open to the sky. The quiet pool had filled his mouth up to its level.

Jonah cupped each boy's head as he rolled them over. Then he wrapped his arms around his own son's narrow chest. He looked around the silent forest. He looked upstream and down below the dam. He looked up to the mountain. He looked for strength to bring his son to shore.

PART I

1

MICAH BERNT OBSERVED the beach park from the edge of the forest: a gravel road, a potholed parking lot, five ragged tents under sunworn tarps. From this height, the ocean looked completely still and very far away, a flat blue desert one shade darker than the cloudless sky.

He heard a truck and slipped the pack from his shoulders into the tall grass. The driver never glanced his way, but he felt the eyes of the teenager sprawled in a beach chair in the bed. Bernt's father was a Missouri Rhinelander, his mother Filipino. In California, people assumed he was Mexican. Here he could pass for local, as long as he didn't open his mouth.

Bernt nodded and the boy nodded back.

He waited for the teens to carry their spearfishing gear under the ironwood trees. Then he shouldered his pack and followed the edge of the field until he found a narrow path leading into the forest. The tracks of dirt-bike tires interlaced in the hard-packed dirt. When the trail crossed a stream, he turned and followed the thin flow of water between mud-caked boulders. In a few minutes, he reached a spot where it pooled deep enough to dip a bottle without stirring any silt.

He scrambled out of the stream, dropped his pack and sank into the ferns, drank a liter of water in two gulps. No birds called in the forest. The stream was silent.

From his rucksack, he pulled an eight-by-eight tarp, twelve carabiners, and three rolls of 550 cord. He staked out a simple A-frame,
hanging the tarp over a line between two trees. He took the second
length of 550, tied one end to a grommet in the tarp and stretched it
to a tree ten feet away. He wrapped the line from tree to tree until he
had a rough perimeter at shin level. He strung a second line a couple
feet outside the first, then clipped the two lines together with ten of
the carabiners at equal distances. He hung the last two carabiners
from the line in his tent.

Finally, he unstrapped his sleep system and laid his patrol bag
under the tarp. He forced his heavy bag into a stuff sack for a pillow
and laid it below the carabiners, where he would hear them jingle if
anyone tripped the cord.

It was easier to go through the routines than resist them.

He left camp before dawn each morning. There were always people
up early at the beach park: GT fishermen with their elaborate gear,
uncles stopping by to throw net for an hour before work, kids in the
tents getting ready for school. Bernt would walk up the road to wherever he'd left his car—a different place each night—then drive south
to Kealia and park at the restrooms.

On windless mornings, glassy sets rolled in at Kealia like ripples
on a pond. One or two at a time, surfers would tilt onto a peaking
wave, coast down the face with a few laconic strokes, stand high near
the collapsing water. Bernt came to recognize a few who caught more
than the others. One, a woman, was the best. Seeing her flash along
a fast right then carve her board three hundred degrees to extend the
ride a few more seconds before gracefully topping the wave and reappearing with her feet high in the air, her arched back accentuating
the slim cut of her bikini against her brown skin, was the high point
of Bernt's day.

He used shampoo and soap under the outdoor shower, wrapped
a towel around his waist to strip off his wet shorts and dress him-

self, propped a mirror on the hood to shave, ran a dollop of product through his hair. He had no illusions that the runners and dog-walkers on the trail, the surfers pausing to read the water before dashing down the beach, the handful of tourists up this early, didn't grasp his situation with one glance.

If it was depressing to know the best part of his day was already over, he tried to take comfort in knowing this, the worst part, was almost over, too.

On his eighth day in the woods, Bernt interviewed for a job selling mowers and marine engines. The manager who interviewed him was barely out of high school. His grandfather had founded the shop His great grandfather had been an indentured laborer. Lining the walls above the kid's desk were faded photos of families in crisp ki-monos posing stiffly in front of plantation houses. Bernt asked the kid to drop the hourly by a buck fifty and increase his commission five percent, and he agreed. He'd catch hell from his grandfather when the old man found out.

That evening, Bernt drank a six-pack of Heinekens on a picnic table at Kealia. The waves were breaking cleanly, but he never saw the woman.

It was nearly dark as he walked toward the beach park. The parking lot was empty except for three ice heads lingering around a rusting pickup. He'd seen them before and given them little thought, beyond the operational concerns of the attention they might draw. He had a professional opinion on how they handled businesses—selling so blatantly and so close to the families in the tents—but this wasn't his community. Anahola was a Home Lands area. He assumed their disrespect was noted. Someone would take care of it eventually.

He was moving through the shadowed tree line when a rusty van pulled into the lot, a wooden rack screwed straight into its roof, a pile of battered surfboards and random junk roped haphazardly on top, one rear window jammed askew. A bearded man unfolded from the driver's seat, his head darting until his gaze froze on the baggie that flashed in an ice head's palm. A woman watched keenly from the passenger seat, surveying them all with a vigilance bordering on hatred.

Haoles.

Just a short time on island and the word came automatically. Whether they lived out of a van or owned ocean-front property, they all reminded him of the outnumbered white kids at his high school: pitifully eager to fit in or resolutely oblivious to anyone outside their tiny circle.

He was about to turn his back and step into the forest when he saw the woman frown and twist in her seat, speak angrily to someone. A spark flared in his brain. In ordinary situations, threat assessment was automatic and unconscious. But an error—even as minor as the occupancy of a vehicle—set off alarms. He looked more closely. Then he stepped out of the tree line.

He reached the group as the bearded man was passing over the folded bills. Bernt caught his hand and threw the man's fist back at him, easily causing him to stagger back toward the van. "If I see you here again," Bernt whispered, "I'll keep the money. And I'll cut you."

Anger boiled somewhere behind the man's eyes. But only fear was strong enough to cut through his confusion. The woman was more collected.

"Fuck you!" she screamed. "You need to mind your own fucking business. Who the fuck you think you are? You better get your ass up, Omen, and—"

Bernt opened the door and shoved Omen into the driver's seat. The man gave his woman a terrified glance and tried to bolt back into Bernt's arms, but Bernt slammed the door on him.

"Get the fuck out of here!" he screamed, banging the van. It rolled forward, and for a moment Bernt locked eyes with the little boy standing between the two rear seats.

"I never knew they had one buk buk superhero. You get one magic bolo knife or what?"

Bernt turned. One of the ice heads was just a few feet away. His cheeks were hollow and his lips scabbed over, but he was still good-looking, vaguely European, with a deep tan and curly black hair. He wore work boots and jean shorts sagging from his skinny hips. His forearms were ropy with muscle. He had the hands of a carpenter. His hair was cropped close. A few Army tattoos, a few prison. Three inches on Bernt, at least.

"I not going give you no humbug for harassing my customers. I never like that haole bitch. But you need finish what they started." He flashed the baggie in his palm.

"No thanks," said Bernt.

The man turned to his friends. He was clearly the leader of their little gang. "*No thank you.* This Flip talk like one haole, an' fresh off the plane, too."

Bernt turned to walk away, but the man stepped with him.

"Where you from?"

"Kapaa," Bernt lied.

"You stay Kapaa but you sleep in the forest? You must get trouble with your wahine."

Bernt said nothing.

"Yeah we seen you." For an instant, Ice Man's eyes turned keen and piercing. "And we know you never like no pilikia. Just pay up. One hundred only."

He walked as he spoke, drifting right, making it harder with each step for Bernt to keep all three in front of him.

"Nah."

Ice Man grinned, his teeth black stubs. "So what then, you like spar?"

All three were moving now, fanning out. The other two didn't look like fighters, but they didn't need to be.

Ice Man raised his hands.

In one motion, Bernt slipped the pack from his shoulder and lifted the heavy steel ASP from its sleeve. He let his wrist drop with the weight, flicking just enough for the baton to telescope and lock with a satisfying *click*.

The stranger grinned. There were plenty of nights Bernt would have been happy to see him pull a blade. But he was glad when Ice Man gestured for his boys to stand down.

After he'd watched the headlights bump across the bushes and sweep down the road, Bernt returned to his camp. He could bug out with his essentials in under two minutes, but he took the time to remove all trace. Then he walked deeper into the forest, through clearings cluttered with burnt-out cars, until he reached the ocean. He chose a small cove to wait out the night and settled into the moonshadow cast by a tall boulder.

It was always lonely, to be awake and alert in the darkness. But he was never alone.

At Benning there'd been a Weapons Sergeant who'd spent years living out of a van, climbing mountains. One night, waiting for a jump, he told a story about a time he had to down-climb a two-hundred-foot face without a rope. When someone asked how he didn't panic, he said whenever he felt it coming on, he imagined the sound of a carabiner snapping shut.

Bernt didn't see him again after Jump School. He'd heard the guy drove his van into the mountains after his discharge and swallowed a bottle of pills. But the click of the ASP always reminded Bernt of his imaginary carabiner. *The sound of safety,* he had called it.

2

MOMILANI AND CLIFTON Moniz lived in a one story house with a metal roof and a long lanai overlooking the Anahola hills: blunt Hokualele and Kalalea tapering like a shark's fin. A neighbor kept goats in the field on the hillside. There was a small orchard in the backyard: avocado, Meyer lemon, tangerine, breadfruit. An old mango shaded the 'ohana house out back, a single spacious room they'd built for their daughter and granddaughter. It had a full bed in one corner and a wooden counter with a sink and propane stovetop. There was an outdoor shower and a toilet in a little stall against the wall, one side cut low to give an ocean view.

Bernt found the room through a note on the bulletin board outside the general store. The rent was reasonable. There were other applicants, but they offered him the lease on the spot. In hindsight, Bernt realized, this was a warning sign. His life ran relatively smoothly as long as he maintained clear boundaries. He preferred transactional relationships with officers, coworkers, bartenders, and landlords. But Clifton and Momilani were not that type of people.

For the first week or so, they gave him space. They'd told him he could help himself to anything from the trees, and they must have been watching closely enough to know he never had. On the tenth day, he found two ripe avocados on his doorstep when he got home from work.

The next Wednesday was Bernt's day off. He was scrolling through a course catalogue for the island's community college when he heard Clifton calling from outside.

"Ho Micah, you like smoke meat or what?"

"Yes sir."

"Today my birthday, and Momi like throw one small kine party. No need bring nothing, just come and eat with us."

Bernt had enrolled in college many times, but it still took him most of the day to track down all his transcripts and VA paperwork. It was late afternoon when he finally registered. He drove down to the general store and bought one six-pack for himself and another for Clifton. A few dozen people had gathered on his landlords' lanai. Men tossed horseshoes in the yard. Clifton sat on a white marine cooler, tending a wok on a tripod above a propane burner.

Bernt sat on his own small cooler at the edge of the lanai. He smiled broadly whenever anyone addressed him or made eye contact. He resisted the urge to pull his sunglasses down over his eyes, except when he walked to the fence to smoke an American Spirit. The goats trotted expectantly forward, but he had no scraps to throw them.

When Kalalea's long shadow reached the house, Bernt thanked Momilani and Clifton for including him. He drank the last two bottles in bed, watching videos on his phone.

The next evening, Clifton was sitting on the lanai when Bernt got home from work. He gestured at the cooler, and Bernt took a seat in one of the empty chairs against the wall. It was easy, sitting with Clifton in the dusk. On Friday, Bernt picked up a six-pack on his way home.

It became a routine. Often, they sat in silence. Momi would laugh when she came out to grab one of her Coors Lights. "Now I see why he rather drink with you than me."

Sometimes Clifton was a few beers in by the time Bernt joined him. Then he told stories about his days as a fishing boat captain, if he was in a good mood, or what had happened that day in the fields, if he wasn't. He worked for an international agrochemical company on a small test plot in the mountains outside Kilauea. He and Momilani had raised their kids on the west side of the island, where the company leased thousands of acres. The transfer to Namahana had given them the chance to move back to the family property.

One night, Clifton's eyes were red and his voice hoarse. His boss had ordered a spray upwind of the field where he was working. "That young Japanee had try blame *us*," Clifton rasped. "He thinks 'cause we been round long time, he can do things old school. He better watch out. Maybe we never file no grievance, but we know some pilau shit going on. We all seen it."

Bernt asked why he didn't just retire and go back to fishing.

Clifton laughed—the sound of ripping Velcro—and popped another beer. "'Cause you cannot beat the benefits, 'as why. One day I get Momi show you my 401K. *Mean,* da buggah."

3

B ENEVOMENT SEED HAD licensed distributors in seventy countries and corporate offices in Brussels, Basel, Lagos, Durban, Phnom Penh, Sydney, Beijing, Mexico City, São Paulo, and New York. But its headquarters were still in the hometown of the company's founder, formerly a railroad stop outside the cities, now an outer ring suburb where an ancient glacier had dug deep kettle lakes marking the end of the boreal forest and the beginning of the prairie.

Michael Lindstrom's second-floor office overlooked a swale of brilliant green turf ending at a row of ornamental pines. Beyond an overpass, two identical glass towers threw loops of setting sunlight from their upper stories. Lindstrom had been in this office six years, but the amber tint and cinematic dimensions of the windows still had the power to mesmerize. Pale brown clouds drifted across a golden sky. The cool whisper of climate control completed the sensation of standing outside the world.

His door was closed, and Miyake was on speakerphone. Since the investigation, Lindstrom had been taking his calls privately.

"Growth rates in field three continued at the same rate," Miyake was saying.

"How about the inputs?"

"Soil pH keeps dropping so we're replenishing lime faster than we want."

"All within budget?"

Silence.

"How far over then?"

"Five thousand, more or less."

"Unacceptable."

"I've shown you my books. I can't control the weather. I can't regrade those fields. I *can* shut down field one."

"Not yet. But I want you to supervise the next application."

"Roger that."

"How about the situation with the community?"

"Less people showing up, but they're getting more aggressive. I tell the boys just drive slow and don't respond. But it's getting to them. I just had one guy no-show, didn't even call in sick. We need those security cameras."

"I told you it's not in my budget. Are you planning any more orders this month? Your boys were burning through anhydrous this summer. It raised a red flag over at Compliance. I had to personally sign off on it."

"Thanks boss. We accidentally over ordered. There's plenty on-site now."

"We just need to get through the next few weeks. You're saying growth is still at plus three eight?"

"Three point eight four."

"Perfect. And sorry you're down a man. I hope he turns up. Don't forget we froze hiring through the end of the year."

At a whiteboard scrawled with abbreviations and percentages, codes for germplasms, cultivars, field numbers, Lindstrom changed a three to a four. He stared at the board. There were more than a thousand plants represented on it—six varieties of corn, five of soy, as well as beans, millet, wheat, arabica—the most valuable crops in the world. He knew their average growth rates to the millimeter. The yield weight to the gram. He could pull every peptide in their DNA.

These seeds had grossed nine billion last year. Nearing a trillion over the life of the patent on the pesticide they'd been bred to resist. A patent that was about to expire.

His phone chimed. "Mr. Lindstrom? The team is ready."

Brady, Erin, and Pierce were standing with their backs to the window. A team from Agricultural Productivity was shutting down the projector and unplugging laptops. January was two months away, but everyone was already gearing up for their End of Year presentations. The conference rooms were booked out for weeks. AP left without exchanging a word with Lindstrom's people.

"We may as well do a quick status before your pitches," said Lindstrom. "Erin."

Erin Shields had been with Benevoment when it was still Midwest Seed. Her experience had been invaluable to Lindstrom when he arrived at HQ fresh from the field with no experience in the moral mazes of corporate management.

"Crude is off seventeen cents a barrel," said Erin, "and the forecast is continued decline. We're predicting corn to come in at $3.65 for the year, unless there's a shock."

"Brady?"

"DeKalb is seeing negatives in every field where they planted Gen Two."

"How about in soy?"

"Nothing in Gen Two is standing out. If anything, there's a downtick in moisture tolerance."

"Pierce?"

"I believe you had a one-on-one with Miyake today, so you know more than me about Namahana. Looks like Blue Mountain strains are still the standouts. Growing successfully in all fields and all conditions. It's only the, uh, externalities we have issues with."

"Miyake briefed me on that."

"His boys are getting pretty rattled."

"Miyake briefed me. We've got a game plan."

"I hope you reminded him that Benevoment facilities are gun-free zones."

Pierce had arrived six months ago from tropical R&D. Before that, he'd been in one of the chemical plants. He'd raised red flags at every stop, and Barrett still refused to explain why he'd dropped the man in Lindstrom's lap.

Lindstrom looked patiently at Pierce. "There's a plan. If you have further concerns we'll address them in our next formal status."

He let his gaze fall on each person, one by one. "All right. We have eight weeks before End of Year. In our last meeting, I asked each of you to mock up a pitch for our presentation. I have my own ideas about strategy, but I want to hear yours first. Erin."

Erin stood. "To thrive in the twenty-first century, this company must leverage its advantages. That means protecting our global brands from baseless accusations and overregulation. For a quarter century, Benevoment has been synonymous with effective, affordable crop solutions *because of* Efloxiflam. It's true Gen Two hasn't seen the gains we'd hoped for, *yet*, but Michael Lindstrom is still the best this company has ever had, and that makes him the best in the world. At this stage, it would be irresponsible to undermine his work or the Efloxiflam brand."

Erin sat down without looking at anyone.

"Pierce."

Pierce checked the knot on his tie, then stood. "Benevoment remains the industry leader, but the competition has never been fiercer: not only hostile governments undermining patents, but individual actors with gene-sequencing and production capabilities that were science fiction just five years ago. To maintain dominance in an asymmetric market, we must innovate. Gen Two research has been stagnant. With Gen One's patent imminently expiring and generics on the verge of flooding the market, I recommend we immediately suspend all investment in the Efloxiflam family and shift resources to its most promising successor: Morzipronone. Its current team has failed to lower volatility or demonstrate upside to justify a widespread consumer switch. Clearly, fresh blood is needed. Our advice is to transfer lead on Morzipronone to Michael Lindstrom."

Pierce sat down. The AC hummed.

"Are you fucking—"

Lindstrom ticked the point of his pen against the table. Erin did not finish her sentence.

"Brady."

"We buy time," Brady said, without rising from his seat. "We extend the patent on Gen One a few more years and keep working Gen Two."

"How?" said Erin.

"Namahana," said Brady. "The small-use crop incentive. The patent office will extend us three years if we can get Gen One approved on coffee bushes."

"That's a tough case to make."

"Coffee has some of the highest margins in agriculture, and demand is only going up. Cultivation is already so restricted it's the only legal crop in the world that can still turn a profit in war zones. And climate models say we'll lose fifty percent of *that* land in a few decades. And it's *addictive*. You all know how much I'd love to get into poppies, but until the optics change, coffee is the next best thing. On Namahana, we have bushes that are drought-resistant, rain-resistant, temperature-resistant: climate-proof. And the dosage upside is huge. We can immerse a seedling in Flox Plus Firewall for three days."

"And the beans taste like lighter fluid," Erin interjected.

Brady laughed. "They said no one would buy the Cavendish. Now people think that's what a banana is."

"What about the investigation," said Pierce. "I thought we were going to lay low."

"The investigation is over. We've been cleared. Everything this company has ever done has been opposed by the grass-fuckers. Yes, a few protestors are still showing up, but that investigation is the last thing anyone above us is worrying about."

Someone from Fertilizers rapped on the door. They were five minutes over time.

In his office, Lindstrom allowed himself the indulgence of letting his mind wander freely over a problem. He knew Erin hadn't just been telling him what he wanted to hear, but that didn't mean she believed it, either. She'd simply made the strongest argument available to accomplish her goal. Which was, what?

Numbers were the reason everyone gave for every decision. But they weren't anyone's goal. Was it power? That felt like too crude a term. Freedom was better. Or force: the ability to shape a path through the company. But the farther you pushed, the more resistance you met. At some point, the only way forward was to shape the company's path to fit your own.

As the scientist who invented Efloxiflam, then the executive who managed it, Lindstrom had long been shielded from this reality. Only now, with the patent on Gen One expiring, was he finally feeling the full pressure. So far, Gen Two had showed nothing in corn, soy, wheat, sugar beets—the profit drivers. To complicate matters, Bloomberg had reported that a Chinese conglomerate was in negotiations to buy Benevoment. Their own specialties were in rice, potatoes, cotton—it was a natural fit. Nothing official, but C-level executives were already trimming their lines, hoping to keep them—and the force they carried—intact.

Erin understood these dynamics better than anyone. For years she'd been the only non-white—the only *person of color,* he corrected himself—in senior management. In most meetings—like the one they'd just had—she was still the only black person in the room. The fact that *he* was the clincher to an argument her career depended on was probably the biggest professional compliment Lindstrom had ever received. But that didn't mean it was the right one.

He'd dismissed Pierce's pitch offhand. Now he wondered whether he needed to turn the problem around. Instead of defending his position, he should be asking who else was vulnerable.

4

ONE TUESDAY EVENING, there were already four empty bottles at
Clifton's feet when Bernt arrived. He took two Kirins from his
six-pack, used one to open the other, and put the rest in the cooler
between the chairs.

"What you know about GMO?" Clifton asked.

"Not much," said Bernt.

"Genetically modified organisms."

Bernt nodded reflectively. He watched the wind toss the trees on
the ridge.

"You think one GMO went kill those kids?"

"What kids?"

"The three boys in the sugar ditch?"

"It's what they say."

"Who say?"

"I don't know. The hippies on the farm I used to work at."

"One *organic* farm?"

Bernt nodded.

"Jonah guys come by again today."

"Who's Jonah?"

"Da faddah. The one who found 'em in the water. Came today
with one bullhorn. Six guys with him and three wahine. One dressed
like da kine, da skeleton what comes for you."

"The grim reaper."

"Da grim reaper brah."

Bernt could only nod.

"It's our fields they say had poison the stream."

"What do you grow there?"

"Different kine stuff. Coffee, cane, corn, soybean."

"You spread a lot of chemicals?"

"Pesticide, herbicide, fertilizer. Same as any farm."

Bernt said nothing.

"We stay careful. We read the warning labels, follow the PPE and REI. I never get sick."

"What about the other week?"

"That? Was nothing. Just one small kine mistake."

"It looked like you'd been gassed pretty bad."

"You was in the service," said Clifton. "You know how it is. Sometimes your eyes water or your bell get rung a little. Nothing bad as first week full contact drills, Waimea High, banging helmets like tap, tap, tap. Just some headaches is all."

"Now they have concussion protocols."

Clifton laughed. "Why you think they give us da gold-plate health insurance?"

"You don't think that stuff could have poisoned the kids?"

"No can. Those boys had drown. Jonah, he never went in the tunnel with them. Da buggah stay sleeping in his truck. And he go blame us. Now we get dreadlock haoles banging our cars, calling us killers."

Clifton drained a bottle, opened another. "You ever been in one riot?"

"Yeah."

"Already, one guy had left. I worked with him twenty years. Never even gave notice. You watch, sooner or later, someone going catch cracks."

Bernt didn't answer. Clifton didn't say more.

The college offered three classes that met on Wednesdays—his day off—and filled his prereqs. He wasn't taking Contemporary Prose Forms, so he signed up for physiology and something called Cultural Economics. On the first day, he took an empty seat between a stoned haole boy and a woman in her twenties with a fresh pink burn over creamy brown skin. Her shiny black hair was chopped short at the neck. When she smiled at him, Bernt pictured what she saw: a thirty-year-old man with no paper, pen, books or a knapsack, just phone, wallet, and keys lined up neatly on his desk. Like every other guy in the room, he wore board shorts and slippers.

She rolled her eyes, dug in her bag for a ballpoint pen, then ripped three sheets from her notebook and slid them toward his desk. She had strong hands, he noticed.

The teacher introduced himself as Dr. Higa, then launched into a story about Captain Cook, who'd gotten along with the indigenous people on his first visit to the islands, but returned unexpectedly to harvest more food and timber from a bay that had been put under kapu by the gods and was stabbed in a melee after trying to kidnap their king in order to regain a stolen rowboat. "The historians call this murder," said Dr. Higa. "As economists, how do we explain these events?"

No one answered. Bernt watched the clock on his phone. He couldn't believe how long it took each second to change. Finally he broke the silence.

"Obviously Cook failed to gather proper intel on the disposition of the population in the operational environment. He went in with too light a footprint. This was a warrior people, but he thought he could march in with a few sailors and kidnap their commander."

"In Cook's defense, they did seem to believe he was the incarnation of the god Lono."

"But how did they feel about this god? Was he a shark or something? Maybe Cook assumed it was like his own god, someone benevolent. Maybe the people didn't want to see Lono land on the beach and exfiltrate their king."

Bernt's neighbor raised her hand. "The bay was under kapu,

right? Which was religious, but also ecological? They had to pre-
serve limited resources. But Cook thought it was just, like, primitive
superstition." The teacher nodded. "And what was he doing out there
anyway? I mean, he was from an island too, right? But they didn't
stay on their land. They were building an empire. He was looking
for a Northwest Passage to transport, like, beaver pelts or whatever."

"Excellent points," said Dr. Higa. "We have a conflict between
two economic models, one based on sustainability, the other on re-
source extraction. Now I want you to pair up and discuss how this
relates to the concept of gift economies that was in your assigned
reading."

In his peripheral vision, Bernt sensed the stoner swiveling his way.
He shifted in the other direction.

"I'm Nalani," said the woman.

"I'm Micah."

"What were you talking about earlier?"

"Just basic counterinsurgency theory."

She nodded. "Um, do you have any theories about gift economies?"

"How were we supposed to read something before the first day of
class?"

"Didn't you log into the portal?"

Bernt stared grimly at his phone, wallet, and keys. His paper had
one word written on it. *Cigarettes.*

"Okay," said Nalani. "So the gift economy used to be the only
kind there was. They were always throwing big luaus or giving each
other feather cloaks and stuff. And everyone was kinda keeping track
of who owed what to who, so it gave them all a way of relating to each
other. But finally someone invented the exchange economy. In, like,
Iraq or somewhere. And it was super convenient, because you could
just get something from someone and give them something else and
walk away. You didn't have to be friends."

"The Iraqis I knew weren't like that."

"It was thousands of years ago, when it was the fertile crescent."

"It just seems pretty cold."

"Well it's the reason we have all this stuff. Otherwise it's like you'd have to know a bunch of Chinese people just to get them to make you an iPhone."

"So now we have iPhones, but no one helps each other? Great trade."

"You sound like my uncle."

"I bet he was in the service."

Nalani laughed. "He's always talking about brothers in arms or whatever."

"It's not just in combat. It's the culture. If you get pulled over on base, the MP doesn't just give you a breathalyzer and lock you up. He might ask about your combat experience and what's going on with your family. He'll determine whether you're a danger to yourself. He'll try to understand your situation."

"It's the same way here. That's why we get so many drunks driving around. The cop finds out their aunties are cousin to each other and lets them go. All this 'ohana stuff is the reason we've got no economy. Outsiders won't invest because of nepotism and corruption."

"Yeah, well, people here seemed to be doing fine before Cook showed up."

"Maybe ali'i. But the Kanaka Maoli were practically slaves. Getting sacrificed all the time and giving everything to the kings."

"So you wish Cook had got away?"

"I have mixed feelings. Which makes sense I guess, since I'm mixed."

Bernt's concentration reached its limit; the rest of class passed in a blur. As he walked to the parking lot, Nalani caught up. "By the way, Lono wasn't a shark. He descended to Earth on a rainbow and dispensed fertility."

"How did he do that?"

"I don't know. Maybe like my uncle on the ranch: just grab the boto and jam 'em in."

"You saying your people needed help with that?"

"You know how it is with these local boys," Nalani said, glancing across the lot where the blond stoner and a skinny brown kid with a wispy beard were leaning deep into the engine of a battered pickup, "just 'cause they get the equipment no mean they read the manual."

5

I WAS A brilliant autumn afternoon, unseasonably warm. From the dining room's floor-to-ceiling windows, orange elms glowed before the cheerful, wind-chopped lake. Leaf-shadow flickered on a white tablecloth, where Barrett sat pecking at three phones fanned in front of him.

Lindstrom thought Barrett's choice of restaurants had less to do with the view than the two o'clock happy hour. It was a show of power. Not only could he be at a bistro in Excelsior on a near-daily basis, but he could squander the afternoon of anyone he decided to invite, up to and including the CEO, who was rumored to have a standing weekly appointment.

"Just hold your nose and work with him," Barrett said without looking up. "Once we get you in there, we'll find a way to take it over."

"My people told me the same thing," said Lindstrom. "One of them, at least."

Barrett looked amused. "They say Morzipronone's a sure bet. Wrigley's got it locked in."

"But what do you say?"

Barrett stared fixedly at his phones.

"So you're not sure."

"Have you seen it?" asked Barrett.

"I've seen numbers, nothing recent."

"I mean, have you seen an application. Seen the plants?"

"I haven't been in the field for months."

"Wrigley says the numbers look very good."

"Are you talking growth rates or dollars?"

"I think we're talking yuan," said Barrett.

"So it's happening."

"They've gone through my books already," said Barrett. "Compliance says they have a team of lawyers going through every EPA report."

"That'll take years."

"Let's hope so."

Barrett still hadn't looked up, except to take a gulp from his wineglass. He swiped his finger across a screen every few seconds, reading and dismissing a barrage of messages, rarely typing a reply. He'd been this way before smartphones existed, before laptops, before email. They'd met in the field, thirty years ago, when Lindstrom was a research assistant and Barrett was overseeing six hundred acres in northern Iowa. Then it had been binders, field journals, manuals. He was constantly consulting notes or taking new ones in a manner that made clear whatever he was writing had nothing to do with anything you were telling him. He was antisocial, arrogant, a pure prick. But he was loyal to his scientists. He'd brought Lindstrom with him when he was promoted to oversee the islands; he'd vouched for him as a lead scientist, and, when the time came, he'd paved the way for his transition to corporate.

"Have they started combing your shop yet?" Barrett asked.

"You would know before I did."

"True. Did you ever get a resolution to that school incident in Waimea?"

"We brought in a professor from Mānoa. He said the symptoms were consistent with stinkweed exposure. I guess there was a big patch growing up the hill."

"So stinkweed sent ten kids to the hospital."

"The state and the feds were satisfied. Our papers were clean. All the protocols had been followed."

"What's the on-site monitoring like out there these days?"

"State Ag has three inspectors. None on our island."

"Running ops in a banana republic does have its benefits."

"Yeah well, my guys are spooked. You wouldn't believe the conversations I'm having with my lead out there."

"Guys in masks still threatening his men?"

"You know how it is, the majority of the locals appreciate what we do. They understand that agriculture is their only chance to have a real career."

"And the case is definitely closed on the incident?"

"Accidental drowning. I gotta be honest with you, I know he's been through a lot, but at this point I'm wishing they'd charged the dad with negligent homicide. As it is, he can still play the victim card and convince his dead-enders to keep showing up."

"And the police won't clear them out?"

"Working in a banana republic has its drawbacks. They're all cousins to each other. I'm thinking about flying out Pierce to check on things and talk my lead scientist off the ledge."

"Do you trust him?"

"Ha. More like I can spare him. He's a smart kid. But not as smart as he thinks."

"I mean your lead, Mr. Miyagi."

"Miyake. I trust him. He knows his people. He's one of them, for better and for worse."

"Send the kid. Make sure the case is as closed as you think it is."

"Okay. But don't worry about Miyake. He just doesn't understand how it is here."

"Ignorance is bliss," said Barrett.

"Do you remember," said Lindstrom, "a few months after I got promoted, you called me into your office and told me, 'Quit being such a selfish little P.O.S.' It took me six more months to figure out you meant I was being too nice."

"Some people never figure that out."

"Being an asshole doesn't come as naturally to some of us."

"It isn't easy," said Barrett, "doing what we do. Look at those protestors. They'd rather believe zombie fucking corn is going to end life on the planet than live with the idea that maybe the world is a complicated place, corporations aren't completely evil, and feeding ten billion people means growing crops in ways our grandparents couldn't."

Lindstrom nodded and kept eating.

"But that was never your problem," said Barrett. "You were always capable of making tough choices, as long as it was for *science*. I remember when word came out the budget of some artisanal niche you were excited about was being shifted to a bigger profit driver, you were so self-righteously pissed off I had to talk you out of calling HR and quitting."

"It was cassava," said Lindstrom. "A staple crop for millions of people."

"Anyway, what I'm saying is you've grown up. I've seen you make plenty of hard choices—kill good projects, fire good people—for the *right* reasons. To save your ass. And mine. To give ourselves a chance to save an even better project one day."

"Am I detecting a moral in this story?"

Barrett drank off his pinot, signaled for another. "You know Wrigley's gunning for you."

"For me or Efloxiflam?"

"For you, for Efloxiflam, it's all the same. He's got the numbers. I've seen the deck they're building for their EOY. It'll play well in China."

"Yeah but what about brand equity. We have ten million customers. Actual farmers. They're not going to switch to an inferior product."

"They won't have a choice. He's going to kill the whole line. Flox Plus, Flox Sentry, Flox Defender. If it starts with F, it's done."

"That's a PR disaster."

"He's got an angle." Barrett paused. "You'll love it. 'Corporate responsibility.' The Benevoment Green Initiative. He's going to say we are phasing out synthetic chemicals and going with products 'derived from nature.'"

"If Morzipronone's derived from nature, what's Flox derived from, comets?"

"You have to admit. It would be nice to push a brand without so much baggage."

"There's never been a single peer-reviewed study linking Flox to—"

Barrett waved his hand. "That isn't stopping California."

"Those regulations could be years away."

Barrett glanced down at his phone, and did not look up.

"Anyway," said Lindstrom, "they still haven't solved for volatility and drift. Any farmer who sprays it will kill half his neighbors' crop."

"You haven't heard?" said Barrett. "That's not a bug anymore, it's a feature."

"What are you talking about?"

"Think about it."

"You're saying Wrigley is pitching a product that will ruin farmers who don't buy it? Legal will never sign off. Too much liability."

Barrett shrugged. "Wrigley's got a great pitch. His problem is no one trusts him. But if you're on board, the project gets blessed. The Chinese want to make a splash. You can save your people. You'll have unlimited resources. You may even science it into a half-decent product."

"I might save my people, but they won't let me touch the science."

Barrett laughed. "I'm just saying, the train is rolling. This is your chance to jump on. Derived from nature? It'll kill."

6

SUNDAYS WERE THE hardest.

They began all right. Coffee and cigarettes as the shadows pulled back from the hills. But the empty hours yawned. Clifton and Momilani always had somewhere to go. If not visiting their granddaughter, there would be a wedding, graduation, first birthday, or some other excuse for a party among their vast network of friends and family. They invited Bernt, but he never accepted. He was already too close to them. And he was uncomfortable accepting favors he couldn't balance out. Beyond keeping the cooler stocked and bringing Clifton's mower in for a tune-up, he could offer nothing they needed. Their lives were rich.

One afternoon, he heard the familiar drone of a C-130. He walked around the side of his house until he could see it from the hillside: cruising slowly over the ocean, low and parallel to shore, its tail painted Coast Guard red.

His phone vibrated with a message, from Momilani, "Clifton missing. We at da crack."

Crack 14 was a surf break down the highway. In the spot where cars lined the shoulder on days with a big east swell, he saw Clifton's F-150 and Momilani's Pathfinder, a few more muddy vehicles, a fire engine, two cop cars, and a county lifeguard truck. He followed the path to the cove, where the ocean poured disorganized and heavy, the wind a wall from the northeast, pressing his T-shirt tight to his chest and chattering it beneath his arms. The bay was a mess of rebounding waves and hissing foam.

It was obviously a misunderstanding. Clifton would never dive in these conditions. But there was the lifeguards' red ski, darting through the danger zone by the point. Farther out, he saw one small hull, then another, at least half a dozen fishing boats daring the breakers and disappearing in the troughs, rising and dropping like rice grains in a boiling pot.

He walked the trail to the tiny beach. Among the firemen, cops, and lifeguards clustered on shore, Momilani stood out in a billowing muumuu. He waited until she caught his eye and gestured. She enveloped him in the muumuu, kissed him on the cheek.

"On a day like this, he went out."

"How do you know?" he asked.

"He left his things on shore." She tilted her head. He saw the small pile. "A boy saw them. Thought it was one tourist. Called the lifeguards."

Bernt walked around the bay onto the headland. The ocean sucked itself into gray, heavy waves that slammed into sizzling foam against the rocks below. Whitecaps bunched thickly out to the horizon. The entire island seemed fragile. The tumbled boulders had been cliffs once, and before that, smooth ridges rising to snowy peaks.

Bernt looked methodically across the water, letting his eyes relax and unfocus, trying to catch the thing that didn't belong. Lines of white birds glided in the troughs between swells. A breaking wave left a white scar on the gray water. At any moment, a hundred points were calling his attention. It was unnatural to look for human life out there.

Now and then, a new searcher came up from the beach, saw him in that spot, and walked further down the path. They kept coming. Dozens of them. Clifton's 'ohana. They watched the coast until the boats returned to the harbor, until all they could see was the blinking red lights of the helicopter, its searchlight illuminating one flickering circle of wave and foam in a vast and roaring darkness.

He stopped at the general store and bought a liter of rum. The last time he'd been drunk at a bar, he didn't make it through happy hour before a bouncer hit him in the back with a softball bat, probably saving him from a murder charge. So he drank in his car, watching lifted pickups and rusted-out island cars pull in and drive off: a stream of kids out cruising, locals grabbing ice, beer, and poke, homeless haoles from the mainland, alcoholics, addicts. All with somewhere better to be. All but him.

Drinking dulled the anger. But it came back deeper and more general. What had been a focused self-loathing for putting himself in this position returned as holy rage at a world in which so much loss was possible. When he finally pulled out of the parking lot, all he knew was that this anger could not say inside him any longer. It needed to become real pain.

He drove down to Anahola Beach Park and did a slow turn through the parking lot. Then he crossed the highway and drove up and down the blocks of the village. A floodlight was still shining on the wall of the community center. Three familiar figures slumped beneath it.

When the high beams lit him up, Ice Man squinted into the glare, then pushed himself up onto his heels. The others never stirred.

Bernt kept the headlights at his back as he walked through the damp grass.

Ice Man squatted with his elbows on his knees, hands dangling, wary but unthreatening. Annoyance flashed across his face, followed quickly by the wolfish grin. "You not one cop."

Bernt hurled the empty bottle of rum so it shattered above the man's head.

Ice Man delicately lifted himself to his feet, picked up the broken neck of the bottle, and stepped out of the light. Bernt stepped sideways as well.

"I don't have a knife," Bernt said, which was true. He'd left it in the truck.

He glanced at the wall of the community center. Tweaker Dum and Tweaker Dee were still slumped against it in a daze. Ice Man was alert enough. He had the longer reach and stepped sideways toward Bernt's right hand. Bernt stepped toward him. He knew he was going to be cut and he wanted to control how it would happen.

Ice Man feinted with the shattered bottle. Bernt flinched but gave no ground.

Any doubt if Ice Man could fight was laid to rest by the man's deliberate, patient circling, forcing Bernt to reveal clues about his own training. If Ice Man had been an amateur, Bernt would have been aggressive, pressuring the other into making a mistake. Instead, he'd have to be patient and minimize the risk of serious injury.

They were close enough to touch. Bernt held his hands open and high to protect his neck. He squeezed his biceps to his ribs to protect the axillary arteries in his armpits. He circled to his left, toward Ice Man's right hand, trying to regain the initiative. The plan seemed crystal clear in his head, but the execution was complicated by the alcohol still rising in his bloodstream, making him clumsier by the second.

Ice Man checked with the bottle, a careful, controlled flick of the arm, a boxer's jab. He expected Bernt to avoid the blow. All his thoughts were with the punch he was going to deliver as soon as Bernt lunged sideways. So there was an instant, as the glass carved into Bernt's forearm, that Ice Man was unprepared and Bernt stepped behind his ankle and almost managed to hip-toss him before Ice Man slammed his heel into Bernt's shin and both went down, tearing at each other's arms, trying to find an opening to the neck or at least a point of leverage.

Even with one hand, Ice Man was able to hold Bernt off. He had three inches and fifty pounds on him. When he chopped Bernt in the base of the neck, then used his forehead to break his nose, he thought he'd killed him.

At that moment, a police siren whooped; blue lights flickered behind a spotlight. Ice Man glanced around for the broken bottle, but it was somewhere in the darkness.

He lay down in the wet grass and clasped his hands behind his head. It had been self-defense, after all.

Bernt came into his body with a snap, his hands cuffed to a restraining point in the back seat of a cop car. Ice Man was on the seat beside him, loudly and profanely telling his side of the story.

Both men looked so bad the cops didn't hesitate to sit them on the same bench while they went through booking. "You crazy fucker," said Ice Man, ruefully.

"Why didn't they take me to the hospital?"

"'Cause you started crawling around on your hands and knees calling him Lieutenant and saying you was okay. You no remember?"

Bernt didn't answer.

"I tell 'em already was self-defense. And I get two witnesses."

"What's your name, anyway?"

"Vierra. People call me Sunny."

"I'm Micah. Where'd you learn to fight?"

"I think you know." For a moment, Vierra let Bernt glimpse the cold intelligence that ran below the surface.

"How long since you left the service?"

"Long enough for get two priors already. I get one more I go jail, automatic."

Now Bernt had nothing to say.

"Just tell 'em the truth," said Vierra. "You get one diagnosis, right?"

Bernt stared at the linoleum tiles below his boots. He'd remembered the dark ocean. The tiny pile of clothes on the rocks.

Vierra misunderstood his silence. "If not, you need ask the VA for one new evaluation."

7

LINDSTROM NEEDED ALL hands on deck in the run-up to the End of Year. As irritating as Pierce could be, it had been a real sacrifice to fly him out. His only job had been to offer Miyake an encouraging face from corporate, but apparently even that was too much for him.

"This guy you sent me," said Miyake, "he's a spy or what?"

"What do you mean?"

"I keep telling him, whatever he needs, just ask. If he wants to see the fields, I'll take him out personally. But he never comes to me. My boys say he just pops up asking questions. He's going through old budgets, archived logs. He's a snoop."

"Is there anything you're hiding?"

"Plenty! You know that. I keep saying, if USDA or HDOA showed up, they'd find a dozen violations. We got yards of silt fence washed out and all the catchments overflowing. We were down one man already, and last week one of my applicators drowned."

"Can they loan someone out from Kekaha?"

"They're dealing with MCMV in four fields that side."

"I just need you to hold things together a few more months. After that, you can spend whatever it takes to clean up the backlog."

"That's what you told me last year. You think the Chinese gonna pay for it?"

"I need you to look at the bigger picture. What do you think is keeping us on this island? We're running the same shops in Belize, Malawi, Vietnam—places where acreage is cheap. I'm fighting for Namahana. And unless you feel like moving to Ho Chi Minh City, I need you to fight for it, too."

"What if I send your boy out with Junior Silva tomorrow? They've got a big application in field three."

"Go ahead if it will keep him out of trouble. Just make sure he reads the labels before he sprays anything."

Lindstrom looked around his office. Tomorrow, his team would make their final pitches on End of Year strategy. He wanted to be certain of his choice before he stepped into the room. He'd asked Brady to pull together everything he could on Morzipronone, but Lindstrom hadn't learned anything he hadn't already known or guessed. The compound had been in the pipeline for years. No matter who managed it or what scientists were assigned to it, they couldn't get its PIs on par with Flox.

The newest version was the most effective yet, but the tweak in chemistry had made the volatility worse. Morzipronone wouldn't stay where it was sprayed: a slight breeze carried it miles. It didn't matter what they put on the label; no application guidelines could prevent drift onto neighboring fields. Any crop that wasn't genetically modified to resist it would cup and die after just a few exposures.

It was obvious that if any regulators or independent scientists ever saw that data, there'd be huge lawsuits. But Wrigley was going to argue, plausibly, that this would never happen. Benevoment was a major donor to every university program that could do that kind of research, and the acting head of the Department of Agriculture had been the president of the Commercial Growers' Association. The farmers would be harder to convince. But Wrigley had the best marketing shop in the business, and they'd outdone themselves on this project.

The winning play was obvious: throw his own reputation behind a flawed but inevitable product and try to work it up into something decent. There was no way the board would say no.

There was nothing more to read. No information yet to process. The only thing left was to convince himself.

It was only six thirty when Lindstrom pulled into the garage. He'd left the office early to get in a seven-miler. Char was shuttling the kids to various practices. In minutes he was running down the street to the path that curved into the forest. He followed it down to the lakeshore and under a railroad trestle, where it connected to a trail that ran for miles. As he found his rhythm on the pavement, his mind eased back into the stream that had preoccupied him for weeks. It was ridiculous, he knew, expending so much effort on a few hundred coffee cultivars on a hill so steep it wouldn't hold its soil. But something had gone right with those Namahana bushes. They'd bet double zeros and hit.

Of course Lindstrom had never had a breakthrough that didn't require luck. It was the nature of the business. You bred two thousand plants to get one seed. You maintained facilities in twenty-five countries so a hybrid could flourish in a single field. Benevoment had succeeded over and over because it had the resources to manufacture luck on a scale that no one on the planet could match. Its double zeros were inevitable.

But that didn't take away the thrill. Lindstrom had loved the field, lived for it: squeezing pipettes in a climate-controlled lab, packing down handfuls of exquisitely processed soil on a chilly North Dakota dawn. And he'd loved what that work accomplished: his seeds fed millions of people, allowed hundreds of thousands of farmers to make a living. When they'd offered him a promotion and asked him to manage the entire line, they'd told him he would go from helping millions to helping billions. And he had. But despite the field visits and the PR tours—shaking hands with small-scale farmers in Madagascar who'd formed a village co-op to borrow money for Flox Plus Defender—it was impossible to feel the visceral satisfaction he'd felt as a scientist.

The trail ran through acres of tall grass prairie, big bluestems already bending under the weight of their seed heads. In the last few weeks, the sky had receded from the close thickness of summer to the remote and brittle dome of autumn. Only the satisfying puffs of his warm breath marred the clarity of the thin, cold air.

It wasn't that he had no sympathy for Miyake. He knew how it felt to receive an objective from Golden Valley with only the vaguest directions on how it should be implemented, so if a transport fate miscalculation caused an application to poison a neighbor's herd, or an ROI came in below projections, it would always be the mid-level manager who owned the responsibility. If the EPA did look at Namahana, which was unlikely, they were sure to find compliance issues. But these were technicalities, fines, impossible to avoid. The field hands knew the risks. They all had full health benefits. Lindstrom felt worse about the nitrogen. Given the slope of the fields and the rate Miyake was ordering lime, it had to be impacting water quality.

He crossed an aluminum footbridge. Nothing was pristine. Every rainstorm sent a torrent of petrochemical runoff from the road through a culvert directly into the streambed below him. No one had intended to destroy this watershed. It was simply what regional planners with the best of intentions had considered best practices. By the time they learned better, it was too late.

The upper windows of the distant skyscrapers flashed with the last sunlight. Night drifted up like smoke. His watch beeped. He turned his back on the city, running easy and strong.

When he was a boy, Lindstrom had read a book about the samurai. Besides the specificity and variety of their blades, he'd been struck by their philosophy: that every moment—from serving tea to severing heads—should be approached with the focus and discipline of a sculptor making an irrevocable cut. With the cruel clarity of a child, he'd decided that anything short of this approach to life would be a failure. And of course he'd eventually forgotten all about it.

He wasn't sure if one of his books on corporate leadership had mentioned Bushidō, or if he'd just dredged it up from wherever he'd repressed it, but he'd realized, recently, that at some point in the process of becoming an executive, he'd actually achieved something resembling the standard he'd once set for himself. In the office, he led people and delivered world-changing products without indulging in sentimentality. At home he became the empathetic, compassionate man his wife and children loved. The man God loved. He went out in all seasons to train his body to function at its highest level. He held no delusions, saw clearly the world was uncertain, outcomes conditional, purity an illusion, compromise the only constant. He could see all of this and still act decisively, make short-term sacrifices for long-term goals, assess probabilities and take risks. He could trust the team he'd assembled and the product that had defined his working life. And he knew that he could trust himself, its creator and its shepherd.

In the last hundred yards before the trestle, certainty arrived. Erin was correct, of course. Efloxiflam had built Benevoment. Morzipronone was fool's gold. Only Lindstrom could protect the company from its own worst instincts. Without breaking stride, he reached up and clicked off his headlamp. A half-moon had risen in a cloudless sky. His aluminum ID bracelet flashed on his wrist. The grass glowed silver, every stem and seed visible. His feet were light; the endorphins streamed in a steady flow. It wasn't just his own life he was carving every moment: there were thousands of people in his company, tens of thousands of dealers and distributors, millions of farmers. He'd understood this responsibility intellectually, but he'd never fully embraced it, not until now. For years, he'd gathered force. Now he would exert it.

The company would follow him or it would cast him off. But he would bet on Namahana.

8

THE COUNTY PROSECUTOR had neither the capacity nor the inclina
tion to press felony charges on every drunk and ice head that
managed to knock each other out. Vierra had a sprained thumb;
Bernt had a concussion and a laceration on his arm. The assistant
prosecutor was visibly relieved when Bernt backed up the other men's
statements and took responsibility.

After she'd made some calls and verified he was a disabled combat
veteran enrolled in college, she offered him a plea bargain: one year's
probation and the assault charge would be dropped. The only thing
on his record would be a citation for public intoxication.

He never told Momilani about the arrest. Clifton was still missing.
The compound was always full of people, but Bernt was as solitary as
he'd been in his first weeks. If he bought anything from the general
store, he drank it in his room alone.

He was closing a sale on a Kubota 54-inch Zero-Turn when a me-
chanic named Brydon edged into the room and started wandering
among the trolling motors.

"I get one personal-kine question," Brydon said, after the customer left. "My uncle, he had go hunt pig in Namahana Reserve
and no one seen him for two days. We organizing one search, and I
thought maybe you could help. Uncle say we can shut down early."

"Of course," said Bernt. "Let me just log this order in the system."

For the first time in days, he felt something besides disciplined dullness and rage. He would have a place to put his energy, an opportunity to be useful. Gratitude surged through him.

He followed Brydon north until they finally turned at an open gate posted KAPU: PRIVATE ROAD. A gravel track ran toward a broad green mountain. They crossed a close-cropped pasture dotted with monkeypod trees, drove briefly beside a stream, then climbed above. In the forests of the upper ridge, Ōhiʻa and curly koa grew so thick their limbs formed a tunnel above the track.

The old forest gave way to a meadow where twenty or thirty cars were parked in rows. They walked toward a one-story house with a corrugated metal roof. Beyond were a smaller building and a stable. Cop cars, fire trucks, and a white pickup from the Department of Land and Natural Resources were pulled up in front. There were half a dozen rocking chairs on the covered lanai, but no one had ventured up the steps. People leaned against their tailgates, stocky men and women in Carhartt overalls, Realtree camo, mud-spattered boots.

Brydon introduced Bernt to an old Japanese man with a pleasant, round face. "This is Uncle Joe. One legend up here."

"Nice to meet you braddah. How you stay?" Uncle Joe bowed slightly, clasping Bernt's hand in both of his. He held a tube of long papers in the crook of his elbow.

"Ho braddah Joe!" someone called. Two riders on horseback had emerged from the forest. Uncle Joe raised an arm and waved the paper tube—topo maps, Bernt realized. As the riders came closer, he saw one was a man: lean, tall, deeply tanned, sixty at least, though it was hard to tell with haoles who'd spent a lifetime in the sun. The other was Nalani.

They tied their horses to the lanai. Nalani stopped to chat with a young fireman. The older man walked over to Uncle Joe. "How you stay, old friend?" They spread the maps across the hood of a truck. Firefighters, police, and a DLNR man joined them.

Uncle Joe pointed out the key zones for the search and how to access them. He offered to lead a group, but the horseman said, "More better you stay back and coordinate."

"I not so much older than you," said Uncle Joe.

"I never say you cannot handle, but no one know these valleys like you. And we need someone for stay back and manage the grids." After a few minutes of discussion, Uncle Joe rolled up the maps, and the men dispersed. The horseman remounted, put his fingers to his teeth, and blew a whistle that froze everyone.

"Aloha kākou," he said, "and mahalos for your kokua. You all know braddah Kimo stay missing. Auntie Sylvia went call police yesterday and we had find his truck parked up the road toward Kalaupala. His dogs had come back already and was cruising under the truck. We going make teams. Whoever know these hills or get search and rescue experience, step forward now."

A mix of hunters and firefighters walked to the front. Bernt joined them.

"What kind experience you get?" the horseman asked.

"John F. Kennedy Special Warfare School. Jungle Training Phase Two. Pathfinder and Tracking courses."

"Shoots, welcome braddah Ranger. I like pair you with someone knows the area." He turned to the crowd. "The rest of you join one of these guys. You and your party going walk at an even pace in one straight line. We get plenty flags for marking trail. No forget, you in deep country now. We no like send search parties for our search parties."

Nalani came to Bernt's side. "I'll take him, Uncle." She held out her arms for a fleeting hug and kissed Bernt on the cheek.

The crowd was forming into clusters. Only two men didn't move to join a group. They were obviously brothers, each over six-two. One had a round, powerful belly and a column of precise black triangles tattooed down the right side of his face. The other had the lean, slabbed physique of a pro linebacker or a Navy SEAL. A sleeve of triangles covered his arm, shoulder to wrist. Bernt had already seen a few men like these around the island, warriors who seemed to have stepped straight from an era before European contact and the epidemics that followed.

Two middle-aged women stood beside them. Stern and thickset, with matching Carhartt coveralls, they could have been siblings too, but something told him they were a couple. They split off from the brothers and introduced themselves to Bernt as Doreen and Mahea. Doreen carried a double-barreled shotgun, while Mahea had a seven-inch Ka-Bar strapped to her hip.

"This is my uncle's property," said Nalani, as they walked toward the edge of the forest. "It's easy to get lost if you don't know the valleys."

A trail appeared beneath the trees. The group followed it in single file. The forest was gray and fragrant. After twenty minutes, the dense canopy opened to a vast field of black stones.

"What is this?" Bernt asked.

"A heiau."

He saw a flash of color on a dark cairn: a scattering of fresh flowers and what looked like a pile of salt.

"Your people still come up here?"

"Who says they ever left?"

Nalani brushed her hand along a stone as she passed.

*

The trail ended at a muddy clearing with rusting farm equipment and a sagging Quonset hut. Nalani guided them onto a gravel road, then a faint track that ended at a stream. She hopped across the rocks to the other side. "This is where our grid starts. We'll walk two miles upriver, then come back on the other bank."

Doreen squatted by the stream, looked up and down the valley, cupped a handful of water. Mahea tied a pink plastic ribbon to a branch on the bank where they crossed.

Vines and bushes grew thick in the valley. The trunks of huge Albizia lay fallen across the ground. As Bernt strode and slithered, he catalogued the equipment he'd have brought—at least a jungle knife and a can of dip. The forest felt chaotic, both massively undifferentiated—

millions of leaves, thorns, rocks, and shadows—and maddeningly specific, no pattern or shape ever repeated. At first, he toggled from one mode to the other: floundering through a sea of green and brown or tunneling on a patch of hog-rooted mud, a dusting of purple blossoms, a green shoot growing from the soil cupped in a living tree. Gradually, he found the patterns. He was back in Tracking school, the Alabama swamp where he'd waded waist-deep for six kilometers, the pine forests of Fort Bragg. He began unconsciously sorting the forces that shaped wild places: rain and wind, plants and microbes, animals with goals and plans, their trails tracing the points of least resistance.

In a grove of hau, he saw a patch of bright red mud on a branch high off the ground. It could have been left by a hunter's boot. As he pushed closer, a faint rustling he'd heard in the leaves became a rattle, then a shake of branches, then a wild-eyed boar on open ground, twenty yards ahead and coming at him.

It startled when it saw him, bunched its barrel-thick body, bared its tusks and groaned. Bernt froze, seeing instantly how the underbrush boxed the boar in. He felt its energy, not wary, as a wild animal should be, but roaring, wild and rushing.

No time to find a weapon.

He dropped into a crouch.

At full speed the boar was a charging black shadow, its massive head aiming straight for Bernt's legs. Its plan was simple: to hurt him before it could be hurt.

Bernt dropped his fists to defend his groin. To his left, he heard a faint mechanical click, then the unfocused bang of a shotgun. The boar staggered. A second blast sent the boar crashing sideways into the bushes.

Mahea ran past him. Bernt felt a hand on his shoulder, Nalani. He realized he was on one knee, but didn't try to rise. To his left, Doreen was jamming ammunition into her over-under.

"You like me bang him with another slug?" she called.

"No need," said Mahea.

The boar lay on its side, plowing its delicate pink nose through the leaves. Its flanks rose and fell. Bernt could hear it breathing. The pig feebly churned its front hooves through the mud as Mahea positioned herself behind its dark bulk. She grabbed a rear hoof and stretched back the leg, exposing pale skin beneath black bristles. Pinning its thigh against her body, she hoisted the pig's back end off the ground, stretching until its stomach arched taut and exposed. The knife was in her right hand. Upside down and helpless, the boar craned its neck. When it found Bernt and Nalani, it fixed their eyes with an expression profound and unreadable.

Mahea punched the blade into the flesh behind the foreleg. The boar sighed. Mahea's forearms flexed with effort. Finally, a spray of black lace materialized on her arm, and she released the pig's weight, stepping away roughly. Struggling to catch her breath, she watched with a clinical expression, as the pig shuddered and its eye became a bright, black pearl.

"Must be one sow around here," said Doreen.

"I never smell her."

"That buggah sure did."

"Thanks," said Bernt.

"Eh, next time I shoot better."

Mahea was still examining the pig. "You had barely brush him with the buckshot."

"Was enough though. Where's the slug?"

"Went through the back and caught the spine."

"See? My kill then."

Mahea laughed. "What we going do with him?"

"Carve him up."

"Only if you like carry."

"What, you just like leave him here?"

"One search party this."

"You know I never like waste."

"We take the backstrap then and leave the rest."

Mahea began carving at the boar's haunches, slicing through skin and membrane as Doreen got a grip on the hide and peeled it back. Nalani and Bernt sat on a log and shared a bottle of water.

"Do pigs roar?" asked Bernt.

"That one did," said Nalani.

"Pua'a just like any other man," said Doreen, over her shoulder. "Make big humbug when they think they close to poking something."

Finally, the spine was exposed and Mahea could slice the thick flanks of meat from either side. Doreen had found a burlap sack, and the women took turns carrying the blood-soaked bag as the four of them pushed through the last of the hau until they arrived back at the stream.

Here, the walls of the valley rose steep above the trees. On a boulder in the middle of the flow, someone had left a waxy green ti leaf folded beneath a smooth river stone. A sound echoed off the cliffs, quiet, urgent, unceasing. Bernt rounded a corner and saw the falls dropping forty feet in one smooth arc from a cleft where the walls converged. A gray cloud had settled on the black cliffs. Bright ferns dripped thin streams of water. This was not a neutral place.

Nalani crouched on the small stones that ringed the dark pool below the falls.

"Cold, the water." She scooped a handful and poured it over her face. Bernt did the same. Ten minutes earlier, it would have been refreshing. Now it only added to the chill. "My uncle guys used to catch plenty 'o'opu from this river, but they're no more."

Bernt looked into the water. It was clear and bottomless.

"There's a cave behind the waterfall."

"Should we search it?"

"Can try!" said Nalani. "My tutu told us how. You take a stone in your arms and sink to the bottom, then walk in the dark where the water is quiet."

Bernt shivered.

"There's a mo'o down there, a lizard. He hid a princess from her enemies during one of the wars. My cousin guys used to dive down and look. But they never touched bottom."

Mahea clipped the corner off a plastic bag of poi, and they all took

turns squeezing the pounded kalo into their mouths. Doreen tore a
ti leaf from the bank and used it to whisk away the flies circling the
bloody bag. The smell reminded Bernt of foot patrols past village
butcher stalls, flayed goats hanging behind wire screens.

They rose, spaced themselves, and began walking back on the
opposite bank. Shadows climbed the treetops. They moved in twilight, then in darkness. Bernt saw flashes of light. Will-o'-the-wisps.
Optical illusions. Finally, they crossed the stream and found the trail,
a pale glow running through the trees.

Suddenly they were surrounded by low shapes and bobbing wires,
a pack of dogs at full speed, GPS trackers attached to their collars.
Bernt heard engines and saw headlights through the branches. One
four-wheeler, then another. The two brothers. The first leaned down
to Mahea. She shouted something in his ear, handed up the bag, and
they rolled on.

Nalani led them on a longer route back to the house, skipping the
trail past the heiau. "More better this way, after dark."

Doreen and Mahea made their goodbyes.

"Like come inside?" asked Nalani.

Lights blazed in the empty house. Two thinly cushioned couches
and a water-marked coffee table faced a huge stone fireplace. A dozen
finely carved and polished chairs sat around an antique dining table.
Portraits hung on the walls, a few simple paintings of white people in
black robes, a dozen black-and-white photographs of white and brown
people, formally dressed, unsmiling. Above one couch, a blurry photo
of a small church in a forest clearing. A long rifle sat on brackets above
the mantel—a breech loader with a percussion cap. Bernt spent a moment taking it all in before following Nalani into the kitchen.

She filled a glass and held it out. "Straight from the spring."

He drank the cold water, walked to the deep ceramic sink, and
refilled his glass.

"You spend a lot of time up here?"

"Whenever I could, when I was a girl."

"You didn't get bored?"

"I loved it. I rode my horse, helped out on the ranch. This is my home."

Bernt gestured toward the portraits. "It's been in your family a long time?"

"From Kamehameha days."

"Is he one of your ancestors?"

"Not directly. This land is from my haole side."

"How did they get it?"

"They came as missionaries. Their kids bought land and started industries—ranching, pineapple, sugarcane. Now we lease most of it. No one wants to work the land anymore, except my uncle."

"You don't want to be a cowgirl?"

"The cattle don't even cover the taxes."

Bernt nodded, stared into his water glass.

"So how did you end up here?" Nalani asked.

"Uncle Kimo's nephew asked me to come."

"I mean, on island."

"I got a job on an organic farm."

"You don't seem like the type."

"A girl I knew back home sent the application as a joke. When the guy emailed back, I figured, What the hell . . ."

"She really wanted to get rid of you." Nalani laughed.

"I never thought about it that way."

"Sorry. I was only kidding."

"It's okay," said Bernt. "It wasn't serious."

Silence.

"You're right though. I wasn't the type. Some of those hippies are sharper than they look, but most of them think they've seen shit because they bought acid in Amsterdam and spent a month backpacking in Thailand."

Nalani shrugged. "You don't know what they've seen. Maybe they had their reasons for leaving home."

"I guess. I mainly hung out with the Filipino aunties who bused in every morning. They all claimed I was their grandson and tried to talk to me in Tagalog."

"So you quit?"

"Not exactly. Eagle, the operations manager, asked me to work the Kilauea farmers market with this girl, Cassie."

"Okay."

"Market started at three o'clock, sharp. People could line up, but no selling until the lady blew the whistle. Our farm specialized in tuberoses. When supply was low, things could get tense. One day, we had ten flowers and six women in line. I had a bad feeling about the first one. She was wearing a shirt that said SPIRITUAL GANGSTER. And sure enough, when the whistle blew, she grabbed every flower in the bucket. The other ladies wanted tuberoses, too, and they were regulars. So Cass asked her to share, at which point the lady said something about staging a house for a client flying in by private jet and stuck a wad of cash in Cass's face."

"Haole attitude."

"I figured this type of situation must be the reason Eagle had asked someone with my background to work the market. So I reached over and took her arm like this." Nalani stepped closer as Bernt lifted her hand. He eased his thumb into the soft skin of her wrist, found a notch, and pressed firmly. She watched her fingers open.

"The radial nerve. So the lady dropped the tuberoses, I told her she was banned because of her disrespectful attitude, and the other women got two flowers each. The next day, Eagle started lecturing me about how there was no place for aggression at Tender Roots Farm. I was packed and gone in fifteen minutes."

"That's screwed up."

Bernt shrugged. "It was probably for the best. I'd have gotten fired for something worse eventually."

He let go of her hand, but Nalani didn't step back.

His eye fell on the flintlock. "She was a good shot."

"Doreen? The best. We were lucky they decided to go with us."

It was amazing, how a millimeter could be the difference between standing comfortably beside someone and being dangerously, intimately close. Bernt loved it. Sometimes he loved it more than what followed: fight, flight, something else.

Nalani had gone quiet. He could see she was ready to take another step and end the tension. But he dragged it out a little longer, saying the first thing that came to mind. "You think that's what happened to Kimo, without Doreen to help him?"

Something slammed shut behind Nalani's eyes.

In the final months of his final deployment, riding with the Special Missions Unit, Bernt had become highly skilled at reading people's faces. He'd never grown numb to the intimacy of that brief moment when he knew what someone was feeling before they knew it themselves. It made him feel protective, an inconvenient feeling, considering what usually came next.

He stepped back.

"You can stay," said Nalani, uncertainly. "We've got plenty of beds in the bunkhouse."

"I don't want my landlady to worry."

She let him see her confusion. But she didn't ask again.

When he found his car in the pitch-dark field, he looked back at the house: a cozy row of yellow windows below the black silhouette of the mountain, the universe so bright in the biting cold, he could have sworn he was back in the Korengal, dregs of adrenaline and cortisol still rinsing from his system, the blood-stink still in his nostrils.

All the way down the mountain, he wondered why he wasn't still back in the cabin. If he was protecting Nalani, who was it from?

There was only one answer: himself.

Early the next morning, Momilani knocked on his door. Two spear fishermen had found what was left of Clifton's body hung up on a reef outside Pilaa.

9

I TRUST YOU ENJOYED your trip to the islands?"

Pierce moved to open his laptop. Lindstrom gestured him to stop.

"Just tell me about it."

"Where do you want me to start?"

"Namahana."

"The coffee bushes look good. The growth rates are phenomenal."

"The same in every field? All conditions?"

"More or less. The numbers vary. I can pull them—"

"I know the numbers. Tell me what you saw."

"They're healthy plants."

"What did you expect to find?"

"I wouldn't say I had expectations—"

"Of course you did. Think about it. Did you believe the numbers?"

"I didn't *doubt* them. But I didn't believe them, either. Brady's whole pitch about the next banana or whatever."

"And now?"

"It seems possible."

"Good. Now tell me what else you saw."

"The maize hybrids?"

"No."

"You mean compliance."

"Is that what you were asking my agronomist about?"

"I documented several violations. The—"

"Documented?"

"I have photographs."

"And where are these photographs filed?"

"Currently? In my files—my personal files—and on the camera."

"So I wouldn't go so far as to say anything has been 'documented.'"

"These are clear violations. Record-keeping, off-label applications, failure to provide proper protection equipment, mishandling of Restricted Use Pesticides. I saw workers without detection devices or ventilators in fields that had just been sprayed. There are severe runoff issues, which, considering the stream involved, is obviously a sensitive—"

"Did you measure any of this?"

"No. I didn't. It was obvious—the visual cloud, the soil erosion. I'm not naive. I know no one wants to know this. But—" Pierce stopped. He thought about what he was about to say. If he'd looked into Lindstrom's eyes at that moment, his career might have taken a different course. But he kept staring at his laptop, possibly for courage. "Miyake has lost control."

"That is not your evaluation to make."

"Do you have any idea what's happening over there? It isn't just documenting RUPs and the environmental stuff. There's a circus going on outside the gates. Hippie girls in bikinis twirling Hula-Hoops. I saw Death riding a bike."

Lindstrom let himself lose his composure. "I am updated on it daily. And we are taking it exactly as seriously as it warrants. I spent seven years on that island. The people there, they aren't like you or me. It doesn't matter if they're doctors, lawyers, deadheads, or meth heads, none of them came because they are following the highest calling of their professional occupation. They are lost souls looking for the navel of the goddess, or the perfect wave, or a talking dolphin that will tell them to stop hating themselves. They are freaks. And they are harmless."

"There were natives too, with guns."

"What kind of guns?"

"I don't know. Rifles."

"But not threatening anyone?"

"I guess not. They just stood there."

"Look—" Lindstrom paused, thinking about how to phrase this. "These are rural people. The aloha hula stuff, it's good marketing, but the guns, the pickup trucks, that's their culture. If they were going to do something, they would have done it already. All of this, it's a distraction. And we are going to drop it, now, so you can explain to me why you were requesting files in Waimea on projects terminated while you were still in elementary school."

Pierce looked down at his computer. Lindstrom knew he was longing to end the awkwardness of this face-to-face communication and open up a screen between them.

"I wanted to understand the full scope."

"The full scope of what exactly?"

"The full scope of our, um, exposure."

"Whose exposure?"

"This division. R&D."

"You can't pull a few files and 'understand' what we've done in this division for the last twenty-five years."

Pierce shifted in his chair. Lindstrom let the silence gather force. He'd found the rhythm; he was enjoying it.

"So why are you here?" he asked.

"To tell you how the bushes look?"

"I mean, why are you at Benevoment?"

Pierce considered this question.

"Because it's the best."

"Best what."

"Best products. Best scientists. Best paycheck. Biggest market share."

"Is that why you're here now, or why you took an offer from us five years ago?"

"It's why I'm here."

"Good."

"But being the best doesn't mean we can't be better."

Lindstrom smiled. "Every day, each of us wakes up with a chance to make things better. I know you think this company has done some pretty F-ed-up things. And you're right. I've been here thirty years. Every day I remind myself I chose this. I knew I'd been given a particular set of gifts, and I wanted to do something that mattered. I could be tenured at a research university, buying out my teaching responsibilities and churning fifteen journal articles from every data set. But I wanted to be in the action. Do you know what that means?"

"Generating value for the company?"

"It means having the strength to do the necessary thing. The way you make this company better—the way you make the world better—is by doing your job. It doesn't always make you feel good. But the right thing to do isn't always the thing that feels right. It takes discipline and fortitude to learn that, more than most people have. I think you have it. That's why you're having this conversation with me instead of sitting at HR reading the terms of your severance."

Pierce plucked his shirt cuffs out of his jacket sleeves, looked Lindstrom briefly in the eye. Nodded.

"So thanks for being my eyes over there. Shoot me those numbers when you get back to the office. And don't forget to give your computer an end-of-year cleaning, delete unnecessary files and whatnot."

10

NALANI USED HER forearm to pin down her notebook as she covered the page in tight, indecipherable squiggles. They were talking about ants. "To quote Dr. Wilson," said Professor Higa, "'Selfishness beats altruism within groups. Altruistic groups beat selfish groups. Everything else is commentary.' Can anyone explain?"

Silence.

"It was in last night's reading."

Nalani looked around the room one more time before she spoke. "He's saying evolution might not end at the DNA level. Like, a single ant that takes all the resources for itself is more likely to survive within its group. But a tribe of ants that cooperate could wipe out the selfish ant's whole colony and pass on genes for teamwork instead."

"So if Wilson is correct, what does that tell us about our own society?"

"That we need socialism?" said a pale girl with dark purple lipstick.

"That's not cooperation," said Nalani. "It's redistribution!"

Someone muttered something from a corner of the room.

"What'd you say?" Nalani asked.

A local boy leaned forward, skinny and dark brown, his black hair reaching to his shoulders. He was a teenager but had the stern face of an older man. Bernt had never heard his voice. He usually spent class tipped back in his chair with an ironic smile, a pair of shades hooked over his ears and resting under his chin.

"I said, easy for one Winthrop to say."

"What does that mean?"

"It means, the only people worried about *redistribution* are the ones get something to distribute in the first place."

Nalani turned red. Bernt wasn't sure if she wanted to cry or throw punches.

"What it means," said Bernt, "is if that guy is right, we're *all* fucked. Because the only society that's truly unselfish is motivated purely by religion, and there is only one like that on Earth, the Caliphate."

The room was silent.

Their teacher spoke up. "Let's turn back to the ants for a moment."

Nalani found Bernt in the parking lot. "If you think ISIS is so altruistic, why'd you fight for this country and not for them?"

"Fuck ISIS. And fuck this country. It's not why I fought."

"You don't sound like my uncle now."

"This society has killed just as many of my friends as any hajji did."

"Are you all right?"

"Just having a hard day."

"Work?"

"An anniversary."

He waited for her to walk away. When she didn't, he opened a small compartment in his dashboard and took out a tightly rolled joint. "You burn?"

"Shoots," said Nalani. "But not here. And I'm driving."

They parked on a dirt road surrounded by grass taller than Nalani's truck. Bernt lit the joint, rolling it so the flame didn't run up the seam. He passed it to Nalani.

"I never asked what you're studying," she said.

"Nursing."

Nalani exhaled. "I'm studying Business Management."

"What kind of business?"

"Any kind. Agriculture, tourism, solar, logging. I'm honestly hoping to find something no one's thought of yet. My family just sits on all this land. They don't want to sell but cannot stay the way they are now."

Bernt waved his arm out the window. "Is this yours?"

"My cousin's, all the way to Kipu. Have you always wanted to be a nurse?"

"No."

"What then?"

"A soldier."

Nalani shook her head when he offered the joint back.

"Do you wish you were still in the Army?"

"You said you come from ranchers, right, and missionaries?"

"And Kanaka Maoli."

"Well I come from grunts. My dad met my mom at Subic Bay. My grandfather was in North Africa and Italy. My great-great-grandfather rounded up Blackfoot Indians. He married one. None of us ever earned a commission. None of us were ever good at anything else."

"So why did you leave?"

"I got on the wrong side of some stuff. It got fixed, but it came with a discharge."

"What happened?"

Bernt scanned the grass. "I'd like to tell you," he said, "but to be completely honest, it's top secret."

He took a long pull from the joint, then noticed Nalani staring and became too self-conscious to exhale. His eyes darted back and forth above his puffed cheeks.

"I'm serious," he finally said, smoke streaming from his nose.

"I know," Nalani said, fighting back laughter.

He started laughing, too. "I sound like an asshole."

"No," she said. "Well—"

It took them a minute to recover.

"Seriously though," said Nalani, "is that what happened today?"

"What? The classified—? No. Fuck no. That shit doesn't bother me. Today is just a date when one of my friends passed."

Nalani's truck had good AC. It swirled blue clouds of smoke. Outside the windows, the grass bent and tossed.

"Who was he?" Nalani asked.

"Our combat medic. He saved our asses after we got ambushed helping a crew of civilians retrieve a broken-down crane outside Nasiriyah."

"What happened?"

"Halliburton got its crane back."

"I mean—"

"We were driving in convoy when the lead vehicle blew up. Doc was running to it when they detonated the second charge. He was alone in the kill zone with half his leg gone, but he wouldn't let any of us come for him. He applied a tourniquet and crawled up to see if he could save anyone."

"But he didn't survive?"

"They flew him to Ramstein, gave him a new leg and a bronze star. He shot himself in his parents' basement."

"Oh," said Nalani. "Do you know why?"

"Yeah."

Bernt stubbed the smoldering joint, wet his fingers, and carefully pinched the edges.

"My landlord's funeral is in three days."

"What happened?"

"He drowned."

Nalani stared out the window, watching the acid-green stems bow and wave.

"You stay maka'ala," she said. "Something pilau passing over this island."

They held the funeral at Anahola Beach Park. Cars lined the road for a quarter mile. Bernt found a spot in the back of the crowd. He saw Momilani at the waterline. She beckoned him closer, just as the pastor said something barely audible above the wind and the slap of the small shore break. A tall brown woman with silver hair raised her arms and invoked something, then began to sing, stepping from side to side and tracing images in the air—waves, mountains, rivers. Her hips and shoulders moved in sequence the way steeper waves follow a gust of wind.

Bernt met Momilani's eyes again. She gestured more sharply. He walked slowly around the edge of the crowd. The woman spoke in the lovely, unhurried language Bernt had heard only a few times. She chanted and the crowd responded. She sang again, but did not dance. Bernt felt something slip, and in the next gust of wind there were two cool ribbons on his cheeks.

There was silence. A gust made the palms above them stream and rattle. "Let us pule," said the pastor. People stepped back and began clasping hands, patiently maneuvering on the crowded beach, folding the circle in and out until every hand connected.

As the pastor spoke about the lines of Clifton's ancestors, watermen who made their lives on the sea, Bernt closed his eyes. In darkness, he felt the warm, dry palm of his landlady in one hand, a stranger in the other. Then the entire chain of lives came down the line, like a sunbeam through a cloud. He opened his eyes. The day was overcast. A squall drifted off the ocean and spit rain on the mourners. Momilani's purple muumuu billowed. Her shoulders were thrown back; her face was stern. Finally, the crowd mumbled "Amene" and they all dropped hands.

Bernt followed everyone's gaze toward two fiberglass canoes resting in the sand. Dozens of people put hands on the canoes and pushed them down into the surf. Momilani lifted a carved wooden bowl from a table near the water. She waded in, the muumuu drifting in the foam. She handed the bowl off and boosted herself into the middle of the canoe. Five more people hauled themselves in. A small woman in the final seat called, "Paddles up," and ten arms lifted, with a gap where Momilani held the bowl. "Huki," cried the woman and the paddlers rocked forward, plunging their blades with one motion in the water.

The canoe slipped through a gap in the reef and climbed the incoming waves so the bow rose high and the first paddler swung through nothing but air until the bow slapped down and the stern lifted. The last paddler pressed her long, flat blade along the gunwale, steering down the backside of the wave. Eventually, the canoes came together out in the bay, the silhouetted paddlers almost indistinguishable from the seabirds that flew in lines through the wave troughs, disappearing and reappearing in the gray-green ocean.

Under a forty-by-twenty-foot tarp on a frame of galvanized pipe, four tables were set end-to-end, covered in dishes. Aunties lined up behind chafing pans, gently waving ti leaves to keep away the flies. Slack-key guitar played from a speaker. Men sang about the windward mountains, Koʻolau and Waimānalo, birdsong at dawn, places that no longer existed, memories that felt like dreams. Eventually someone switched to reggae.

Bernt drifted toward the sand, where children were playing in the water while their mothers ate off paper plates. He watched a few men unrigging the canoes, unwinding rachet straps from the curved wooden spars that connected the hull to the outrigger.

"How did you like this local funeral?" asked Momilani.

"It was good," said Bernt.

"I want you to meet my granddaughter. She's going to stay with us."

A skinny, serious girl held Momilani's hand. "Anuhea, say aloha to Uncle Micah."

Anuhea lifted her arms and Bernt squatted down so she could kiss him on the cheek.

"Now go find Auntie Lei," said Momilani. The girl looked around, then ran off.

"He was going to help his brother guys clean aholehole," Momilani said. "But he never showed up. And then a boy found his clothes on the beach."

"It's strange."

"It is. It's actually—I don't actually believe it."

"It's hard at first."

"I mean, I don't believe it. I don't think Clifton went diving for one lobster."

"Did they do an autopsy?"

"He was in the water long time. My cousin identified him. They told me not to look."

"So there's no investigation."

"It's pau already. They ruled it 'accidental drowning.'"

Bernt looked at the mourners around the tent and thought of the cousins and friends who'd been at the house the last few weeks. Why was she coming to him?

"If there's anything I can do . . ."

"There may be. But I never like mention it yet. Small island you know. Now go make one plate while still get lomi lomi."

11

CAN DEAL WITH him, you know." It was another 2 P.M. lunch meeting, Barrett drinking greyhounds this time.

"Thanks," said Lindstrom. "It would be a shame though. He's sharp."

"Lord protect me from promising employees."

"You must have had a conversation like this about me."

"Which time?"

"I *was* a risk."

"A calculated one."

"I'm serious. I appreciate it."

"Maybe my calculations were a little sloppy." Barrett swept his eyes across Lindstrom's without making proper contact. For him, the equivalent of a bear hug.

"These are the times I miss fieldwork."

"Aw Mike, is that what this is, a pity party? If you're not ready to make a call on the kid, think it over a day or two and let me know."

"Sorry, that was a tangent. Pierce is a distraction. I need to save my line."

Barrett bobbed his head. "This is true."

"What are they saying about Morzipronone?"

"You mean Greenbelt? Well. It's not in the bag, yet."

"Whose call will it be?"

"That's the five-billion-dollar question. Maybe the China Co-Op. Or the Politburo Standing Committee, who knows?"

"So that's how it's going to be? A neutral handoff and let them make the call?"

"Officially, it has to be. But context is everything."

"And only one of us has a marketing campaign."

"Wrigley plays the game with politics, you play it with product. You've done pretty well so far, and made a lot more money."

"Yeah, but somehow he ends up with all the friends."

Barrett shrugged. "He's a friendly guy."

Lindstrom's phone chimed. It was Neeka. She knew he was having lunch with Barrett. He muted the phone. "Sorry, what was that?"

"Your product," said Barrett.

"We're bust on everything except Namahana."

"The coffee bushes."

Lindstrom nodded.

"The kid-killing coffee bushes. They still protesting?"

Lindstrom nodded.

Barrett cast a meaningful glance at the table. Lindstrom's phone was lighting up. Neeka again.

"I should take this."

He weaved awkwardly through the crowded tables toward the bar, a finger plugged in one ear. "It's Miyake," said Neeka. "I can't calm him down. He's not speaking English."

"Can you put him through?"

"Of course."

"Dennis?"

"One more of my guys had go missing. And one found dead. That's two of our old boys in two weeks. And a third disappeared a few weeks before that. Cannot be one coincidence."

"Well, what can it be?"

"My men are dying."

"And you think someone killed them?" Lindstrom looked around. The bartender was rinsing glasses and the TVs were turned up. "You still there? Have you spoken to the police?"

"Not yet."

"Well they're the ones who deal with murder."

"And what you like me tell 'em? That all these uncles had work together years ago on one project I no can discuss?"

"I don't see how that's relevant," said Lindstrom, carefully.

"Or maybe they doing it for those young boys. Maybe it's Jonah guys."

"You think a bunch of hippies are killing our men?"

"Not hippies, those local braddahs."

"How old were your boy—those men? In their sixties?"

"'As right."

"And what were they doing when they went missing?"

"Well Clifton, he had go diving. And Uncle Kimo was hunting pig on the mountain."

"So two seniors had accidents while engaging in highly risky activities. And if I recall, those men weren't in the best physical shape."

"I need you to come out." Miyake was calming down, code-switching back to standard English. "We're in full crisis mode."

"We're in a crisis here, too. I'm actually at a meeting right now, trying to save our jobs. Look, we've got the data. If you can make one more spray and take a final reading, we'll call it good and luck those numbers in. I'll fly out after the EOY, and I'll get you whatever you need. Namahana will be Benevoment's top priority."

The line was silent.

"I'm sorry about your men," said Lindstrom. "Thank you for bringing these serious concerns to my attention." Without waiting for a reply, he slipped the phone into his pocket and dragged his mind back to the crowded bistro: white tablecloths and a blizzard raging silently beyond the windows, nearly obscuring the dismal gray lake.

"How's Miyagi?" Barrett asked.

"Furious. His field workers are having accidents, and I froze hiring through end of year."

"That's the spirit. Those are our old boys over there, aren't they?"

"Yeah I guess so. To be honest, I hadn't thought about it. I knew Miyake put them out to pasture somewhere."

"So it's coming back full circle."

Instinctively, Lindstrom glanced around the room. There were still nights when he'd dream entire conversations, word for word, that had happened during the worst months of his life. He'd wake up shivering in clammy sheets. Char had diagnosed him with PTSD, and he hadn't even told her the full story.

Barrett had spoken lightheartedly, but Lindstrom watched his eyes flicker around the room as well. The two men sat in silence as the server refilled their glasses. Barrett gestured at his highball, still half-full. The young man nodded. Barrett's eyes followed him through the tables a second or two, then swung back and flicked across Lindstrom's. His phones chimed but he didn't look.

"It's still there, you know."

"Of course," said Lindstrom. "It has a half-life of six hundred years."

"I mean legally. There is no statute of limitations on this."

"The circle is a lot smaller," said Lindstrom.

"Getting smaller by the day, apparently." Barrett drained the pink dregs of his greyhound.

"Wrigley's data is bullshit you know."

"Of course."

"No, I mean bogus. It's faked."

"Can you prove?"

"I was thinking about that. We could give his datasets to one of our friendly university departments and ask them to write up a memo."

"You can't get to the academics without going through Community Relations. And nothing happens in that shop without Wrigley knowing."

"I have a few connections."

"Don't try to go around CR. The professors all know who signs the checks on their unrestricted grants."

"What about the volatility? I've heard we have internal numbers showing it's as bad as ever, maybe worse."

"Wrigley says the regulators will slow-walk any investigation.

Farmers who don't adopt will have to carry brown fields for two or three years at least. No one can hold out that long."

"So what would happen if that strategy leaked to the media?"

Barrett met Lindstrom's eyes and held them, the equivalent of a knife against the ribs. "Is that why you invited yourself to lunch?"

"I thought it might come up."

"You're actually considering it."

"Don't I have to—"

"Of course not."

"—if I want to save my line, save my team."

The server set down another greyhound. The old man winked at him and the server looked amused. Barrett's expression changed as he swung his gaze to Lindstrom.

"After all these years, you're still a risk."

Lindstrom gazed back, expressionless. He'd prepared for this moment.

"I shouldn't have to tell you, what you are proposing, there is no upside. You'd be starting a reaction no one will be able to control."

"You don't have to tell me," said Lindstrom.

Barrett smiled. "So you just wanted me to watch you pull the pin out of the grenade. You needn't have bothered, I know you're capable of it. You were always an idealist."

"Don't insult me," said Lindstrom. "It's not just my lines Wrigley wants to kill, it's our way of doing business. If we compromise on product, we can't get our reputation back. Not in the time I've got left, maybe not ever. I didn't think I'd need to explain to you that I have nothing to lose."

"What's nothing to you these days, Mike? Fifty thousand? Five hundred? A million? You're in line for that, at least. Most likely more." Barrett's phones had been chiming intermittently; now the messages were coming in a stream. "Don't worry. I take your point. And I even agree with you. I wasn't sure you had the balls for this. I assume it means you're sure you can extend the patent with those coffee plants?"

This was the other moment Lindstrom had been preparing for. He stared hard and silently until Barrett met his eyes. "Completely," he lied.

Barrett held his gaze so long Lindstrom began to doubt himself. He didn't like to do this for self-serving purposes, but as he looked into the older man's eyes, he thought of the Creator: waiting patiently in darkness, then pushing through the soil to unfurl from a million limbs, expressing Himself into a lonely human being, nailed to a tree in a corner of the empire. It was a meditation he'd honed over many years, worn shiny as a lucky coin, the only thought capable of giving him that particular, absolute certainty that from time to time he desperately needed.

Finally, Barrett glanced away. "I'll put in a word," he said. "You'll have a chance to make a case at your End of Year. But in exchange for an even playing field, you have to promise not to blow it up. If Wrigley wins, you do it his way, and you do it cheerfully. It's only fair. He's been doing it your way a long time."

"All right," said Lindstrom. It was the deal he'd been hoping for all along.

Barrett was tenderly swiping the face of his phone. He did not look up. "In a few days, your boy will be getting a lovely promotion," he said. "Please explain to him why you felt he was ready for these new opportunities. We can't have him wondering about our motives, can we?"

12

WINTER ARRIVED WITH downpours that turned the land to mud and sent foul-smelling red plumes down the rivers into the bays. The highway was backed up for miles by tourists in rental cars looking for sunshine. Bernt was in the mechanics' bay, helping Brydon disassemble an outboard motor head. A few days earlier, dirt bikers had found Uncle Kimo at the base of a cliff.

"The police made the report already. Said Uncle's neck all buss. Ruled it one accident."

"Strange his dogs never found him."

"Probably chasing one pig when he fell."

"Did he know the area?"

"Been hunting it three, four years, ever since he start working that side."

"Where did he work?"

"One of the ag companies. Benevoment Seed."

"You think it's strange, him dying like that?"

"My mom say he always was one clumsy buggah."

That evening, Bernt knocked on Momilani's door. The girl, Anuhea, opened it. Momilani was in the kitchen. "Tonight you eat with us," she said. "I made oxtail soup."

In the small dining room, Momilani asked her granddaughter about her day at school. The girl glanced shyly at Bernt. After he returned her smile, she turned to him more often. Her gaze was searching, open. He'd been looked at like that many times, but never by a child.

After dinner, Momilani sent Anuhea into the kitchen to do the dishes.

"How long is she staying?"

"Always now, I hope."

"What happened?"

"It's this boyfriend. Our daughter had her troubles, but she never smoked batu before he moved in. At first we let them stay because of Anuhea. But in the summer, it got worse. All of a sudden she was bringing us her problems—she could not find da kine, ice, prices had gone up, she needed money, very pilau stuff. Then one night her man came shouting in our window. Said she was in withdrawal. I tried to take her to the hospital, but he drove off with her. For one week we never knew what happened. Then they came for Anu, and we called the police."

Momilani leaned back and glanced through the kitchen door.

"The police said only CPS could take Anu from her mother. First there would have to be an investigation. That was months ago. They were staying in a tent behind one cousin's house. Lots of people going in and out. We took food every weekend. Then last week, the school called, said Anu told a boy on the playground she like see his ule. Finally, CPS made one home visit and interviewed the girl. And now she's staying with us—with me."

"Where is he?" said Bernt. "The boyfriend?"

Momilani glanced at his eyes. "No."

She spoke with a sharpness that silenced him.

"It would be different," she said, apologetically, "if Clifton was here."

Bernt absent-mindedly touched the dent in his nose, still tender. "This uncle that went missing in the reserve. Did you know him?"

"Braddah Kimo."

"He worked with Clifton?"

Momilani nodded.

"How many more guys work over there?"

"Not many. It's a small field for that big company. What, his family has suspicions, too?"

"I don't know," he said. "Suspicions about what?"

Momi glanced into the kitchen. "We talk tomorrow," she said. "You're up early?"

It was barely dawn when Momilani knocked on his door. They sat on the lanai of the main house, in the chairs facing the mountains. The sun was rising over the ocean. Hokualele and Kalalea shone red in its light.

"Do you ever get really angry?" asked Momilani.

"Yes."

"I'm angry all the time. With Clifton, mainly. I know that makes no sense."

Bernt shrugged.

"I've thought about it so much," said Momilani. "And I still don't understand."

"Understand what?"

"Any of it. But I know he never went diving for one lobster that day. Not unless he went pupule since I last saw him."

"Is that possible? That he had some sort of breakdown?"

"He seemed normal that morning."

"What did that mean for him, normal?"

"You knew him."

"Not as well as I thought."

"Well. He was like you, about that boyfriend. He would have tried to handle it himself if I'd let him. But everything was happening all at once—first the boys, then the pilikia with our daughter, then the investigation and the protests. When we met you, I saw right away you could understand. I was glad you two were sitting together. I knew he needed to talk. But I never for a moment thought he could not handle. He was bull-headed, the guy."

Bernt decided to be direct. "So there are three possibilities. He could have misjudged the water. But you're sure he didn't. So either he went in on purpose or against his will."

"I know," said Momilani. "I've thought it through."

"And?"

"I just cannot believe my husband killed himself."

Bernt watched the mountains. They were golden now. He was tired of these conversations. For some reason, girlfriends, wives, and parents always seemed to think he was the one who could explain what had happened to their men. Sometimes they searched his eyes as if expecting to see the dead man looking out. Sometimes they looked at him as if he was the one who'd killed him.

"No one says it to my face," Momilani went on, "but I know there are people who believe that my husband, all those guys, they were responsible for what happened to those boys."

Bernt looked away from the mountains and met her eyes.

"What's your belief?"

"I never liked what those men had to do in the fields. I thought they'd be the ones in the hospital one day. So how can I say those chemicals could never—"

Bernt shook his head, silencing her. "I'll help you," he said. "Whatever I can do."

"There is a man," said Momilani, "named Junior Silva. He was Clifton's supervisor. If something happened in those fields, he'll know."

Bernt lay in bed with a yellow notepad, drafting an interrogation plan.

The first objective, he decided, was to develop a more detailed estimate of the situation. He wrote down the data he had to work from. Clifton dead in the ocean. His coworker dead in the forest. A mob who'd accused them of killing three boys. Laid out like that, the situation seemed obvious. But killing someone was hard. Killing someone discreetly much harder. And killing multiple people discreetly was nearly impossible, even for someone trained to do it.

Killing yourself, on the other hand.

He looked back over his last few months with the Moniz family and felt ashamed. Clifton had told him exactly what was happening, and he hadn't listened. He hadn't wanted to know.

A gecko on the ceiling chirped.

Bernt looked down at his scrawled notes. They didn't inspire confidence. Fortunately, the stakes were low. Nothing was bringing Clifton back. No one was under fire.

He dropped the pad on the floor and sank into the bed. A fly landed on the ceiling. The gecko walked up to it and chomped. It stared at Bernt as it chewed the wriggling insect.

Bernt wondered, as always, how it was possible to walk right up and eat a fly.

Kapahi reminded Bernt of the neighborhoods he'd grown up in: three-bedroom bungalows, chain fences, chained dogs, ragged tarps stretched over trucks with propped hoods. Few houses had lanais, but all had a carport, a concrete pad, or a patch of dirt with at least a few plastic chairs and a table where people could gather after work. In the yards were clusters of banana trees. Rows of ti bent and fluttered like green banners when the trade winds gusted.

Junior met Momilani and Bernt at the chain-link gate and led them to the carport, where plastic chairs were lined up in front of a flat-screen TV. He rearranged them energetically, then sat and lit a cigarette, flicking the lighter several times before it caught. On his forearm, a faded Navy tattoo.

"So what you like know?"

Bernt had decided to open with a Direct approach and transition to Emotional if an appeal to old friendships seemed necessary. Beyond that, the interrogation field manual wasn't much help. Fear was obviously off the table. Not that it mattered. He was less sure than ever what he was looking for. In the night, it was always obvious that everyone carried the same dark star inside them. But in the light of morning, it still seemed possible Clifton was the uncomplicated man Bernt had thought he was. And even if he had killed himself, one thing was clear: he hadn't been murdered in some bizarre conspiracy.

Bernt's goal for this meeting was simple: to expose the simple facts and clear Momilani's head, so she could start learning how to live without the bullshit people tell themselves to give meaning to their loss.

"Why don't you start by telling us about your work. Describe the personnel and facilities."

Junior turned to Momilani. "He sound like one cop."

"He's not a cop," said Momilani, her voice even more lyrical than usual. "He's a military veteran. He rents a room on my property."

"You was in the service." Junior tapped his cigarette against the chair, flicked ash on the concrete floor. "That explains it. Me and Clifton, we had work together long time. Lately was on this small field, what we call Namahana, after the mountain. They had use 'em for test chemicals on all kine crops at elevation. But a few months ago, they tell us no more the others, just coffee bush."

"And Uncle Kimo, too?"

Junior nodded. "We had all work together, twenty years at least."

"Who did you report to?"

"The field scientist, Dennis Miyake. One local brother, same as us."

"And him?"

"He report to one haole named Lindstrom. He back on the mainland now, but I knew him when he stay out here."

Bernt had brought his legal pad. He wrote the names. "How many on your crew?"

"Was four. Now me."

"Clifton, Kimo, who else did you lose?"

"Braddah Anson. Another old-timer. He left a few weeks back. Never even give notice. They say he on Maui now. Hana side."

"So he's alive."

Junior picked up an empty beer bottle and pushed his cigarette inside, not seeming to notice it was still burning. "Buggah go Maui don't mean he's dead."

Bernt watched creamy smoke fill the mouth of the bottle and seep out in a pale blue line.

"Is that unusual, for so many guys to work in the same place so long?"

Junior snorted. "My father was one sabedong man. Guy had to carry one herbicide tank for the same plantation his whole life. I was born Camp Nine, same as him."

Bernt considered this. "Do you think it's strange how they died, Clifton and Kimo?"

Junior squirmed the pack from his jeans, shook out a cigarette, flicked the lighter four times before it caught. "Strange? Sure. Two guys mahke li'dat, so close together."

"But you think they were accidents, like the police said?"

"You heard different?"

Bernt said nothing.

Junior drummed his fingers on the chair. "Ocean dangerous. Braddahs think they know 'em, but can change fast. Same with da kine, wild pig. Mean, the mama sow. And the boar too, when he smell da kine, estrus. Experience no matter, neither. Sometimes the buggah who think he seen everything never see what stay in front of his own face."

"So it *was* strange, or it wasn't?"

Junior glared at him. "You sure you ain't one cop?"

Bernt held up his hands. "Sorry. Just trying to keep it all straight." He pretended to read from his notes. "The protestors, did they ever threaten you?"

"Jonah guys? They some punchy fackahs. But they never tried scrap with us."

"Can you be sure?"

This time Junior sucked the cherry down to the filter before dropping it in the bottle. "I know his family. They good people. I'm sure some buggahs stay mad at him. Them boys was his kuleana. And since you asking me, I think he no can handle. He like find somebody for blame. But he ain't going round murdering kanaks."

"Clifton told me about the protests. He said it was like a riot."

Junior pushed himself out of his chair. "You like one beer or what?"

Bernt shook his head.

Junior opened a fridge beside the washer-dryer and came back with a silver can. "Now what was you asking me?"

"About the protests."

"Look, the braddah lost his boy. I never like those haoles he hang out with, but most of them just pilau hippies smoking too much pakololo."

Bernt looked at his notes; nothing was written but the list of personnel. A breeze lifted the paper, rattling the palm fronds out in the sunshine. He remembered an evening on Clifton's lanai, a dry laugh, like something being torn in two. Junior was flexing the thin walls of the beer can with his fingertips. Why was he so anxious?

"We just want to lay this to rest," said Bernt, "for Momilani's sake. Nothing you tell us will ever be repeated. If there's any chance something on that field could have hurt those boys. An accident. Something that could have left Clifton feeling—"

"What?"

"Responsible."

Junior kept flexing the can. Fast at first, then settling into an oddly familiar cadence—*creak-pop, creak-pop, creak-pop*.

"It would mean a lot," said Bernt, "for Momilani to know what really happened."

Creak-pop. Creak-pop. It was the rhythm, Bernt realized, of a heartbeat.

Finally, Junior spoke, slowly and reflectively as if working something out in his own head, rather than answering Bernt's question.

"Working test fields ain't like growing cane," he said. "Every day we get a work order. Plant 'em, spray 'em. But we never harvest. Now and then the agronomist comes with his little leaf punch and takes away his samples. No one ever tell us why we doing what we do. Until one day they say till 'em up, or burn 'em, an' we start all over."

With a final *creak,* Junior flexed the can until it crumpled. He spun it and pressed it flat between his palms. "Bottom line," he said, "we don't get paid to grow nothing or know nothing. If Clifton make himself mahke, it wasn't 'cause of nothing that had happen up on Namahana."

After a few weeks with the SMU, Bernt had learned to predict when an interrogation would turn. It wasn't anything he could put into words, just a change in the energy of the room, right before a civilian from an unspecified agency, or an operative with Velcro fuzz where his patches should be, stepped up and slapped the bound man in the face or backhanded his abdomen. Once, he'd actually asked one of them—CIA he thought—how she decided when to go off-manual. She'd thought for a minute and said, *When they start believing their own bullshit.*

A good answer. But one he took with a grain of salt. They'd just finished a bottle of Johnnie Walker Black, and she was a trained liar.

Now, Junior tapped the aluminum puck impatiently, the way he'd tapped his cigarette, tapped his fingers, tapped his way through the entire interview. "You got anything else?"

Bernt glanced at Momilani, then shook his head.

The energy in the room had definitely changed. But the man's face was composed, as if the roles were reversed, and Junior was the one who'd learned exactly what he wanted to know.

Bernt wasn't surprised when Momilani seemed to avoid him for the next few days.

"He was lying to us," she'd said, when they were back in the car. "But I don't think he was lying about Jonah and those boys."

Bernt knew that however low her expectations had been, he'd failed to meet them. He'd gone in soft and unprepared. The result had been predictable: an untrained civilian stonewalling him with humiliating ease.

Then, early one morning, Momilani called from outside his door.

"Junior's sister just called. He isn't answering his phone. His truck is at his house, but he's not there. And his supervisor says he hasn't shown up in days."

She paused. "I'm sorry," she said. "I don't need to bring you this. It's not your kuleana."

"No," he said. "Thank you. Come inside."

He uncapped a half-empty bottle of Mountain Dew and chugged it as he dug out his notes. There were six names on the list. He crossed off Junior's. Two disappeared. Two dead. Two left: the field scientist, Miyake; his boss, Lindstrom.

He looked up and caught Momilani looking wistfully around the room. She and Clifton had been careful not to enter since he'd moved in.

"Do you know this guy, Miyake?"

She shook her head.

"That's all right," said Bernt. "I'll find him."

He spent most of the day on the shop computer. When he searched for the Namahana field, the top results were corporate press releases and a social network page for a group called 'Āina Defenders, with photos of tattooed, brown-skinned warrior types mingling with skinny hippies holding signs. In one, a black-robed skeleton strode on stilts above the crowd. Bernt had an old profile. He got the password on his third try, typed a short message, and hit SEND.

He found a link to the company's Twitter feed: a North Dakota farmer was hosting a real conversation on GMOs, Brazil was a net ag exporter thanks to biotech. He searched news stories. LOCAL TEEN A BENEVOMENT SCHOLAR. BENEVOMENT, INC. WINS U.N. AWARD. He opened an article in *Environmental Breaking News*. China had lifted its GMO ban with no explanation. BENEVOMENT was hyperlinked and brought him to a scroll of stories: in Nicaragua, DEA planes spraying

Flox Plus Defender over the jungle to wipe out coca plantations; in D.C., the EPA suing California over its decision to label Efloxiflam a carcinogen; in Berkeley, Benevoment sponsoring research on a robotic bee.

When he googled "Benevoment controversies," the first hit was an article—MEET BIG SEED'S BIGGEST NIGHTMARE—about a retired engineering professor now studying the correlation between rising Efloxiflam sales and autism diagnoses. "The deeper we dig," she said, "the more we find. Diabetes, Parkinson's, cancer. Depression, aggression, suicide. Economists may be mystified by so-called 'deaths of despair' among privileged whites in the U.S., but we believe the explanation is quite simple: decades of exposure to the bestselling lawn care product in history."

Bernt googled the professor. He started with her faculty page but soon fell down a rabbit hole of accusations and counter-accusations. HAS AGROCHEM ALARMIST HOODWINKED MAINSTREAM JOURNALISTS? asked an article full of indecipherable charts and tables. The reporter worked for a nonprofit called the Genetic Literacy Project. When Bernt clicked "About Our Team," he saw it was advised by a dozen professors at famous universities. But an article in *Mother Jones* said the GLP was a PR front for the Big Ag companies.

He set down his phone with a sensation like mild seasickness. Somehow all this information had left him feeling more ignorant than when he'd started. The bell over the door jingled and a man came in carrying a chain saw.

An hour later, Bernt was waiting as a fisherman and his son debated whether the old man really needed twin 150s for his Force 21 or just a new pair of 115 horsepower outboards when an image appeared in his head, a graph from the professor's website: three lines—herbicide sales, autism diagnoses, subscriptions for antidepressants—rising in eerie parallel, year over year.

What if the chemicals had poisoned their minds, not their bodies?

Bernt let the two men walk out without even buying the 115s. As soon as the shop was empty, he looked up the Namahana facility in satellite view. The compound would clearly be a challenge to surveil. It sat about a mile down a long gravel road, surrounded by fields. He began outlining a plan: hike in before dawn, conceal himself near the gate, observe Miyake's vehicle, wait at the highway and follow him home. And then what?

He wouldn't make the same mistakes he'd made with Junior. He'd give the man a chance with an Emotional approach. But Fear would be on the table.

At closing he was still tweaking his contingencies. Staying covert would be the hard part. He didn't know the disposition of the security systems at the facility and had to assume there would be trained personnel on duty. He felt the pleasant thrill of adrenaline slipping into his bloodstream.

Finally satisfied, he leaned back and stretched. His eye fell on a filing cabinet half-hidden under the counter. He pulled out the top drawer and dug through stained invoices and creased business cards until he found the shop's copy of the island's slim phone book.

He flipped through the floppy pages, took a grim look at the reconnaissance plan he'd just spent hours drafting, then typed an address into his phone.

There were just a few minutes of daylight left when Bernt parked on a residential street above Kalaheo. It was a cool evening; his hoodie wouldn't draw attention. He walked past a gated driveway with the bronze numbers he was looking for, then kept going until he found a break in the hedges that lined the road. He cut through an undeveloped lot with a FOR SALE sign from a fancy British auction house. Grass grew to his knees. Chickens clucked over a pile of rotting mangoes at the base of a gnarled tree.

The lot fell steeply down to a barbed wire fence. Beyond was a pasture with a few cows grazing flank-deep in the grass. Bernt pulled two strands of wire away from each other, stooped, and stepped carefully through. He walked directly into the field, his back to the line of houses, as if he was cutting through to some place beyond.

He was high on a hill overlooking dry plains planted with neat rows of dark bushes that ended at ocean cliffs. He could see for miles and saw no one. He squatted on his haunches and swiveled. Here and there, freshly built homes were hidden by living fences and automatic gates. But most of the houses had plywood walls, tire-rutted lawns, and lines of ti instead of ornamental palms. In one, a fishing boat sat high on a trailer, brass reels gleaming in the twilight.

Miyake's backyard was obscured by a thick hedge of areca palms. In the twilight, all he could see was the smooth darkness of the lawn, a few bright windows. A plumeria tree created a cone of slightly deeper darkness, which Bernt stepped into. In one window, he saw a kitchen faucet, copper-bottomed pans. There was no sign of Miyake or anyone else.

After fifteen minutes, he began a slow circuit of the yard. There was a small lanai on the second floor. Bernt walked into the bushes below, rustling more than he'd have liked. He leaped and grabbed the balcony with outstretched arms and hoisted until he could grab the railing with one hand. From there he was able to swing sideways, rest a heel on the floor, leverage himself to standing. The maneuver hadn't been as easy as it used to be. Nor as stealthy.

He stood beside the door, listening, then took a few steps back until he could see into the bedroom. A dresser drawer hung open; a polo shirt lay on a rumpled quilt. Quickly, he slid the door eighteen inches and stepped into the room.

"Step foot again, I shoot."

Bernt stopped, resisted the urge to turn his head, slowly spread both hands. Now that it had happened, he realized it had been his plan all along.

"Who are you?"

"I'm a friend of Clifton Moniz."

Now he turned. The man was standing in the tight corner between the bed and the wall. He held a small pistol in one hand, a cell phone in the other. Bernt had already coded Miyake 2B according to the intelligence interrogation manual—moderately cooperative and not necessarily knowledgeable of any pertinent information. Now he reclassified him, 3A.

"Why are you coming into my hale like a thief?" Miyake's voice cracked in the middle of the question.

"I'm helping Clifton's wife, Momilani. She just wants to know what happened to him."

"Who do you work for? Don't move!"

Bernt had taken a long step toward the foot of the bed. Now he stopped, raised his hands even higher, lowered his eyes. He had an intense urge to move quickly and resolve the tension. But he resisted. He was back in his favorite state of being—all-consuming situational analysis—one channel monitoring spatial relationships and nonverbal cues; another responsible for tactical decisions to be made very quickly: freeze, fight, retreat; the remaining bandwidth furiously analyzing the knowledge that Miyake seemed perfectly willing to blow someone away in his own house, which could mean Clifton really had been murdered or none of these guys was playing with a full deck. *Aggression, depression, suicide.*

Two options emerged. He could have the conversation he'd intended, with the power dynamic reversed. Or he could change the dynamic, which might leave one of them dead.

Bernt slowly raised his arms higher. Then he took a step toward the foot of the bed.

"Stop!" shouted Miyake.

"I'm not going to hurt you," said Bernt. "I just have some questions." He took another step as he spoke, keeping his eyes down and reading Miyake through his peripheral vision.

Miyake drew his gun closer to his body.

"You don't need to be frightened." Another step. He was past the foot of the bed.

"Don't move!" shouted Miyake. Bernt watched the tip of the pistol. It wavered up and down, back and forth. He kept his hands up, his head down.

"I can shoot you in my house," said Miyake. "They won't arrest me."

"Are you sure?" Another step. "I'm not a threat to you." Another.

He'd turned the second corner, five feet from Miyake, one step from the gun.

"Who sent you?" said Miyake.

"Momilani Moniz. She just wants to know what happened to Clifton."

"What you think happened?"

"I think he was sick," said Bernt. "I think you might be sick, too. I want to help."

For the first time, he met Miyake's eyes. A final step. He took a breath and let the weight of his upper body fall against the muzzle of the pistol. The small, cold nose dug hard into his breastbone. He felt the slide push back. One millimeter. Enough. A shift in tension. He clapped his hands together at the same instant Miyake pulled the trigger. He felt the dull clicks deep in his chest, one after another. Miyake tried to yank the gun back to let the slide spring forward. Bernt would not let him. *Click, click, click.* With his right hand, Bernt cupped Miyake's fist around the grip of the pistol. It was like holding a thrashing fish. He pulled the weapon toward his heart. Then he released his hand. Instantly, the pressure on the muzzle eased. He heard the click of the gun re-cocking. But his hand was on the slide now. He pushed the slide back to its limit, twisted, tore the gun from the other man's grip.

Miyake lunged and Bernt slapped him away. He walked backward out of the narrow slot between the bed and the wall, stood in the center of the room and gestured with the pistol—still holding it by the slide. "Let's go downstairs."

❧

They sat on stools at the kitchen island, beneath the copper-bottomed pans. Miyake had been crying as he grabbed ineffectually for the pistol, but now his face had settled into a sullen glare.

"I'm sorry I scared you," said Bernt. "I know those men were your friends, too. I thought you'd want to understand what happened to them just as much as we do."

Miyake was staring at the gun—a Glock 26, barely large enough to fit two fingers around the grip. Bernt had set it on the table, between his flat palms. He followed Miyake's eyes, picked it up by the barrel, and set it on a stack of saucers on a shelf behind him.

The tension eased slightly. "Yeah they were my friends," said Miyake. "They thought they were still young bulls."

"What about Junior?"

Miyake shrugged. "Maybe he needed some time off."

"So when did you buy the gun?"

"A long time ago. I don't remember."

"It's still packed with factory grease."

Miyake's glare deepened. "You know about the protestors?"

Bernt nodded. "If I was in your shoes, I would have bought a lot more gun than that."

"I got a good deal," he said, defensively. "They said it has plenty stopping power."

"Look," said Bernt, "I'm not a highly educated person like yourself. I need you to explain what I'm missing here. You are afraid for your physical safety. You've even gone so far as to buy a firearm for self-defense. Everyone on your crew has died or disappeared. But you're telling me you don't think *they* had anything to be afraid of?"

"You want me to say I think Jonah guys had kill my men?"

"Not if you don't think that's what happened."

"I don't think that's what happened."

"So tell me what you think."

"I think one old man had jump in da ocean and drown. I think another old man had fall off a cliff and broke his neck. And I think another old man got too much stress and took an unannounced vacation."

"So maybe you bought the gun for another reason, then."

"Like what?"

Bernt waited, delicately.

Miyake shook his head. The pout was gone.

The saucers clinked as Bernt reached back to lift the gun. He removed the magazine and set it on the table. He pinched the release pins, pulled the slide from its rails, and set it beside the clip. He set the empty frame on the table, squarely aligned to the clip and the slide.

"I like to take an optimistic view toward people," said Bernt. "I give everyone a chance to live up to that expectation. Unfortunately, in my experience, the majority of people do not earn that optimism." He picked up the pistol frame. "They are self-centered." He pressed the slide into its grooves. "They are weak." He pushed the magazine into the grip. "And they are prideful." He set the weapon on the table, beneath one flat palm. "And the biggest victim of their weakness and pride is themselves."

Miyake stared at the gun.

"I know it's not a coincidence, what happened to your men."

Miyake was looking around the room as if he'd never seen it before.

"And I know it's affecting you, too. You don't feel like yourself anymore. You haven't for months." He paused. When Miyake said nothing, he continued, slowly, as if checking items off a list, "You've been under stress and isolated. You're thinking about death." Bernt glanced at the gun. "And you're making a plan."

Miyake stared at the gun under Bernt's hand.

"You can trust me," said Bernt. "I'm going to help you."

Finally, Miyake met his eyes. "How?"

"I'll keep this until we meet again. I want to get a sample of the chemical you've been testing on those coffee bushes."

"What for?"

"So we can understand its effects."

"I mean, why are you taking my Glock?"

"It's just for a few days."

"You just said I could trust you. Now you're robbing me."

"I'm protecting you."

Bernt stood and walked to the door, his eyes on Miyake. He let himself out into the backyard, felt the dark envelop him, found his way through the bamboo into the field and back to the street. He didn't think Miyake would call the police, but he crouched in the shadows for half an hour, watching. And in the darkness, on the silent street, he felt all that he'd suppressed in the intensity of action. He cradled the little weapon and stared into the black trench that had opened each time the trigger bar clicked dully against the slide.

13

DRESS REHEARSAL WAS two days away, End of Year less than a week out, the team was down a man: Lindstrom had every excuse to cancel. But both kids had evening ice times and rides from other parents. And when Char had made reservations at Bar La Grassa that morning, she'd given him that look. So, at a quarter to six, Lindstrom told Erin to email him the deck once they were done for the day.

He drove freely on 394 for three minutes before traffic stopped: a river of red taillights, bright for long minutes, dimming for a few satisfying seconds. The radio was playing a block of Led Zeppelin. Lindstrom turned the volume up. Miyake had called that morning to tell him Junior was missing. The police were involved.

He got off at Penn and took it to Plymouth. Char didn't like him driving through this part of the city, but he wouldn't tell her. He was only on the fringes of North Minneapolis, and it was noticeably darker. Fewer streetlights, more of them broken.

He relaxed as he crossed a bright overpass and entered the North Loop. The temperature had dropped ten degrees since he left the office. On the sidewalk, snowflakes drifted yellow in the light from floor-to-ceiling windows. Char was sitting just two feet away, looking straight at him, but he was invisible behind the glare. He paused for a moment and simply looked. At this stage in her life, it was impossible to conceal the work required to keep her figure. She wasn't just thin now, she was fit. Her bicep flexed as she lifted her martini. It was a pleasure to watch her in the silence behind the glass, skin glowing in the reflections from copper and chrome, an aura of sexy, professional calm amid the chaotic bustle of the restaurant.

She gave him the look as he snaked his way to her table. "Have a drink at least."

He shook his head. "I've still got to deal with some emails."

He asked the waiter for an ice water. "Pierce left today."

"Where?"

"Brussels."

"Maybe you should have requested that transfer."

"Chief Compliance Officer for E.U. Statutory Management Requirements?"

"Maybe not."

"Should be a good fit for him."

"It would be nice to get away."

"Get away from what? The kids' school? Your practice? We had a chance to go to Europe before the promotion. You said you wanted to come home."

"And now I think it might be nice to travel again. The kids are a good age for it."

"I'm afraid that window's closed. Unless the Chinese fire me."

"Or promote you."

"I'll be lucky to keep my job."

"You could move out of R&D."

She really meant this, Lindstrom realized.

"It's tempting."

This surprised her. She smiled, took the last, long sip of vodka, and offered him an olive. "Since when?"

"A few weeks, maybe longer. It's not like I'm doing science. I'm managing people who manage people who do science. I'm tying my career to a twenty-year-old technology whose greatest selling point, at the moment, is that its numbers don't have to be cooked, which is a point I'm not even allowed to sell."

"Is something wrong?" asked Char. "Besides all the usual things?"

"No. Well, maybe. I got another call from Miyake today. He thinks someone is murdering his workers."

"Can that be true?"

"What motive could there be?"

Char didn't answer.

Lindstrom couldn't contain his irritation. "Say it if you think it."

"Some people believe that field killed those boys."

"You can say it. They believe I killed them."

"Not just you."

"The company."

She said nothing.

"You know nothing we used on those fields could possibly kill adolescent boys in a body of flowing water."

"I know that. But the poor futher clearly doesn't."

"What more can I do? I flew over there. I spoke to the police and the state investigators. I had a personal conversation with the father. I even gave him my number. He's never called."

"So how is Miyake doing?"

"He's extremely stressed. I've placed a lot of pressure on him. There's a lot of pressure on all of us. This isn't a normal review. Our whole line is at stake."

Char was silent. These were the times he hated being married to a psychiatrist.

"I'm tired of it," he admitted. "No matter how much profit we bring in, no matter how much we innovate, they still see us as a problem. They want to sell bright bottles of patented chemicals but don't want to own the externalities. And that goes double for everyone outside the company. They eat our food and condemn us for growing it."

"I'm sorry," said Char. "I know it's frustrating."

"I know you know it's frustrating! I just wish I knew you disagreed with them."

"I think your work is incredibly important. You've helped feed millions of people."

"And you think we're poisoning them, too."

She shook her head.

"I know you do. You get your news from NPR."

"I'm not the bad guy," said Char.

"No, I am."

"Who are you really talking to right now? The father of that boy? Your bosses?"

"All of them," said Lindstrom, disgusted with himself. "Everyone."

"You don't feel appreciated."

"No. I don't. And now I'm ruining dinner."

Char laughed. "You ruin dinner when you don't come home for it. You ruin dinner when your mind is somewhere else. You don't ruin dinner when you tell me how you're feeling."

This was what Lindstrom never ceased to need reminding of, that vulnerability was the path to strength. That this self-pity, which felt like the exact opposite of what he needed to function, was part of discipline, too. He had learned this a long time ago, yet these conversations always had to follow the same arc: frustration, anger, self-pity, and, finally, honesty, clarity, perspective. "I'm worried about the prototype."

"Has anyone said anything?"

"Barrett brought it up. It's still a liability, a big one. Big enough to affect the sale, I think, if the Chinese knew about it."

"But it's always been there."

"Yeah. Nothing's changed. This thing with Pierce, the snooping around, must have got me thinking about it. And these workers, dying and disappearing. They were all on that project. That little field, Namahana, was how we got them out of the way. We never thought those coffee bushes would amount to anything."

"You've made your peace with what happened," said Char. "You're doing everything you can."

Lindstrom thought about this. Miyake would certainly disagree. *Who you think going disappear next?* he'd asked Lindstrom a few hours earlier.

The waiter set down their plates. Lindstrom asked for a glass of Pinot.

His wife smiled.

"They warned me I would miss the field," he said, after a few minutes with his risotto. "But they promised me control. Instead of hoping some MBA at headquarters would appreciate what we were doing, I could be the one making those decisions. I could shape my own lines and I could shape my own destiny. But it wasn't true."

"Well you always knew the company serves its shareholders."

"That's not what I'm saying. They talk about shareholder value because they need to call it something. But there's no accountability, not to shareholders, not to anyone. It's chance. You can do everything right, but if there's a drought in India and orders drop ten percent, you'll be blamed. Unless you can get transferred in time for the blame to hit the next guy. And it goes all the way up. No matter what anyone tells you, or what they believe about themselves, all anyone is trying to do is make sure there will always be a chair for him to sit on when the music stops."

"What are you saying, Michael?"

"I'm saying," said Lindstrom. "I'm saying."

He stopped and thought about what he was saying.

"I'm saying I'm tired. I need to take better care of myself. Mentally, I mean."

Char reached for his hand again.

"I need to see the kids more. I need to take us all on a vacation."

She squeezed.

"I'm sorry," said Lindstrom. "How was your day?"

14

IT WAS WEDNESDAY, Bernt's day off, a school day. He hadn't been to class in weeks, and he'd never turned in an assignment. He knew he wouldn't be earning any credits. But he wasn't prepared to spend the day alone.

They were talking about real estate.

"Land and power," said their teacher. "Pre-contact, there was no distinction. To rule a people was to control the land, or vice versa. Paradoxically, even as their rulers came and went, generations of Kanaka 'Oiwi remained rooted on land they held no right to. So what changed?"

"They all died of yellow fever," said the boy with the sunglasses under his chin.

"They got their ownership rights," said Nalani, "in the Great Mahele."

"Maybe they got rights, but they never got ownership." The teenager had leaned back so far he was talking to the dusty ceiling tiles.

"That's not true," said Nalani. "There was a process. Any Kanaka Maoli could register—"

"The process wasn't made for Kanaka, it was for haoles like the Winthrops who—"

"Nainoa—" said Professor Higa, with an edge in his voice.

Nalani talked right over him. "Getting the right to own property means getting the right to sell to anyone you choose. I won't apologize for—"

"Yeah. You won't apologize."

Bernt remembered why he'd quit coming to class.

🍃

She found him sitting in his car.

"You ditch class for weeks then just sit there like a ghost?"

"Me and everyone else. Except you and your friend Maui Jim."

"Never mind Nainoa. I known him his whole life. He's my girlfriend's little brother."

"Even the professor couldn't get a word in."

"He's worse than Noa. Acts like he's the expert, but it's always so one-sided."

"Maybe you should ask yourself why you're always on the wrong side."

She glared at him. "I just think things are more complicated than he admits sometimes."

"Well, I gotta go take care of some stuff."

"Then why have you been sitting here waiting for me?"

Bernt shook his head and stared through the windshield.

Nalani was still glaring at him. "You want to buy me coffee or what?"

🍃

They drove to the Starbucks in the new addition to the mall. Nalani chose an outside table, with a view of Petco and the green cliffs of Haʻupu.

"What happened to you?"

"I got busy."

"At the mower shop?"

"We sell marine engines, too."

"You like working there?"

"I like being useful."

"But it's not like being in the Army."

He shrugged.

"There must be some things you don't miss about the military."

"It's hard to explain to civilians."

"What is?"

"Why people like me are drawn to certain professions."

"People like you how?"

"People who like violence."

"Isn't that just being a man?"

"I don't mean watching MMA. I mean risking your life to take someone else's."

"Well you shouldn't feel bad about that. We need people like you to protect the rest."

"I think I need to clarify something, because you seem to be under the impression that I am a good person."

"Just because you're an asshole doesn't mean you're a bad person."

She smiled at him, inviting him to laugh. This made him angrier. "And what puts you in the position to make that judgment? Because we've spent a few hours together? My first priority every day is to avoid situations that could cause me to kill someone."

"But that's the point, right? You were only doing what people around you were doing."

"No, I was doing what the people around me couldn't do as well as I could."

"So why are you in school to be a nurse then? Shouldn't you be a cop or something?"

"I have education credits with the VA. If I don't use them they go away."

Nalani rolled her eyes.

"And why are you there?" Bernt asked. "Couldn't you just be a cowgirl on your family's ranch?"

"That's not the kind of help they need."

A gleaming pearl passed behind Ha'upu, a 737 descending toward the airport.

"I think you'd be a good nurse," said Nalani. "You can still turn in your final paper. I can help you."

"Like I said, I'm pretty busy."

"At the shop."

"It's more of a personal matter."

"I thought you were here alone."

"It's my landlord. His wife, his widow, thinks his death was suspicious, and I told her I'd try to find out what happened."

Nalani leaned forward, unable to keep the delight out of her voice. "You're solving a murder? What happened?"

"At first it seemed like a swimming accident. But that guy we were looking for, Uncle Kimo? It turns out they worked together. And then their supervisor disappeared, too. So there's a pattern. I think maybe they were exposed to a chemical that made them suicidal or something."

"People here usually just hang themselves."

"Well, suicide is just a theory. Murder is a possibility."

"By who?"

"You know those boys who were killed in the stream a few months ago?"

Nalani's mouth tightened. "What about them?"

Bernt realized he'd brought up the subject too abruptly. Dead uncles was one thing, dead kids something else. "It was just, some people blamed Clifton and those other guys, because of where they worked."

Nalani's expression didn't change, but she seemed to relax a little. "Well, let me know if you find anything. You've got me curious."

The next day at the shop, Bernt returned to the scientist's website. He couldn't understand the technical jargon or molecular diagrams, but he printed two reports that mentioned Benevoment.

That evening, he drove back to Miyake's house, parking up the street and walking back to ring the buzzer. There was no sign of police. He assumed if Miyake wanted them involved, they'd have found him already. Just in case, he'd hidden the gun in the forest near Momilani's.

When Miyake opened the door, Bernt had the uncanny feeling he was meeting the man's identical twin. There was none of the anger or despair of the other night. If anything, he seemed almost cocky, narrowing his eyes and suppressing a smile, as if he knew something Bernt did not. Miyake led him to a stone patio with two chairs in the shade of the plumeria. Purple and white flowers were scattered across the weathered rock.

"Did you bring what I asked for?" Bernt said.

"What was that?"

"Samples of what you've been spraying."

Miyake laughed. "You can buy it at Home Depot. We're testing new plants, not new pesticide."

"What about you," asked Bernt, angry at himself, "how's your mental state?"

"What do you think? I got people breaking into my house. Stealing from me."

"That was for your own protection."

"It must have worked. I'm still alive."

"I'm just asking you the same questions I asked Junior."

"Were you protecting him, too?"

"I'm trying to learn anything that might help us understand what happened to your team."

"What can I tell you? Flox Plus has been on the market for twenty years."

"So if the product is safe and everything is fine, why were you carrying a gun?"

"Because of people like you. Local people already know how important agriculture is to these islands. Always has been. Walk up any valley on the North Shore, you'll find the old kalo lo'i. Ask anyone you meet this side, they'll tell you what camp their grandfather grew up in. This island's best times was plantation days. Now you get transplants protesting GMO. But what do they do for the island? Sell real estate? Grow pakalolo? They call *us* a threat. The real threat is suicide and drugs, kids born and raised here who don't see no point in getting one diploma if they need go mainland just for find one house and get one decent job."

"That may be true," said Bernt. "But it's beside the point."

"So what's the point?"

"The point is to learn the truth, so we can make sure no one else dies."

"You never like know the truth," said Miyake. "You like make someone pay."

Bernt practiced self-control for a moment. Then he handed the printed pages across to Miyake. "You said you've been making that stuff for twenty years. Well that's exactly what these papers show, a correlation with disease, including mental illness."

Miyake squinted in the fading light. He frowned, licked his thumb, and began flipping through the pages. Bernt watched him closely.

"Who gave you these?"

"I found them in my investigation."

Miyake folded the stack of papers in half and shoved them back at Bernt.

"This shit makes me so angry."

"You don't agree with the conclusions?"

"What conclusions? It's bogus science. How can I disagree with nonsense?"

Bernt shook his head.

"Don't believe me? Show it to one middle school chemistry teacher. They'll tell you same thing. It's kapakahi. Gibberish."

They were sitting in cold shadow. Shamas in the branches exchanged their evening songs.

"What if I told you I killed those boys?" said Miyake, unexpectedly. "What if I dumped a drum of poison in that stream. Would you protect me?"

"It's not about the boys."

"Then what if I had ordered those guys to spray without safety equipment?"

"Is that what happened?"

Miyake rolled his eyes. "We follow the application labels."

"So why do people get sick?"

"What people? Sick how? This is what you people do. Boys drown. People get sick. And you say, 'They were killed by the corporation.' But we never invented cancer. We never invented death. You'd rather spend a lifetime looking for a bad guy than a second thinking maybe none of it means anything. You keep saying I'm afraid. I think you're the one too scared to see the truth."

In another time and place, this would have been the moment to backhand Miyake in the ribs and take the breath out of him. But whatever frail thread had brought Bernt here was now unraveled. He couldn't interrogate someone when he didn't know the next question to ask.

The birds were silent; the light was gone. Miyake was a pale shape in the darkness.

Bernt stood without a word and left him in the chair under the plumeria tree.

"I need that gun back," Miyake called out.

"You're safer without it," Bernt answered. "Trust me, I know."

15

THE NIGHT BEFORE the End of Year, Lindstrom dreamed he was standing outside his house. The sky was overcast. He started walking down the familiar street. It wasn't until he stepped on a neighbor's flagstone path that he understood the rules. He could not touch the grass, the flowers, the bushes or trees, any growing thing. Fortunately, there were a series of slate pavers running around the side of the house. He hopped from one to the next until he could step onto the brick patio and from there the concrete slab beside the still, black water of a swimming pool.

He was cautious, at first, but that soon felt absurd. There was no one watching. He got a running start and leapt onto the cedar fence, stepped onto a railroad tie bordering a flower bed. It was like the game they used to play on rainy days. The floor was lava that would burn you to a char. It was not a game they played when Mom and Dad were home.

He walked the tie like a balance beam, used a crescent of Adirondack chairs arrayed around a fire pit, and pulled himself up the plastic slide of a jungle gym, which brought him within stepping distance of the next fence, a split rail. He peered over the edge.

It must have been the height of summer. The lawns were thick, the bushes unruly. Flowers bloomed profusely. It was hard to believe it was all dead, everything outside and everyone inside. The dead leaves tossed in the breeze, still firmly fixed to dead branches.

It was 3:40 in the morning. Lindstrom stared into the darkness. He knew he wouldn't fall back asleep. He never did after that dream. He brought his face to the warm and distant body of his wife, inhaled her. She did not stir, and he did not want to draw her out of the depths. The winter solstice was a few days away. Four A.M. was as dark as it would ever be.

He associated this hour with the opening of deer season, when his father would shake him awake and he would grope his way to the dungarees and flannel shirt laid out the night before. They took the old highway through the center of town, familiar buildings made exotic by the solitude of early morning. Lonely neon signs. Now and then on the long drive, his father would ask him to uncap the green Coleman thermos and refill his travel mug.

He carried a rifle, just like all the men, but the only time he'd ever taken a shot, his father had to track spoor for hours. As a boy, he couldn't understand how his dad and uncles could treat the act of killing so matter-of-factly. They'd grown up on a small dairy farm on the Iron Range. His grandparents had always been very old. He understood now that they had loved him, and even been tender with him, but his memories were vague, apprehensive. They were simple, stern people living in a simple, stern house that was steadily falling apart around them.

The house was still standing; he owned the land. But it wasn't safe to go inside. When his children were small, he'd brought them in while Char waited angrily outside. They'd climbed through a window because he'd forgotten the key. It had been a grand adventure, lifting the lids and peering at the ashes in the iron stove, climbing the stairs and pacing the tiny bedrooms where his grandparents had raised five children. The basement stairs had collapsed. All they could do was shine the flashlight across the junk piled on the bare dirt floor. Mason jars. *Reader's Digest*s.

It had been a young buck. A three pointer, its ribcage rising and falling where it lay in the alder swamp. He'd found the rack in his father's basement, his name and the year on a little plaque. It must have ended up in one of the countless dump runs he'd made after the funeral. What he remembered best from all those hunting trips was the long ride north, pouring his father's creamy coffee, steam swirling from the thermos, the headlights illuminating a tiny arc of the long highway, pale stands of aspen glowing blue at first light, winter coming nearer with every mile they traveled.

He always gave himself time for a long, luxurious shower. He shaved in the steaming bathroom, walked downstairs in his towel to start a pot of coffee, letting the cool air close his pores. Then back to the bedroom, a starched shirt from the dry cleaner's hanger. He wore this suit only two or three times a year. There were some conventions of corporate life he felt were truly ridiculous, but the confidence of wearing a well-tailored suit wasn't one of them.

Finally, he slipped on the ID bracelet his wife had ordered after an NPR story about a runner who was hit by a car and died alone because no one could locate her family. He'd been self-conscious about it at first but had come to see it as good luck. He'd never bought himself a proper, engraved wedding ring, and he liked having his name and hers together on his wrist.

Before he left the house, he checked on his children, staring into the darkness of their bedrooms until his eyes adjusted. He saw his daughter curled into a ball with two blankets wrapped tight around her, just like her mother; his son, sprawled like a starfish, one arm flung extravagantly above his head, the sheets thrown back revealing his slim bare chest, his mouth open as if he could not possibly take in too much air.

The parking lot was exactly as he had left it six hours before. The same few cars, though in a different configuration, clustered near the door instead of scattered at random. Only Erin's was in the same spot, at the far end of the lot. Either she'd spent the night at the office, or she'd parked there to make everyone wonder if she had.

A cold snap had set in the day before. Ten below, according to his dashboard. That was fine. He even liked it. The sky was so clear he could make out a few dim stars. He didn't bother to put on his overcoat, simply slung it over his arm and walked quickly toward the low darkness of the building, BENEVOMENT glowing tastefully in sky blue letters beside the front entrance.

As he stepped onto the curb, he noticed someone in the lobby: Erin, scrolling through her phone of course. She looked up when he pushed open the outer door, an expression on her face that he had never seen.

"Miyake passed away," said Erin. "The police called the office a few hours ago. They haven't offered any details. He was at home and it's under investigation."

Lindstrom stopped short.

"I'm so sorry."

He refocused. "Who's the contact?"

"Hansen," she said.

He was already walking away. He wondered who else was in the loop, and why Erin had known before he did. But when he checked his email, something he'd been too self-indulgent to do earlier, he found that Hansen had sent out a brief message and CC'd everyone who might possibly need to know. Even the secretary of the CEO.

It was 1 A.M. on the island. Lindstrom called anyway.

"I just got the email," he said to Hansen. "Tell me what you didn't say."

"I wrote everything I know for sure. Unofficially, they think it's a suicide. A neighbor heard something and found him hanging from a tree in his yard."

"Thanks," said Lindstrom and hung up the phone.

He called Barrett next. "You need to get on a plane," Barrett told him.

"Is this a heads-up?" said Lindstrom.

"No," said Barrett. "This is your official notification. Neeka needs to book you a flight. Don't worry about a return. The EOY is postponed, indefinitely."

"Should I bring Erin?"

"We need her here. We need your whole team here."

Someone rapped on his door. He didn't respond. The knock came again. It was Erin. "We're all in the conference room."

"It's off," he said. "I'm flying out today."

"Of course. Who do you want to bring?"

"I'm going alone."

He put on his overcoat and walked to his car, started the engine, sat in the cold. He picked up his phone reflexively, then set it down.

They'd been attending Living Water for a few years. It had an excellent youth program. Lindstrom liked the pastors well enough.

The parking lot was much larger than Benevoment's. A single car near the entrance. A single light in one window. He shut off the headlights, put his hand to the keys in the ignition. Then he brought his hands together in his lap, one cupping the other. The facts were unchanged and quite simple. Their work affected hundreds of millions of lives. Their company would soon decide whether to advance an inferior product or a superior one. The pressures on his team had been tremendous. This was the nature of their business—

A tear opened in these thoughts, the sound of a boy, crying, his own voice, Lindstrom realized, the voice of the boy in the swamp beside his father, confronting something he could not undo.

16

WHEN BERNT SAW the unmarked car across the street from the shop, he almost kept driving. An old instinct, but not necessarily the wrong one. Instead, he walked slowly through the parking lot and lingered at the cash register, chatting with Brydon, who'd been covering the sales floor, as the plainclothes detective made his slow walk in the stark morning sunlight.

"I'm looking for Micah Bernt," said the detective.

"How can I help you?"

"I'm Detective Carvalho. I need to ask you some questions."

"Am I under arrest?"

Carvalho squinted at him. "When I arrest you, you know it."

"I'll bet, sir. How can I be of service?"

"Your name has come up in an investigation, and we'd like to ask you some ques—"

"Go ahead."

"—at the station."

Bernt looked at Brydon, who shrugged.

At least he'd been trained for this.

In the station, Carvalho waited for him on the other side of the metal detector. Once Bernt had passed through, he used a swipe card to unlock a door into the back of the building. He escorted Bernt to a small room with a table and four chairs. There were cameras mounted in two corners.

"Have a seat. I get you one bottle water, or you like coffee?"

"Water is fine."

Carvalho left and did not come back for an hour. Bernt crossed his right leg over his left, and breathed deliberately until Carvalho returned. So far, everything right out of the playbook.

"We have a few questions for you. Just standard kine. Shouldn't take long."

"No problem," said Bernt.

"You're from the mainland?"

"California."

"How do you like it, the local culture?"

"People are relaxed. It's nice."

"Yes, it's a very friendly place. People probably think you're one local already. You found one wahine yet?"

"Not yet."

"What you like do, in your free time?"

"I don't do much. Go to the beach. Go hiking."

"You seen much of the island then?"

"Some of it."

"But you stay East Side."

"Yes."

"You rent one room from the Moniz family."

"That's right."

"And you close with them?"

"Somewhat."

"You know I saw you there, at Clifton's funeral."

"Oh yeah?"

"That's right, I was there."

Bernt said nothing.

"Was one tragedy."

Bernt waited, his right leg still on his left knee.

"Clifton was one waterman, you know that?"

"I've heard."

"How you think someone li'dat went and got himself drowned?"

"It seemed strange."

"Oh, it seemed strange to you?"

"From what I know."

"What do you know?"

"I know the ocean was big that day. Very rough."

"Very rough," repeated Detective Carvalho. "One big swell coming in. Ten foot. And heavy trades, too. Not one witness can tell us they saw Clifton Moniz go into the water that day."

Bernt said nothing.

"Did he say anything to you about going diving?"

"No he didn't."

"You know why I asked you to come down here?"

"No I don't."

"But you can guess."

"I can guess."

"What is your best guess?"

"I think you are wondering why I've been asking people about Clifton's death."

"Asking what kind people?"

"His coworkers."

"You been asking Clifton Moniz's coworkers about his death."

"Yes."

"Why?"

"Because Momilani asked me to."

"Momilani Moniz thinks her husband's coworkers had something to do with his death?"

"You would have to ask her. I just know Auntie Momilani thinks something about his death was strange."

"That's what she thinks?"

"Yes sir."

"And that's what you think, too."

"I think death is strange."

"You seen many deaths?"

"Yes."

"And all of them was strange."

"I wouldn't call them ordinary."

"You was in the service."

"That's right."

"You had to kill, what, some terrorists?"

"I killed."

"You tried to kill one local braddah, too, I hear."

"If you're talking about the assault charge, I wasn't trying to kill him. I was drunk. He was tweaking. We got in a fight."

"What about da kine, those coworkers you talked to?"

"What about them?"

"They tell you anything about Clifton?"

"Not really."

Bernt had not moved since Detective Carvalho had come into the room. It wasn't true that you could tell if someone was lying by where they focused their gaze, or if they shifted in their seat, but Detective Carvalho was exactly the kind of person who would think it was.

"All of a sudden, plenty deaths all over this island. People having accidents. People disappearing. And you know whose name keep popping up?"

Bernt said nothing.

"Micah Bernt."

Bernt said nothing and did not move.

"Wait here," said Detective Carvalho, as if an idea had just occurred to him. "I like go check something."

He left the room. Bernt waited thirty seconds, then he uncrossed his legs, reached across the table, and took the water. He unscrewed the cap and took a short sip, then put it back. He crossed his legs the other way. After ten minutes, he got up and stretched his arms. Shifted back and forth a few times. Sat back down. No need to overthink things.

Carvalho was more polished than he'd expected. Bernt decided this was a good thing. He'd rather face a trained fighter than a random brawler. You were more likely to get killed, but less likely to get hurt.

Detective Carvalho came back with a stack of manila folders. He did not sit down.

"Did Momilani ask you to talk to Dennis Miyake?"

"Not directly, no."

"Why you had go to his house then?"

"I thought he might know something."

"About the death of Clifton Moniz?"

"Yes sir."

"You like know what I think?" said Detective Carvalho. "I think you're lying."

Bernt shrugged. "I was worried about his safety."

Detective Carvalho smiled. "Tell me more."

"So many people on his team were dying. I thought he might be in danger, too."

"You must have been very concerned."

"I was."

"And you normally stay very concerned about people's safety?"

"Of course."

"When you was in the service. You stayed concerned about safety."

"Yes sir."

"Now I know you're a liar."

"How's that?"

"Because your record says something different."

"I was honorably discharged after three combat tours."

"You was. But that don't make you honorable."

Bernt said nothing. He knew what was in the folder. He met Carvalho's eyes. The detective smiled, as if the two men shared a secret.

"You was one highly trained soldier."

"Correct."

"Trained to kill."

"I was a soldier."

"I know plenty soldiers. None of 'em ever trained like you was."

"You might be surprised."

"Nothing surprises me," said Carvalho. "You think just because we one small island we don't know how to work one murder case?"

Bernt resisted the temptation to raise his eyebrows.

"Tell me about your last deployment. What kine things you had to do?"

"It varied. A lot of convoy work. Force protection. I worked with ghosts and civilians and didn't ask questions."

"Ghosts?"

"You know, the guys walking around with fuzzies on both arms where their insignia should be." Bernt crossed his hands and tapped his upper arms.

Carvalho's face was blank. "You worked with ghosts. But you weren't no ghost."

Bernt shrugged.

"If you was so worried about protecting people when you was in the service, seems to me you would have one medal. But you didn't win no medals. All you got was charges." He slipped his thumb into the folder, flipped it open and slid it toward Bernt. Personnel files. "Maltreatment of detainees. Assault consummated by battery. Indecent acts with another. But no convictions. And you was honorably discharged."

"I was charged with dereliction of duty and served my punishment. That's in my record."

"All those offenses, and you receive nonjudicial punishment. How you explain that?"

"You'd have to talk to my advocate."

"I smell one rat."

Bernt did not reply.

"And I think you're one sick fuck."

"Are you asking me to divulge details of classified operations?"

"All I'm saying is I know what sick shit you stay capable of perpetrating. Whatever deal you cut in the Army, you won't get no deal like that with us. We don't offer no KP."

"I still don't know what I'm accused of."

Carvalho opened another manila folder. He stared at its contents with hooded eyes, then spun it on the table. It was a grayscale image printed on standard office paper. Bernt recognized the wrought-iron chairs and the small table, the pattern of stones and grass. One of the chairs was on its side. A headless specter hovered above the chair. It was Miyake, Bernt realized, his neck unnaturally bent, his face over-exposed by the camera flash and disappearing into his bright shirt, his dark hair printed in the same pure black as the shadows below the plumeria tree. One snaking branch in the foreground forked like lightning above the hanging man.

It would have been nice to believe the black current of regret that surged through him, frothing with adrenaline, had something to do with the life of the man he'd pledged to protect. But he'd known how worthless those pledges were, so the regret, he knew, was a selfish one.

"We know you killed Miyake. We have you on video walking up to his front door."

"I already explained that. Do you have any evidence?"

"We have a fact pattern. You are linked to the death or disappearance of Clifton Moniz, Joseph Silva, and Dennis Miyake."

"And what was my motive for all this?"

Detective Carvalho had been standing. He finally sat down, gathered the files that had spilled from the folder, pulled them together and squared them up neatly.

"That is the question we are asking ourselves. The simple answer is that you are one homicidal maniac, one serial killer." Carvalho tapped the stack of files with his middle finger. "That's what the boys try and tell me. But I never think you fit the profile. I know you had some troubles in the military. But plenty guys got those. You was dealing with some bad fackahs over there. You did what you had to."

He looked Bernt full in the eyes, searching for acknowledgment. "What I say is, when one braddah get sent to hell, you can't blame him for acting like one devil. I think you were trying to do the right thing. I know you're a passionate person. You want to do what's right. And you saw something was wrong. We pulled your declaration form. We know you moved here to work on one organic farm. And we know you were fired for violent tendencies. Then you saw guys was polluting one stream with pesticide chemicals. You saw three boys was killed. So you decided to solve the problem. Those men were putting other people's lives at risk, you were trying to stop them before any more children could die."

The two men looked into one another's eyes for an uncomfortably long time. Finally, Bernt looked away.

"A lot of people on this island might call you one hero," said Detective Carvalho. "We got judges on this island who might be very sympathetic. But it all depends on how we paint this picture. We know you guilty. We got all the evidence we need: opportunity, ability, evidence that you was with the victims. The boys are all pushing me to bring up your history, to lay out a picture of one sexual pervert, one serial killer. But I never like do that. Because I don't think it's the truth. I think the truth is you were given certain abilities, abilities most people never want and never can get, and you were willing to use those abilities against the bad guys. Over in da kine, and right here on this island. That's the story I like tell the prosecuting attorney. That's the story I like your friends and family to hear. I no gonna lie. Murder is one serious crime and there gonna be serious consequences. But your reputation gonna matter to the sentencing judge, gonna matter to the people in the prison, too. And it's gonna matter to the people that know you, that gotta speak for you. But I can only tell that story with your help. Are you willing to help me?"

"Am I under arrest?"

"We wanted to give you this opportunity to resolve things before they got ugly. This is your chance to make things right before we announce one murder investigation and the media gets involved."

"So I'm free to leave?"

Carvalho looked sorrowful. "For now, yes. But as soon as we get one warrant, this opportunity will be gone forever."

"All right then." Bernt stood. "Thank you for your time."

Carvalho came around the table. "Maybe I was wrong about you."

He stepped forward. His belly touched Bernt's sternum. Bernt went completely still, suppressing everything that training, instinct, and three hours of steadily compressing rage and self-disgust were screaming at him to do. What the detective was daring him to do.

Then the detective met Bernt's eyes.

For the first time, Carvalho's face conveyed something other than boredom and disdain. Reflexively, he brought his hand to his duty holster, then stepped back, clearing a path to the door.

Bernt could feel Carvalho's nervous energy slowly diminish as the detective directed him through the halls. They took a different route, through an open-plan office that fell silent as they entered, every officer regarding Bernt without expression.

Carvalho had regathered his composure by the time they reached the parking lot.

"You will be watched," he said, in the sunlight outside the station. "Go to your home and your job. Tha's it. Don't buy no tickets. Don't try run. This one small island, and we all 'ohana. There's nowhere you can hide."

PART II

17

LINDSTROM ALWAYS TOOK an aisle seat, but on such short notice all they had available in business class were windows. For the first hour, the landscape was laid out like a spreadsheet: county roads intersecting at right angles, 640-acre squares of brown and white fields. Benevoment leased thousands. The checkerboard gave way to ranchland. The ranches gave way to desert: striated badlands and boulder-strewn plains. A narrow road ran straight through a dry wasteland to a mile-wide array of mirrors, all focused on a single blinding point of light. White mountains rose from brown valleys and became green plains. Towns converged into suburbs. Suburbs became cities. The pale strip of a long beach. Cloud-shadow on the silver ocean.

Sunlight flooded the cabin and went dark as people shut their shades. Lindstrom leaned back and shut his eyes. It was no trouble fending off the wild stabs of grief and self-doubt. But there was another feeling. Frustration, he'd thought at first, or disappointment, something to do with the canceled EOY and all it could mean; he tried to game-plan the possibilities. But a quick, cold, liquid throbbing swept away each fragile chain of logic. It was an unfamiliar feeling—not the probing scalpel of conscience or the buzz and rattle of stress and anxiety. It was fear.

When the captain announced their descent, Lindstrom opened

his shade. He saw white foam racing up black rocks, a seawall sheltering a small harbor, the runway rushing up to meet the plane.

It took three minutes to exit the airport, its concourse open to the breeze and humidity. He walked past tour drivers in matching aloha shirts holding armfuls of plumeria leis until he found a young Asian man in a Benevoment polo. As they walked through the parking lot, Lindstrom looked from Kipu to the distant Anahola hills, nearly half the island in one sweep.

On the highway, he asked for a briefing.

The young man's name was Kim. He glanced at Lindstrom in confusion. "I'm not sure—"

"Sorry," said Lindstrom, "I forgot to ask what you do here."

"I'm an intern. On break from UH."

"Ah," said Lindstrom.

Kim dropped him outside the lobby of the Grand Hyatt. None of the company condos had been available on such short notice. Everything had been arranged at the front desk, so it was only a few minutes before Lindstrom collapsed onto the crisp duvet. His phone woke him, vibrating in his pocket. It was Casey Hansen, one of the few managers left from Lindstrom's day. She'd married a Realtor and settled into the lifestyle, trading any chance to make a real impact for a lifetime in paradise. A good person to grab a drink with, if nothing else.

She picked him up in a shiny Wrangler Rubicon with oversize mud tires. "It's technically our son's," she explained. "He turned sixteen this year."

Rick Evans was holding a table for them at Keoki's, by the waterfall. Another familiar face, blandly good-looking, one of the countless Southern Californians who'd migrated to the island with an effortless sense of belonging, as if it were just another stop on Route 5. Evans ordered a mai tai and Hansen had a merlot. Lindstrom ordered a vodka soda. The long torch flames reflected in the black water. The easy greetings had been replaced by silence.

Hansen took a long sip of her wine, then looked seriously at Lindstrom. "Dennis made his own choices."

"It's how he was wired," said Evans. "All of us knew it. None of us thought he'd take it that far."

"It had to be traumatic, his old timers going one after another like that."

"The end of an era," said Evans.

There was a moment of respectful silence.

"The kids we hire now," said Hansen, "file a claim if their eyes water."

"At least they stay out of trouble."

"Or wash out quick. Drinking's not a problem with the young ones, it's meth."

"I worry about some of Kai's friends, and they're from good families."

"By the way," said Evans. "How's he liking Island Prep?"

"Honestly," said Hansen, "I'm a little worried about him. I'm thinking it might actually be a good thing if the Chinese buy us out. Chase ran the numbers and we have our eyes on some potential investment properties."

"Condos?"

"Single family homes. We can pick up a nice three-bedroom, convert it into a duplex and clear as much on vacation rentals as I make now. Then I could be home a lot more—"

"Would you have to do the cleanings yourself?"

"At first, but—"

"Why did an intern pick me up at the airport today?" Lindstrom asked.

The mood shifted.

"Only person they could spare, I guess," said Hansen.

"We weren't looped in on that."

"I'd have grabbed you if I'd known."

"I'm asking where I stand."

After a pause, Hansen finally answered. "I think you know that as well as we do."

"I don't know if I'm here to clean things up or get cleaned up."

"Miyake said you were seeing good things out of Namahana," said Evans. "If that's true, you need to lock that situation down. Get the data and make sure you can verify it."

"You're saying it may not be verifiable?"

"He's saying," said Hansen, "the only people who've been in that field the last six months are disappeared or dead."

18

A T THREE IN the morning, the rain came so loud it was indistinguishable from silence. Bernt had taken the time to carve a runoff channel uphill of his bivouac, so he was dry and knew he would remain that way, a condition he tried to appreciate as he lay awake pondering how he'd gotten to this place.

Ever since Momilani asked for help, he'd wondered why she'd chosen him: a stranger on the island, a solitary grunt, a Ranger, good for kicking in doors and following orders, not solving crimes or analyzing intelligence. But at some point, as he listened to the thin, satisfying impact on the tarp above his head, he understood: that was exactly why she'd asked him. She'd known if she gave him a mission and led him to the door, he would keep clearing rooms and kicking doors until the truth turned up in the wreckage. Or he walked into a situation he couldn't walk out of.

It was the plan of someone who'd run out of any good ideas, almost guaranteed to fail.

So why had he said yes?

Because it was familiar.

And now he'd reached the room he'd always known he'd come to. The one with no exit. He felt around the slick, damp nylon of his heavy bag until he touched the precision-molded polymer of the tiny Glock. Despite its size, all he had to do was wrap his hand around the grip and the familiar density and texture made his heart rate slow, soothed by the narcotic promise of a safety so transcendent it could render any pain irrelevant.

He'd driven straight from the station back to Momilani's. The same brutal discipline that had kept him from assaulting the detective in the station prevented him from stopping at the nearest ABC store, picking up a liter of Hana Bay, and finding a stretch of road where he could let the universe decide what happened next. The discipline stemmed from a new development in his reality: what happened to him mattered now. If he harmed himself or someone else in such a public way, Carvalho would see it as vindication. He would win.

But there was no question of staying at Momilani's and waiting for the investigation to tighten around him. Where had he been when Clifton died? Alone with no alibi. Wasn't this what Nalani had said? The cops here looked out for their own people. Bernt was the ultimate outsider. In the time it took to pack his kit and retrieve the pistol from its hiding place, he had decided on his next step. He was under surveillance, so he couldn't use his car. He needed help. And there was only one person he could ask.

They'd met in a waiting room at the VA. Custis had moved to the island a few years earlier, just in time to buy a house before the apps changed everything. Now he rented out spare rooms and beat-up cars to tourists and spent most of his days spearfishing and exploring the mountains with his German shepherd. One night, after they'd finished a bottle of Old Crow, Custis told Bernt about his bug-out spot in the state land above Moloaa. When things went to shit, he was going to pick up his daughter from her mother's and go there to ride out whatever came next. He had supplies for a few months laid in. He could hunt boar in the forest and fish the reefs when it was safe enough. He'd even started an orchard. He spent one or two weekends a month clearing land and building lo'i. He called it Zion.

Bernt had only asked to borrow a car. But when they passed each other in an aisle of the Big Save, he felt a scrap of paper wrapped around the key Custis pressed into his hand. A set of coordinates, Bernt discovered, when he unfolded it in the driver's seat of the old Mercury Sable. On the satellite view in his app, they marked an indistinguishable point in a vast canopy of trees. The nearest access was an unpaved road that proved to be an overgrown utility spur, dead-ending at a yellow gate. He parked by a rusting pickup with a bush growing through its windshield. In the trunk of the Sable, he found a rucksack, a trench shovel, a case of water, and a box of MREs. A scrap of paper was taped to the shovel blade. *Use me.* He filled the pack, lashed the shovel, and walked into the forest.

He followed the contours of the land. A streambed led him to a clearing piled with monumental boulders. Dense and leafless groves of whip-thin guava gave way to high-branched Albizia and wild mangoes. He climbed the ridge, let his knees go loose on the downslope, leaping rocks and roots. In the next valley, a broken branch led to a boot print. From there, Custis had made no effort to hide his traces: trampled saplings, chainsawed limbs.

Bernt came into the clearing. There were dirty stones piled into new terraces and ancient walls of mossy rock that Custis had been careful not to disturb. In one corner was a fire pit with a small grate resting on two blackened rocks. The sky was still bright above the trees, but the shadows were thick in the forest. However he decided to do it, it couldn't be here, and it wouldn't be tonight.

He began methodically walking the most impacted area until he saw four small rocks arranged in a diamond. He unfolded the shovel. A few inches down, the tip struck plastic: the lid of a large marine cooler. Inside were fresh tarps; coils of 550 line; a machete; hunting and fillet knives; snares and monofilament; a magnesium fire starter; a three-prong fish spear; throw net; collapsible rod; seed packets; a .22 rifle and a few hundred rounds. Bernt organized it all and set up his bivouac with care. When there was nothing more to do, he climbed a boulder, surveyed the campsite, and allowed himself to think, for the first time, about why he'd really come here.

Even with the neatly stowed supplies and tight-pitched shelter, Zion looked like nothing but a muddy clearing in the forest. The idea of Custis and his daughter surviving the apocalypse like cheerful pioneers in the big woods seemed laughable, naive, insane.

Above the forest, Venus was a bright point in the fading blue. His own apocalypse, Bernt knew, had already come. Not with the interrogation. Long before that. And gradually. Or maybe abruptly. He couldn't remember. It must have happened in the hazy time after his discharge, or the less hazy time when he learned to stay alive and relatively safe in the civilian world, to make himself invulnerable by eliminating everything he had to lose.

So why not go back? Would a cell be so much smaller than his room at Momilani's? Could doing time be more monotonous than selling outboard motors? If anything, it might come as a relief, to be surrounded by people who understood violence, to be free of the constant, exhausting responsibility of protecting everyone around him from himself.

Birds sang their final songs. Frogs peeped in the stream. No. He wouldn't talk himself out of it this time. He rose and felt in the rucksack for an MRE. It didn't matter which. A meal, ready to eat, not much better or worse than any other meal he'd ever eaten. He'd let himself care about Clifton. And he'd paid a price. But that was over. He knew now why he'd left Nalani's cabin after the search. It wasn't her he'd been protecting; it was himself.

He was still alone, still unburdened, still immune to the apocalypse.

The night's rain saturated everything. But the morning was bright. At eight o'clock, the heat and humidity were already oppressive. Bernt surveyed his camp: the sagging tarp, the cooler beaded with raindrops and flecked with mud, mud that was everywhere, his feet red with it.

He was holding the gun. It was not what he'd have chosen, but it would do. He wouldn't use Custis's rifle. And he wouldn't do it here. If he left everything just as he'd found it, there'd be no need for Custis to abandon this site. It would be simple. He would reward his friend's trust and re-close the circle, walk into the forest and find a boulder, a waterfall, or a quiet pool, a place that once had a story and a name, now long forgotten, and lay his own story there to be forgotten.

He rose and stretched. He felt serene. He looked around the camp with purpose. In full daylight, the site was more extensive than he'd realized. Jewel-green rows of kalo nodded slowly in their loʻi, beaded water sparkling on the broad leaves. Huge gray trunks of Albizia felled and partially chopped, cords of wood neatly stacked at the edges of the clearing. It would take a twenty-inch chain saw to make those cuts. Custis must have humped one in.

This was more than a weekend project, Bernt realized. It was a mission. There would always be another tree to fell, another wall to build, another row to plant. Custis wasn't preparing for an apocalypse; he was preventing one. The hours he spent clearing brush, lifting stones, hauling gas to fuel the saw and laboriously carve away the stumps, it wasn't to complete some perfect vision of a forest hideaway, it was to create a purpose for one more day of living, one more day with his daughter.

Since seeing the picture of Miyake hanging from the tree, Bernt had barely given a thought to what had happened to him, to Clifton, to any of the other men he'd been so focused on the past few weeks. The obvious answer had seemed more obvious than ever.

Now, a doubt crept in. Why had Carvalho brought him in, if suicide was such an obvious explanation? And why treat the other deaths as murders, too? What incentive did they have to re-open closed cases? Why was he the only one assuming all these men had killed themselves?

He was hungry. He chose two MREs from the pack, rummaged for his phone, and turned it on. The rations tasted like shit. As he forced himself to eat, his phone emitted an unfamiliar chime. A direct message from ʻAina Defender. *Sorry for delay. Important meeting coming up. Can you be in Princeville ASAP? MAHALOS!*

19

PRINCEVILLE. BERNT PASSED blocks of time-share condos and million-dollar bungalows with distant ocean views. Landscaping crews in fluorescent T-shirts trimmed lawns as neat as the fairways bisecting the neighborhood. The sidewalks were crowded with tourists pedaling beach cruisers and retirees walking shaggy Labradoodles and fluffy Pomeranians. Even the dogs were white.

In a lawn care uniform, Bernt would have been invisible. Instead, for the first time since coming to the island, he felt the familiar, exhausting friction of life on the mainland: glances lingered just a beat longer than necessary, no one aware of it, except him, and the dogs, of course, who sensed their masters' unease and loyally tracked Bernt's progress with undisguised hostility.

ʻĀina Defender wanted to meet at an açaí place in the shopping center. He warily scanned the crowded patio, but the blond woman in a sleeveless blouse had to stand and wave to get his attention. He sat down, annoyed with himself. He'd been too focused on his own assumptions, looking for someone else who didn't fit in, instead of noticing the only person sitting alone.

The woman was professionally oblivious to his dark mood. She held her arm straight out from her body and shook his hand. "Aloha! My name's Samantha, but you can call me Sam."

"Have we met before?"

She squinted at him uncertainly. "You've probably seen my signs." She tilted her head and smiled wider.

"That must be it."

"I can't wait to hear what you have to share. My background is in Vaccine Truth, but after we moved here full-time from Orange County, the mana of the ʻāina told me I had a kuleana to mālama this sacred place and help make things pono." She checked the time on her phone. "Sorry to rush, I have a showing in twenty minutes."

Something clicked. Samantha clutching a handful of tuberoses. The Spiritual Gangster.

He put his shades back on. "Thanks for your time. I reached out because I had a friend who worked for Benevoment, in the field you've been protesting."

She nodded along. "I wasn't personally protesting, myself. I manage our social media."

"But you work with the father, Jonah?"

"Yes of course. He doesn't really do computers."

"Well, my friend is dead, and so is everyone he worked with. Dead or disappeared."

"So tragic."

"I think it's possible the pesticides could have affected the workers."

Whatever else Miyake had lied to him about, Bernt believed what he had said about the quality of the professor's research. But it was the only bluff he could think of to make his way into the group, and closer to Jonah.

Sam was still nodding. "I believe our board needs to meet you. We're holding an emergency meeting in three hours down the hill at Black Pot Beach Park. Can you make it?"

"I can clear my schedule," said Bernt.

"Wonderful. You and Jonah will have *a lot* to talk about. Aloha!"

It was a perfect day in Hanalei. Far out at the bowl, surfers rode cleanly peeling overhead breaks. Near shore, tourists on rental boards launched themselves into the whitewash. Bernt had come here a few times, with Cass. She would scrub the red dirt off her calves and pull on a sundress. It had freaked him out, how easily she blended with all the other West Coast girls drinking fourteen-dollar juices as they browsed for two-hundred-dollar bikinis. They'd buy American Spirits and a liter of vodka at Big Save, then walk down the beach, past Pine Trees and Pavilions, to sit on the end of the pier, where they'd let their legs dangle and watch the tourists make fools of themselves and the local kids do backflips into the clear water.

The bay was ringed by mountains. In summer, the sun set in the ocean beside Makana, the last green spire at the end of the road. Cass told Bernt that warriors used to throw burning spears from its summit, drifting like fireworks out to sea. She told him about her parents and her older exes and the gap year she'd spent backpacking around the world. She'd come out to do the island thing because she needed to quit coke and get away from the EDM scene. Bernt knew she liked him because he fit an idea she had about herself—a self-destructive raver chick who wasn't afraid to pass out in doorways or get black eyes. But that was already fading in the weeks she'd spent on the farm. Eventually she wanted to mix acid with her guava juice instead of vodka, and Bernt wasn't going there.

It was hard to believe he could look back at any moment of his life and see himself as naive. But impossible not to when he pictured himself kicking his heels over the bay, laughing at Cass's stories about the drunken Australians she'd "done" Bali with, defending her honor from Sam's disrespect at the market, not even realizing that no matter how much they talked behind each other's backs, Cass and Sam and the hippies at the farm and the Aussie college students would always belong to a tribe that would never include people like him.

He'd been watching rental cars drive tentatively through the rutted dirt lot. Now he heard the roar of two lifted pickups. The first flew two huge flags above its cab: the Union Jack of the official state flag, hung upside down, and the crossed paddles of the independence movement. They drove onto the sand and parked a few feet from a pink family laying out on beach towels.

*

The group gathered by one of the picnic tables. Bernt took his time approaching. From the pier, he could see Sam's blond hair beside a brown man's black buzzcut. Jonah.

He had the broad lats, loose shoulders, and veined forearms of a surfer. But his cheeks were gaunt. His shorts hung loose from his hipbones. When he turned to Bernt, his gaze, for a moment, was raw and unguarded. Bernt knew immediately: he was a man capable of killing.

"Aloha Micah!" Sam said, in her professionally cheerful manner.

"Aloha braddah," said Jonah. He clasped Bernt's forearm and pulled him close until their foreheads touched. It was the closest he'd ever embraced a man he hadn't served with.

"We like hear your mana'o, braddah Micah, just get a few small kine agenda items first."

A skinny hippie with blond dreadlocks twisted up into a beehive set a pair of reading glasses on his thin nose and began reading from a spiral-bound notebook. "At our last meeting, the Active Measures Committee gave an update on their recent activities. The Social Media Chair motioned that the group create an Instagram account. Auntie Mai brought in a dead pueo and the board agreed to investigate the impact of GMO on the island's native species."

"Do we approve those minutes?"

"Move to approve," said one haole.

"Second," said another. They were a couple, a man and woman in their seventies, deeply tanned and dressed in the loose, expensive beach clothes advertised in airline magazines. It was the locals who seemed both out of place and eerily familiar: a woman in an orange work shirt, a man in a T-shirt that read DEFEND THE ISLANDS below two crossed AR-15s. They were the type who walked into his shop every day to buy a chain saw or repair an engine: tree-trimmers, landscapers, fishermen. Then the man caught his eye, flashed him a shaka, and Bernt recognized the black triangles tattooed on his arm. He was one of the brothers from the search for Uncle Kimo. And the woman in the work shirt was Auntie Doreen.

The board moved on to New Business.

"We're hitting a nerve," said the haole woman. "The signs are everywhere. This weekend they launched four rockets from PMRF, and I'm sure you've all noticed the recent increase in airborne activity."

They looked up.

"I count at least four confirmed."

"Possible eight."

The sky was still and nearly cloudless. None of the locals had raised their heads.

"What are we looking at?" Bernt whispered to Sam.

"Geo-engineering."

He looked where she pointed and saw two intersecting contrails, rapidly dissipating.

The conversation had moved on. Bernt heard someone say, "No point showing up to one empty field."

"Then we go to their headquarters in Waimea."

"Some of us get jobs—"

Jonah cut them off. "We discuss 'em later. Micah, you ready for share your mana'o?"

"Thanks to you all for having me," Bernt said. "I know you've been, uh, raising your concerns about the work at Namahana field. And I guess you've heard what's happened to the workers there." He hadn't expected so many familiar faces. Sam was a coincidence, or maybe karma, but he wasn't sure about the others. He wondered whether they'd had their own reasons to join the search for Uncle Kimo, maybe even to shadow him and Nalani. He decided to share as little as possible. "I've done my own research, and I believe the experimental chemicals had psychological effects. It may have made them suicidal, prone to violence."

People were nodding. He was preaching to the choir.

"So what you like from us?" Jonah asked.

"I want to share knowledge. You know the field and the person-nel. I thought you might have a list of Benevoment employees who worked there."

"Like you said, they gone already. So what's the point?"

"To hold them accountable?"

"I'll be straight with you braddah. We had call this meeting be-cause even we don't know what we like do next. The field stay shut for now. They say Chinese might pull everything out. So maybe we had win already. Maybe it's time for quit while we ahead."

"One of the workers was my friend. Clifton Moniz."

Bernt watched Jonah closely, but his face was impassive.

"The only one left is their boss, one haole named Lindstrom. But he never even stay on island no more. Last time I seen him was at my boy's funeral. He gave me one card and say for call him any time. Next day he go tell the newspaper I'm one negligent parent and conspiracy theorist. If you think the chemicals had make those guys mahke, I hope that fackah stay sick, too."

Forty minutes later, Bernt sat in the Sable, facing the street. He'd made an excuse to leave the meeting as soon as he could. When he saw Jonah's truck roll past, he pulled out and followed. It was easy. There was nothing strange about one car tailing another up the twisting road to Haena.

Bernt stopped at Wainiha stream and let two cars cross the one-way double bridge from the other direction. Jonah surprised Bernt by taking a left on the narrow road between the bridges. Bernt kept driving, crossed the second bridge, and pulled over. He waited ten minutes before he turned around.

Less than a hundred yards down the road, he spotted Jonah's truck, parked beneath a house raised off the ground on concrete pillars.

He had another door to kick.

20

WHEN LINDSTROM WOKE, the room was still dark. His head was sunk deep in the crisp hotel pillow. It was almost noon in Minneapolis. He pictured a bright, clear day, ice crystals glittering in the snow. He could feel the humid air rehydrating his cold-chapped skin. Easing from bed, he passed his hand between the drapes and unlatched the door.

The beach glowed blue. A flashlight swept across the reef. The temperature was perfect. Stratus clouds, invisible a moment before, transformed the sky into a potholed desert of searing pink, then faded to ash.

*

This time, it was someone from security who picked him up. They passed through Koloa and the bright green valley of Lawai, topped the hill at Kalaheo and descended to the dry plains of the West Side. No more green hills, just long, dusty vistas rising to the gaping red wound of Waimea Valley and the dim heights of Koke'e at the center of the island.

Little had changed on this side since Lindstrom had lived here, since long before that. The same plantation buildings with corrugated roofs. Dusty trees growing above dusty mesquite thickets. The wooden church on the hill. The old Olokele sugar town: two green streets with shade trees and iron streetlamps surrounded by barren red fields. A little farther, the one-room Pakala post office, lonely beside the highway. On this tiny island, geography was compressed. Every half-mile, you seemed to enter a new place with a new name.

They turned onto a freshly paved drive that wound through acid-green cornfields toward a bright glass building. In Lindstrom's time, headquarters had been a collection of territorial-era buildings with deep verandas and corrugated metal roofs. Now there was a manicured lawn and a long, two-story structure of mirrored glass and creamy white concrete.

Hansen met Lindstrom at the reception desk and brought him to a conference room with a view of cornfields and the distant canyon. Three others were in the room. Maxwell, the security lead, gray hair cut high and tight, ex-military, ex-cop. Another white man, about the same age, his potbelly straining his aloha shirt. And an Asian man, younger than the others, wearing a suit.

"You know Alan Maxwell," said Hansen. "And this is Scott Harkness, our legal counsel out of Honolulu. And this is his guest, Chen Jianlan."

Hands were shaken. Maxwell briefed Lindstrom on what they knew of Miyake's death. Nothing official. But his sources had kept him updated on the investigation. Miyake had been found by a landscaper hanging by his neck from a nylon line strung over a tree limb in his backyard. There had been an overturned table below him, from a matched set of lawn furniture. The police had found bruising on his face and torso, contusions on one wrist. They were trying to establish when these injuries had occurred and requested interviews with Benevoment employees about any workplace incidents. Finding pertinent witnesses had proved challenging, due to the significant reductions in Miyake's team, which Lindstrom was familiar with. For the last week, he'd been working almost entirely in isolation, continuing to maintain the fields at Namahana, even doing the spraying himself, according to the logs.

"So they think he was murdered?" asked Lindstrom.

Maxwell opened his mouth, but Harkness spoke first. "They're going through the routine steps when something like this occurs."

Maxwell nodded. "There is no evidence this was anything but a personal tragedy. Though it would be helpful if we could offer any suggestions as to why our colleague would be capable of taking such an action."

The room went silent.

"I know he was under a lot of stress," said Lindstrom. "There were the accusations. And then the protestors. The tragic accidents that befell some of our team members. The strain that put on him, from a professional standpoint, trying to make up for those work hours. And I'm afraid I put a lot of responsibility on his shoulders, too."

For the first time, the people in the room looked at Lindstrom sympathetically.

On their way out, Casey Hansen casually asked Lindstrom if he wanted to take a tour of the fields. "See what we're up to these days. I've got to show around another visitor anyway."

She hooked his arm and led him down a hallway, out a back door toward the industrial barns. Here things were familiar: the smell of dust, gasoline, fertilizer, and the sweet, sharp odor of the chemicals. A man in a cheap aloha shirt was chatting with one of the agronomists. When he saw Lindstrom and Hansen, he stepped into the sunlight.

"Aloha, I'm Marshall. Just flew in from Durham."

"Aloha," said Lindstrom.

Hansen had disappeared.

"I know you used to run this station. I'm not really on the agricultural side of things, so I'm counting on you to give me the full tour. I think they're bringing around a vehicle."

"Sure," said Lindstrom. "Since we've got a second, I'm going to step aside and make a quick call to my team." He felt as if he were asking permission and had to remind himself none was required.

Moving into the shade of the barn, he called Barrett, while the other man watched.

"Who is Marshall?" Lindstrom asked.

"Someone whose questions you need to answer," said Barrett.

"Who does he report to?"

Barrett didn't answer. He'd hung up.

A worker came around the corner in an open four-wheeler. He stopped it next to Marshall and walked away. Marshall sat behind the wheel and gestured for Lindstrom to take a seat. A wide road of bare red dirt ran straight across the fields. A sign said, MINIMIZE DUST. REDUCE SPEED. Marshall obeyed it. The first fields were fallow, acres of cracked dirt with small weeds taking root. The shadow of the four-wheeler ran across the road. Neither man spoke.

They topped a ridge and rolled down the slope.

"Those are maize seedlings," said Lindstrom, pointing at an endless strip of orange netting stretched low across one field. "I'd have to look at the tags to tell you more. It's probably some sort of Gen Two Flox hybrid."

"It's Morzipronone," said Marshall. "All of it. They went full scale last month. They finally settled on the branding. It's going to be GreenEdge. One word."

Lindstrom did not reply.

"How do you feel about that?"

Lindstrom said nothing.

"Who did you call, back at the site?"

"Tom Barrett."

"What did he tell you?"

"Dropped call."

Now it was Marshall's turn to be silent. They continued driving into the fields, up and down the ridges, passing bare dirt, seedlings under protective netting, green shoots old enough to fend for themselves. Maize and soy, maize and soy. The long ridges once hazy with distance now loomed stark and close. The high land lost its shape as it filled the horizon. Marshall stopped on a hill revealing the full panorama of red dirt fields, ridges and valleys, the pale ocean: a straight blue band that seemed to rise exactly as high as the hilltop where they stood.

"Well?" said Marshall.

"Well what?"

"How do you feel about that?"

"I feel disappointed."

"You don't agree with the decision?"

"I don't agree with the science."

"How can you disagree with science?"

"It's not easy to explain," said Lindstrom, "to someone who's not on that side."

"I have an amateur's interest. On a few subjects in particular."

Lindstrom waited.

"I need to know," said Marshall, "whether anything in your fields could have killed those boys."

"We work with plenty of chemicals that could be lethal. But the concentrations it would take to poison an entire stream? That's more than we order in six months."

"Had you ordered a six-month supply?"

"Not that I know of."

"Would you have known?"

Lindstrom began to answer, but Marshall raised his hand to cut him off.

"Think very carefully about your answer."

"Are you asking me whether someone at the site was working behind my back?"

"I am trying to assess our exposure here, and the more I learn, the less I understand."

"What do you mean?"

"I mean this is your opportunity, your only opportunity, to explain completely and fully what you know."

Lindstrom paused to think. He took another look at the land around them. There were no structures anywhere in sight except a distant cluster of houses, just a glittering flare of sunlit windows perched incongruously high on the ridge up to Koke'e, as distant as it was possible for a place to be.

"I don't know anything you don't. I wanted to buy time for the coffee bushes to prove out. I was starving the project, trying to tighten the numbers before End of Year. Then Miyake's team started disappearing."

Marshall was silent for a very long time, looking intently into Lindstrom's face. Waiting.

Lindstrom hated the man and hated that any answer he gave would be perceived as a surrender. He wondered what else Marshall could be waiting for. "Do you want me to talk about the prototype?"

Marshall cut him off with a short, violent chop of his hand. "Of course not."

He turned back to the four-wheeler, but not quickly enough to hide the first emotion Lindstrom had seen cross his face: disgust. Marshall climbed into the driver's seat and stared at the road ahead until Lindstrom took a seat beside him. They drove through the fields, past the barns, to the glass and concrete building, where Marshall stopped long enough for Lindstrom to get out, then drove away, slowly, so as not to raise any dust.

There was a single door at the rear of the building. A concrete path led to a concrete pad, where a picnic table was bolted beneath a sturdy awning, an ADA-compliant corporate lanai. The door had an electronic lock with a sensor. But Lindstrom had not been issued a badge. He pressed his face to the glass and looked down the long hallway. There was no one in sight.

It took him ten minutes to circle around to the main entrance. When he stepped into the climate-control, the sweat soaking the back of his shirt went instantly clammy. He was suddenly aware of the droop in his clothes and the red dust in the folds of his shirt and pants.

The receptionist smiled as he entered. "I've paged Ms. Hansen," she said.

"I'll just walk to her office."

"That won't be necessary. Would you like to have a seat while you wait?"

Lindstrom did not answer and did not sit. A few minutes later, he heard Hansen's heels tapping briskly across the tile. "Perfect timing. We *just* finished setting up your office."

Lindstrom was thinking of something Marshall had said, about understanding less the more he learned. What could that be? Something here on island. What was on island that wasn't in Durham, or at headquarters? He was still pondering as he followed Hansen. But something kept diverting his focus. Instead of allowing one piece of information to lead him to the next until a pattern emerged—the relaxed but forceful application of concentrated daydreaming he had mastered in his days as a working scientist—he was adrift, his concentration dissolving into empty space, disconnected neurons staying disconnected.

Hansen stopped beside an open door. Lindstrom walked in. Through the windows' tinted glass, he could see the barns, the fields, the distant ridges, cloud shadows moving across them; colors muted and contrasts unnaturally heightened. It was like looking out on an alien planet. The room had two chairs, a desk with a telephone and a monitor, a wastebasket. That was all.

"I'm sure you're eager to get back to work, so I'll leave you to it."

Lindstrom kept staring at the door after she closed it behind her. He sat down at the empty desk. He realized what had been distracting him. It was the alarm he'd been fine-tuning ever since becoming an executive, honed to activate whenever a situation was slipping out of his control. How long had it been going off? Hours? Days? Months? He was frightened to realize he wasn't sure. Not because he'd been exerting his will any less forcefully, but because he'd grown used to having less and less effect.

He'd seen colleagues lose momentum: miss a target, then a promotion, linger in the office a few months, sometimes years, finally accept a transfer or quietly disappear. He'd wondered how they endured the unceasing wound to their ego. Now he knew. They didn't.

They simply let that part of themselves go numb, the part that strove so urgently for more, the part that made them human.

Lindstrom understood he'd reached an endgame from which there was no escape. He might have one or two moves left, but even the best-case scenario still included the end of his career at Benevoment, which meant, checkmate, the end of his career.

In the absolute stillness that followed this realization, two neurons sparked, connected. *Miyake's invoices.* They were in this building, Lindstrom knew, filed alongside work orders, application reports, signed certificates of receipt. He picked up the phone, hovered his fingers over the keypad, set it back in its cradle and arched his butt off the chair to pry his cell phone from his pocket. He called Hansen.

"I need to see all the papers from Namahana."

There was a long silence at the other end. "No problem, I'll get right back to you."

Lindstrom turned on the computer. He tried to check his email, but the computer hadn't been configured yet. He stood and walked through the door. At the end of the hall, the intern who'd picked him up at the airport came walking around the corner.

"Ah, Mr. Lindstrom, can I help you?"

"I'm looking for Ms. Hansen's office."

"Why don't we go to reception and let her know you're looking for her!"

The intern turned 180 degrees and began walking back the way he'd come. Lindstrom started to follow, then stopped. The intern took a few more steps before sensing the change and looking back. An emotion, not quite panic, slipped through before he could replace it with a rigid smile.

"Kim?" said Lindstrom.

The intern nodded.

"Kim, take me to Hansen now."

The two men faced each other in the hallway. There were doors evenly spaced along its length. All closed. Lindstrom wondered if the building was always this quiet.

Kim's eyes flicked toward the ceiling over Lindstrom's shoulder. A

few seconds later, Hansen came strolling around the corner. "There
you are! I take it Kim has been leading you in circles? He's a fine
scientist, but he's got a lousy sense of direction. We're thinking about
geo-tagging him to make sure he ends up in the right field."

The intern smiled weakly.

Hansen took Lindstrom by the arm.

Lindstrom pulled it away. "Where can I find Miyake's files?"

"Plenty of time for that. I've got someone you need to see first."

Hansen started back down the hallway.

"In my office then," said Lindstrom.

"Oh, he's already set up in the conference room. It's Harkness."

"Perfect. I'll see him in my office."

"All right," said Hansen amiably. "Have it your way."

A few minutes later, Harkness tapped discreetly on his open door.
Lindstrom rose and gestured to the chair on the other side of the
desk.

Harkness closed the door behind himself. "I've been contacted by
the KPD. There is a detective who'd like to speak with you."

Lindstrom nodded.

"As counsel, I want to advise you that any meeting with the police
would be entirely voluntary on your part. They cannot compel you."

"All right."

"And it is my recommendation that you do not meet with any law
enforcement representative based on the current state of the investigation."

"Why is that?"

"Because, as I said in our previous meeting, it has no merit."

Lindstrom nodded.

"Are we in agreement then?"

"That the investigation has no merit?"

"That you will decline any requests to be interviewed on the
circumstances surrounding Miyake's tragic suicide. If you are approached by anyone requesting a meeting or a statement, you will
decline to answer any questions and notify me immediately."

Lindstrom considered this. "Are you talking about the police?"

"Certainly. Although I extend that guidance to any interlocutor."

"Including Benevoment employees?"

Now Harkness considered his own words.

"If you have any misgivings about any statements you have made or may make in the future to any employee or agent of Benevoment, I advise you to retain independent counsel."

Harkness reached into the breast pocket of his aloha shirt and placed a business card on Lindstrom's desk. "If anyone reaches out to you directly on these matters, call me."

A moment after Harkness passed through the door, there was another tap on the frame. It was Hansen, with a slim Filipino in a black polo standing close behind her. The man who'd picked him up that morning. "Good news," she said. "Your guesthouse is ready. This is Alden Cabral. He drives for us sometimes. He'll take you there."

"I'll let you know when I'm ready to leave," Lindstrom told Cabral. "It'll be a few hours. Casey and I still have a few things to wrap up here at the office."

Cabral glanced at Hansen, who smiled.

"Since you're still so fresh off the plane, we thought you'd want to work from home for the rest of the day."

"I can't waste an afternoon. My team is still prepping for the EOY. I've got to resolve things here and get back to them."

"Of course! But all the same."

Lindstrom waited, but Hansen said nothing more. Cabral waited impassively.

"What about the files?"

"We're preparing them. They won't be ready until tomorrow."

"No need to prepare anything, just bring me to the file room."

"That won't be possible. They've introduced new protocols. I guess we had one too many people put things back out of order. Now they're very strict about access."

"Who is?"

"Who is what?"

"Who is strict about access? The clerk?"

"Yes, well, no. It is the clerk, but the order comes from above."

"Above you, you mean."

"Yes."

"Well that's all right. I'll take responsibility."

"Above you, too."

This is how it ought to be played, Lindstrom thought to himself. There was no apology in Hansen's tone. And she made clear that if he chose to pursue this any further, there would be no more effort to protect his dignity.

As if he had any dignity left to lose.

"So you're saying someone above me has denied me access to files on my own project."

"That's correct. And since Harkness has spoken to you, there is nothing more you are currently authorized to accomplish here at the office, so we are suggesting you rest in our guest facilities until that status changes."

"I still need to check on my team."

"I've been informed their schedules are full, but I believe you'll have the opportunity for a remote check-in tomorrow. In fact, tomorrow is looking to be a very busy day."

Abruptly, Lindstrom extended his hand. Hansen took it. She smiled pleasantly. Lindstrom did not release his grip and did not smile. Hansen held his gaze. She was not the enemy. She was a professional, treading in waters ever so slightly out of her depth.

This was the game. Though that was the wrong term. It implied there were rules or ethics, when in fact it was exactly the opposite. This was nature itself. People called this reality cruel and structured their lives to avoid it. They wanted the wolf pup to grow fat and healthy and the fawn to roam the forest. But you couldn't have both.

21

THE LANDSCAPE PASSED dimly behind the tinted windows of the
Tahoe. They turned on the Lawai Road and arrived at a development surrounded by cane grass and mesquite. Lindstrom thought
he'd stayed in this house before, but the company owned half a dozen,
nearly identical. Cabral helped him carry his things then idled on the
curb for ten minutes before pulling away.

Lindstrom watched until the Tahoe was out of sight. Then he
walked through the house. He found his suitcase upright in the bedroom, his carry-on beside it. It wasn't the first time he'd been shuttled
from a hotel to a guesthouse. He tried to remember whether they'd
ever packed his luggage.

He sank into a sofa. Hansen was right about one thing. He was
exhausted.

His phone rang. An unknown number. 612. Minneapolis.

"I can't talk for long," said Erin. "I'm not supposed to be calling.
I've been promoted. We all have. New titles. New divisions. They've
been interviewing us all day. Individually."

"Who's been interviewing you?"

"Different people. None I know. None from here. Except Barrett."

"What did Barrett say?"

"He said he wasn't supposed to tell me, but it was probably obvious: they are trying to cover something up. Make you into the fall

guy for someone's fuckup. He said the only way to protect you was to be completely honest and tell him everything I knew."

"What did you tell him?"

"What could I tell him?"

"I don't know."

"The more questions they asked, the more I realized how little I actually know what the fuck has been going on over there."

"Over here?"

"Yeah. The island."

"They were asking about Namahana?"

"About Namahana. About some project you worked on years ago, some prototype."

"Barrett was asking?"

"I didn't tell him anything."

"He already knows everything."

"They're building a case against you."

"I know. I've been shut out. They won't let me access any files."

"I have to go."

"You can tell them whatever you know."

"If you need something," said Erin, "find Evans. He owes me a favor."

There was a bottle of spring water on the counter. Lindstrom found a glass and filled it from the tap. The fridge was stocked with food. Grass-fed steak, vegetarian lasagna, premixed salads, Greek yogurt.

He remembered Kim glancing into the space beyond his shoulder, Hansen appearing a moment later. He turned, slowly, leaned against the granite counter as if lost in thought. Where would the cameras be? He tried to look without looking, then stopped himself. He hadn't turned on any lights, fortunately. So they probably couldn't see his eyes. Did he know that? What did he know? He knew nothing. It was unbelievable, a stunning oversight, that he had never, not once, considered that basic competency in the most fundamental skills of survival—concealment, self-defense—would ever be remotely salient to his life. He'd thought he was a samurai because he'd learned to bargain with men in suits. The urge to leave the house was nearly overwhelming.

He remembered his last conversation with Miyake. *Who they going come for next?*

He stared into the fridge. He needed to eat. Finally, he took out the lasagna, read the label, preheated the oven to 425. Then he walked into the living room. Turned on the TV. Muted it. Could they trace his credit cards? Unlikely. Should he call his wife? God no. Who had he met that day? People he didn't know: Chen, Harkness, Marshall, Cabral.

Marshall and Cabral. A fixer and a contractor.

He slid the lasagna into the oven. The information was there, crowding his mind. Facts butting up against one another, jostling for his attention. It would be easier if he could write them down, lay them out and see the pattern. But he couldn't take the risk. The only privacy he felt certain of at this moment was the solitude of his own mind.

He tried to view the situation as skeptically as possible. It was almost unimaginable: something like that being discussed in the boardrooms where he'd spent hundreds of hours. But of course it could be imagined. They'd do it the same way they handed down a fifteen percent budget cut: mandatory objectives with no directives. There would be a "situation" that required a response with "extreme urgency." How many times had he heard some variation of those words? And who had he told himself they were, the security contractors, paid on retainer, who sat in on the most sensitive meetings and never had anything to report?

But not on American soil, to American citizens.

As if that was how they saw Miyake or the field hands.

And if they'd already taken it this far.

He thought of Barrett, telling him to book a one-way ticket.

The timer buzzed. He took out the lasagna and left it to cool.

Walking into the bedroom, he tried to plan. What would he need? What could he take? Not much. More practical shoes. He unpacked the bag and put away his things, doing an inventory as he went. This made him feel calmer. It was amazing, really, how little you actually needed, when it came down to it.

He ate a cube of lasagna, then forced himself to eat another. He rinsed his dishes, placed them in the dishwasher. Changed into a pair of shorts and a long-sleeve running shirt that could be mistaken for pajamas. Brushed his teeth. It was deep in the middle of the night back home, too late to call Char. He rubbed his thumb across the smooth metal of the ID bracelet. He hadn't taken it off since he'd dressed for the EOY. He reached over and turned out the bedside lamp.

An hour later, Lindstrom felt for his wallet and phone and slipped them into his pockets under the covers. He slid off the side of the bed onto the floor. Lying on his back, he put on his shoes and socks, then pulled on a windbreaker from the spot where he'd discreetly dropped it.

He'd thought about crawling out of the house but had no idea whether this would actually keep him out of view of the cameras, and the idea of someone watching him go from room to room on his hands and knees was too humiliating. Besides, it would sacrifice surprise and speed. So he stood and walked quickly into the bathroom that overlooked the backyard. He slid open the window, felt for the springs that held the screen, then pulled them back and pushed it out at an angle onto the grass.

Down the street there was an easement leading to an ancient path, now a bike trail that connected the beach resorts to Old Koloa Town a few miles away. He ran across the backyards, the grass tight and springy beneath his sneakers. He passed barbecue grills and hammocks, lawn furniture, a trampoline. Most of the houses were dark, their owners on the mainland, probably. A few windows flickered with the blue glow of a television. Lindstrom skipped lightly over the hitch of a jet ski trailer. Ahead was the break in the bushes. Then he was on the path. The night was cool. His body knew the rhythm. He ran for five minutes, ten, fifteen. Down the straight path in the moonlight toward the ocean. The gravel crunched under his heels. He felt better than he had in months.

22

I T WAS MIDMORNING when Bernt waded up the shallow stream below the first bridge. Most of the houses in Haena had been turned into second homes or vacation rentals. It had been easy to find an empty one and spend the night on a covered lanai with an ocean breeze.

After a hundred yards, he entered the forest, stopping now and then to work his clothes free from thickets of wait-a-bit thorn. Finally he saw a roof, then a yard. Near the forest edge, two-foot-tall A-frames were laid out in four neat lines. Fighting cocks strutted, clucked, and preened, tied by the leg in front of each shelter.

Beyond were two plywood sheds and a big Coleman tent. The main house was raised twenty feet off the ground on cinderblock pillars. One column was lined all the way up with dried ahi tails, another with jawbones from dozens of boars. Both formed triangle patterns as if the house's legs had been tattooed. Under a corrugated green roof, a truck rested on jack stands, two muddy ATVs on a trailer beside it. Bushy green plants grew out of black plastic tubs. The skunky smell of cannabis. There were thickets of banana trees and short papayas, their tops crosscut to keep the fruits within reach. In a black plastic livestock tank, kalo leaves bobbed from eighteen-inch stalks, perfectly reflected in the still water.

Bernt settled in to wait. Beneath the house he noticed a wooden rack with a quiver of surfboards, an outboard motor lying across two sawhorses, a stack of wire mesh crab traps, hand-knotted throw nets hanging from pegs, and a battered yellow kayak propped against one of the pillars. In the yard was a rectangular hole, the size of a foxhole or a child's grave, a stack of cinderblocks beside it—an imu for cooking pig.

A door opened at the top of the steep staircase. Two brindle hounds trotted out from under the kayak and looked up as Jonah emerged on the landing and made his way down. He unracked two longboards, lashed them to the lumber rack of his truck, lowered the tailgate so the hounds could hop in, then climbed into the cab, started the engine with a roar, and eased forward down the road toward the highway.

Bernt waited.

The compound was silent and still, except for the strutting, scratching roosters. After a few more minutes, Bernt stepped into Jonah's yard, walked casually to the nearest shed and peered into a window. There were two inflatable mattresses piled with Disney sheets, board shorts and T-shirts, a television with a gaming console plugged into a surge protector, an orange extension cord running through a pried-open corner of the screen and across the yard.

The second shed had one double bed, the sheets pulled up neatly. Women's clothes hung from a rack in one corner. There was a cheap, three-door plastic cabinet, a tiny T-shirt draped over the top drawer. In the big Coleman tent was an inflatable mattress and a big pile of bras, jeans, tank tops, and bikinis. A slim metal laptop sat on a plastic foldout table with notebooks and pens scattered around it.

It was a school day. No one was home.

He walked beneath the main house. It wasn't big. Two bedrooms. He saw where the PVC pipes from the kitchen sink met the line from what must be the only bathroom. Bernt climbed the stairs. If he was found outside, everything was fine; he was simply looking for Jonah, knew him from the meeting, but didn't have his number. He reached the landing, then the narrow porch.

No one answered his first knock. He waited, then knocked again. Then he turned the handle and walked in.

A sectional couch. A glass coffee table. A wide-screen TV with the Surfing Channel on mute. The room was neater than Bernt had expected. The stone counters were spotless. The dishwasher worked quietly away. There were a few pieces of junk mail fanned across the coffee table, two remote controls. A polished canoe paddle hung on one wall. He paused to look at a painting—a fisherman, exhausted and alone, slumped in a wooden canoe on open water, oblivious of the ghostly warriors seated before and behind him, paddling on.

"Hello?" said Bernt, then repeated it, louder. He stepped into the short hallway. There were doors on his left and right. He opened the right-hand door. A boy's bedroom. One twin bed. A bookshelf with toys and cards propped across the top shelf. Posters on the wall of boogie boarders on one knee catching crystal clear barrels. A dresser with a photograph of a woman holding a pudgy brown baby. Another of a young boy lost in shoulder pads and a football helmet. A cheap, particleboard desk covered in stickers—surf shops and Japanese cartoon characters—a rolling file cabinet tucked under one side, a laptop open on the desk and a printer beside it. Exactly what Bernt had hoped to find. He left and opened the door across the hallway. Jonah's room. A messy bed, clothes piled on chairs. A gun safe in one corner. He tried the handle. Locked.

He returned to the boy's room. The cards were condolences. The file cabinet wasn't locked. Jonah had purchased neat manila envelopes with color-coded tags. They hung neatly from racks. But nothing was labeled. Nothing seemed filed in any particular order. Mostly there were printouts: newspaper articles, scientific journals, blog posts, discussion threads, much of it out of order. The topics were exactly what Bernt would have expected: Benevoment, Efloxiflam, toxicology, incident reports, the same stuff he'd been looking at. He knelt on the floor, going through the folders feeling the bottoms where smaller items, business cards, could have slipped.

He was trained for this. Not to analyze intel, but to recognize it.

He was tempted to do what he had done too many times to count—in apartments, caves, palaces, farmhouses—dump everything he could grab into empty duffel bags and get the fuck out.

Then he heard a truck pull into the yard. He peered out the window. It wasn't Jonah's. This one had a welded steel cage in the back. Bernt could see snouts and wagging tails sticking through the bars. The driver cut the engine. It was the brothers. They opened the tailgate, unwrapped a tarp and revealed a hog on its back, its stomach flayed open, the head flat in a dark pool of blood, mouth yawning angry and mournful. The two men heaved the pig out by its bound feet and carried it below the house. The roosters cackled. The dogs yipped and whined.

Bernt ran back into the bedroom, took a closer look at the gun safe. There was a dial lock. They'd spent an afternoon on these at Fort Bragg. He held his ear to the metal and slowly spun his fingers. Faintly, faintly he could hear the mechanism inside. But there was no time. He forced himself to step away from the safe and ran into the large room. He didn't remember seeing a knife block, and his memory was correct. About to check the drawers, he heard voices on the stairs, getting louder. He ran into the Jonah's bedroom, closing the door softly behind him. The window was open. He carefully, urgently pulled back the levers on the screen.

He knew how to fall, had done so from a few hundred feet, his chute deploying just long enough to prevent him from breaking his legs. Where would he go? The highway, not the hills. In the hills the hunters would have privacy and time. And dogs. The dogs complicated everything.

The men were in the living room. He could hear them. What would they do? Shower, probably. Would they use the bedroom? A place to change. He swung one leg through the window, ducked, and straddled the sill. He gripped with both hands and twisted his other leg through. Unfolding his arms as slowly as he could, Bernt slid his elbows off the sill. He'd once been able to do a hundred chin-ups. Now he dangled with his arms at full extension, his feet still more than ten feet off the ground. He felt the windowsill bending under the pressure, creaking.

He fell cleanly for three feet before his foot caught a post in the rack of surfboards. His back was the first thing to hit the hard-packed yard, his head slammed down a millisecond later.

23

BERNT WOKE IN a cage. Overhead, green leaves passed in something less than a blur. Occasionally the slender trunk of a coco palm moved regally across his field of view. The cage was in the bed of a pickup. He watched the trees go by and felt the swaying of the truck's suspension on the smooth road. It was a luxurious feeling, to be helpless and in motion, to curl tight into a fetal position and simply wait. It was a great relief.

The next time he opened his eyes, the situation knitted itself together more coherently. He was locked in a cage. He had fallen on his head. He saw himself hiding in the bedroom, camping in the woods, spying from the bushes. He remembered how he used to feel, anxious, wary, angry, and, always, the great emptiness. He watched himself hide and run and spy. He watched himself sit on the bed in the room he rented from Momilani. Night after night.

Things would never be that way again.

The truck was bouncing. His head was bouncing. He was being driven to the place where he'd be shot. Or beaten to death. Or tied up and thrown into the ocean. He sniffed the air, tried to feel whether they were driving uphill or down. But all he could smell was dust, and all he could feel was the hammer inside his skull.

This was not the first time he'd known he was about to die. The knowledge had always come with a feeling of profound detachment, as if what was going to happen next was the most ordinary thing that could possibly happen, which, of course, in a way, it was. But that wasn't how he felt this time. He felt afraid, angry, and disappointed. He wanted to live.

This was inconvenient, given what was about to happen. But it was also one of the most hopeful things that had happened to him in a long time.

The truck slowed, and then stopped. In the calm that followed, Bernt was hit by a tide of nausea.

As the dust settled, the salt smell of the ocean emerged. He heard the rhythmic collapse of enormous sheets of water. A swell was coming in.

An enormous man opened the tailgate. He crouched a little to see into the cage. He regarded Bernt impassively. Then he said something, and one of the brothers bent down and regarded him with the same non-expression. "This guy had break into Jonah's hale?"

"Da fackah think he hurting now," someone else said. There was no discernible emotion in his voice.

Bernt could see the ocean. To the right was a short point, maybe the arm of a small bay. Volcanic boulders stacked out into the waves, a long reef. Heads and shoulders bobbed in the dark water just beyond. The ocean was supremely still, nothing ruffled it or raised even a bubble of foam. It wove in and out of itself, the entire surface rising and falling in broad humps and bowls, like the rising and falling of a sleeper's chest.

A small edge of the ocean reared up against the far end of the reef and unzipped, folding over into a smooth line of foam, no wider than a pencil mark. The disturbance ran across the broad expanse of the inner reef as another, larger corner of the ocean rose and folded in exactly the same way, then a larger corner, a legitimate wave. Bernt heard that one crash softly and watched it roll across the reef just as the previous wave came back to meet it, so the two met and pushed each other into a pyramid that foamed up and toppled over.

And now the ocean was still smooth but rising and falling out to the horizon, so for long moments none of the people in the water were visible. Then Bernt saw the flash of a white board and the long body of a pale brown woman. She tilted down the sheer face of the water, paddled twice and stood. Her arms swung loose to either side. She glided beside the reef with the white foam licking the tail of her board until she dove gracefully behind the face, her board kicking up and following her behind the veil.

Something bigger had risen farther out; it was impossible to properly understand how big until a yellow board appeared on its slope, this time, a man's prone body. He stroked once with both hands simultaneously and the board skipped down until he stood, settling his weight. He was halfway up the face, and the crest still rose above his head. He rode less gracefully than the woman but seemed to travel twice as fast, until he extended one hand into the face of the water, slowing his board, and the smooth sheet pouring from the breaking crest overtook him. First his back leg, then his shoulder, then his head disappeared, until finally only the man's board tip was visible as the wave poured back into itself and the foam crashed wildly and the man emerged from an exhalation of mist as the barrel collapsed.

"Cheeeeeee Hoo!" Someone pounded the plywood above Bernt's head.

The surfer dropped to his knees, then his stomach, gripped the nose of the board, and let the last remnant of wave push him across the reef and out of sight below the red dirt.

"You bettah stay ready for braddah Jonah."

Bernt shut his eyes. He could hear the big waves breaking on the point. The nausea had its own waves. Finally, Jonah walked to the tailgate and peered in at Bernt.

He looked at him for a very long time without speaking.

"Who you work for then?" he finally said.

"Nobody."

Jonah did not respond. Bernt could not see his face.

Jonah walked away.

The next minutes passed very slowly.

Finally, Jonah walked back into view.

"Who you work for then?"

"Nobody," said Bernt.

Jonah turned again.

"Wait," said Bernt. "I'm telling the truth."

Jonah stopped.

"I'm alone," said Bernt. "I'm not being paid. Not for this. I work at Kiyonaga's Small Engine. I'm a friend of Momilani Moniz."

"And it was Momilani who had tell you for break into my hale?"

"I did that on my own."

"'As right you on your own. And now we decide what for do with you."

Bernt was trying to make a thorough accounting of his options. He wished he'd done it already, but it hadn't occurred to him until now, and Jonah was talking again.

"Things go better for you once you tell us everything."

The first option was the truth. The advantage was that it might ease the pounding in his brain. The disadvantage was that they would kill him.

The second option was to tell them whatever they wanted to hear. It was surprisingly effective, Bernt knew from experience. It might cause them to drag things out, to make sure they learned everything they could. It might even cause them to decide he was worth more alive than dead. But these men didn't want information. They wanted revenge.

A third option—

But this was as far as Bernt got, because Jonah was speaking again.

"Why were you in my house?"

He didn't have time to create a coherent set of alternative facts that could stand up to questioning. He had to come up with the most truthful answer that would not get him killed.

"I was looking for a business card."

Jonah laughed. "You like make one appointment or what?"

"I was looking for the card you mentioned at the meeting. The one from the director."

"The fackah that paid you for spy on us?"

"No," said Bernt. And then, through the nausea, the path appeared. "I came here with nothing. I was doing work trade on a farm. Ask that lady, Sam, the Realtor. She got me fired months ago. I never saw her again until yesterday"

"So what you saying?"

"I moved in with the Moniz family. They had a room to rent. Then Clifton died."

Jonah smiled. "You think we had murder him. I seen. From the moment I met you, I seen that."

"I hadn't ruled it out."

"And now?"

"I guess it depends what happens next."

"You never like trust us, but you thought you could trust da fackah on that card?"

"I thought I could get information."

"How?"

"I used to work with detainees. In combat zones. Collecting intelligence."

"You telling me you was gonna kidnap the buggah?"

"Maybe."

"All because you stay friends with Momilani Moniz."

"Because I was friends with Clifton."

Jonah was crouching now, making eye contact. Bernt lay as he had been for the last hour, his head resting on the warm metal.

"Damn," said Jonah. "You the reason that detective brought me in."

"He brought me in, too," said Bernt. "Said I was a serial killer. I never mentioned you."

"Why they think you was da one?"

"Because I broke into Miyake's house and interrogated him."

"You fackah!" Jonah said, admiringly. "What he say?"

"He said it wasn't their fault."

Jonah nodded. "What you think?"

"I thought the work had given them neurological disorders. Or maybe it was a suicide cluster. It happens. One guy kills himself and his friends start going, too."

Jonah nodded again. "We seen it here, in the schools."

"But now I don't know."

"So what killed my boy then?"

"I want to find out."

Jonah watched a wave stand up on the horizon and roll into the reef. "I be right back."

A few minutes later, Bernt felt something cold touch his skin, a bottle of water, flecks of ice still stuck to it. He rolled onto his side, twisted it open, poured some into his mouth, rinsed, spat, took a long drink, closed the cap and pressed the icy plastic to his temple.

"She remembers now. Said you assaulted her over some flowers."

"Something like that."

"You better not come to no more meetings."

The truck sagged as Jonah sat. "I tell you straight, we know Sam guys stay using us. They the ones try make all the decisions, and we the ones they like put in all the photos. But we using them, too. They get the connections. And they show up. Plenty local people say they like protect the ʻāina and stop this pesticide, then you see who they vote for County Council."

Bernt shifted the water to the other side of his forehead.

"Now the field stay shut. But it don't feel like we won. Only more local braddahs dead."

Jonah pressed something into Bernt's hand, a creased and dirty piece of paper. A business card.

"My boys going take you back. I like let you out the cage, but you seen plenty already. This break ain't called Top Secrets for nothing."

24

INDSTROM HAD FORGOTTEN the island could get this cold. He spent the night hugging his knees at the foot of a well-pruned coco palm, half-hoping resort security would shine a light and force him to move on. He hadn't wanted to draw attention by showing up at the front desk with no car, no luggage, and no reservation in the middle of the night. So he'd followed a path to the silver beach.

The palm fronds clattered. Pebbles rattled in the ocean swell. Tiny crabs ran sideways in the moonlight. At the first hint of dawn, he walked the tideline. Others gradually joined him, early risers: shelling, exercising, screwing umbrellas into the sand.

His phone chimed. A 510 area code. Oakland.

If he'd had anything resembling a plan, he might have let it ring. But he didn't even know if it was safe to buy a cup of coffee, much less what to do with the rest of the day.

So he answered.

"Is this Michael Lindstrom?"

"I'm sorry, who is this?"

"I'm a friend of Clifton Moniz. He used to work for you."

"All right."

"I think we need to talk about what happened to him."

"Why is that?"

"Because someone might have murdered him."

"Who are you?"

"My name is Micah Bernt."

"And you're with the police?"

"I sell lawn care equipment and marine engines."

"How did you get this number?"

"You gave it to Jonah Manokalanipo. He gave it to me."

Lindstrom hung up.

He took a moment to gather his thoughts. He hadn't told anyone but Char about going to the funeral and meeting Jonah. Legal never would have signed off. If it was crazy to return this call, it was less crazy than sneaking out and running away in the middle of the night.

He redialed the number.

"How do we do this?"

"Where are you right now?"

"Poipu?"

"You're on island?"

"That's right."

"Can you get to Kalapaki Beach?"

"Yes."

"Be at the Marriott bar in three hours. If you don't come alone, you'll never see me."

Bernt parked near the canoe club and walked along the seawall. The regulars were gathered at the picnic tables under the ironwoods, their coolers provisioned for another day of talking story and playing horseshoes. He stepped into the stream. The cold traveled up his nerves, churned his stomach, and imploded at the base of his skull, where the headache hadn't let up.

The beach was crowded with visitors laid out on towels, their bodies stark white or bright pink, the shadow of yesterday's bathing suits imprinted on their skin. A beach boy in a yellow rash guard supervised a line of people lying face down in the sand. One by one, they pressed themselves up and slid their feet into a surfing stance. A man in waist-deep water pushed two shrieking girls into the whitewash on their boogie boards. Farther out, a couple on rented stand-up boards poked their paddles gingerly into the water.

Bernt trudged through the sand, his slippers in one hand, scanning the crowd on the hotel terrace. He was on alert, but for nothing in particular. Fight-or-flight hormones cascaded into his system, bringing him to the knife-edge: exquisitely, excruciatingly attuned to the slightest threat, whatever it might be. It had taken him most of his first tour to develop this sensitivity, then most of the next to transform it into second nature, something he could toggle on whenever necessary. He wasn't sure when he'd lost the ability to turn it off.

Across from the poolside bar, he stopped and looked to sea, as if taking in the view. The ridges of Ha'upu rose green above the bay. Beyond the jetty, he could see white masts in the harbor. A tug pulled a towering barge into the open ocean. His eyes moved from the barge to the cliff that protected Kalapaki Beach, the row of houses along its heights. He moved his gaze across the beach, to the grass, onto the crowded terrace, a complete sweep until he was facing back where he'd started. No sign of security. No sign of police.

A middle-aged man was at the bar. He wore running shorts and a T-shirt made of high-tech wicking fabric. He was skinny, with veined forearms and knotty calves, a physique that on the mainland meant you were either a well-off professional or a heroin addict. Bernt walked to the bar. The man's composure was impressive. Only up close could Bernt sense how brittle it was. He caught the bartender's eye and asked for a Sprite, pretty sure he'd throw up anything stronger.

"Are you Micah?" the man asked.

Bernt nodded. "Is there any chance you've been followed?"

"I snuck away last night. I haven't noticed any sign they found me, but I'm not sure I would."

"Who is they?"

"Oh, the company, Benevoment. Or someone they hired."

"And why would they be following you?"

"You really think Clifton Moniz was murdered?"

"Maybe," said Bernt.

"What about the others?"

Bernt shrugged.

"And Dennis Miyake. Do you think he really—?"

"Seems unlikely."

"Why?"

"A detective accused me of killing him."

"And . . . you didn't?"

"I tried to warn him."

"About what exactly?"

"I wasn't sure."

"So you were trying to find out what happened to your friend Clifton, and you talked to Miyake, and now you are a murder suspect."

"Correct."

"Do you think I could be in danger, too?"

Bernt shrugged. "Why would anyone want to kill you?"

Lindstrom looked unhappy and did not answer.

"I hope you realize this situation calls for completely transparency."

"You're not recording this?"

Bernt lifted his shirt up to his armpits, turned in a circle.

"I do have a theory. It has to do with the merger. They're trying to cover something up."

Bernt became more cheerful. "What merger?"

"We're being bought by the Chinese."

"What do you mean Chinese?"

"Well, it's a large conglomerate, but it's really the government."

"You think the Chinese government might be trying to kill you?"

Bernt had lost his cheer.

"No, no. I think it would be someone in my own company. There are a lot of people who are going to be very rich if this sale goes through."

"So how does killing you and Clifton make that happen?"

Lindstrom thought he'd come to terms with what he'd done. But he'd never, not even to Char, actually described what exactly this was. He considered putting Bernt off with a lie or a generality. The silence stretched. Lindstrom picked up his glass, put the straw to his lips. The suction of the straw in the empty glass was louder than it should have been. He felt Bernt staring at him. Until this point, they had been on a roughly equal footing. Now Bernt had the advantage. The only way to eliminate the vulnerability was to bring it to light.

"I was lead scientist on this island for fifteen years. When we were first developing the Flox product line, we went through several prototypes before settling on our current formula. One variant went all the way to predevelopment. What you have to understand is we were under quite a bit of pressure. We were racing to replace a pesticide that had just been banned. It was a very lucrative contract with massive bonuses if we could fast-track it. The approval process wasn't as sophisticated back then. It was possible to go quite a bit farther within the law. Anyway, we invested a significant amount of money and actually launched high-volume production of what turned out to be some pretty toxic POPs."

"Pops?"

"Persistent organic pollutants. It's a technical term. It means they don't break down in the environment."

"So . . ."

"It turned out this variant had unacceptably adverse effects. But by then we'd already produced thousands of gallons, and, given the budget overruns already sunk into the project, a decision was made to dispose of the excess volume on site."

"I need you to say this more plainly."

"Somewhere under Waimea Town is a plume of highly toxic, highly persistent chemical waste with the potential to disperse into the aquifer."

"You're poisoning people in Waimea."

"We don't know that. But there's a near-certain chance the EPA would determine the site requires remediation, and the process would be extremely expensive. And of course there would be lawsuits."

"And you were the one who ordered them to dump it?"

"Not exactly."

"Someone told you to do it?"

"Someone gave me a budget to wind-down the project."

"But you ordered it?"

"Based on the budget I was given, only one option was feasible."

Bernt responded with a long look. "So why do they want to kill you?"

"This is a liability that is not on our books. If it were to come to light, it could impact the sale of the company. And there could be criminal charges. So we took pains to care for everyone with any involvement. Some retired with extremely generous pensions. The rest we transferred to Namahana. As far as I know, I am the only current employee who worked directly on that project who hasn't died or disappeared."

"So Clifton worked on it."

"He did."

"But he has family in Waimea."

"Most of our employees do."

"Did he know they were in danger?"

"I don't know."

"Do you worry about those people?"

"That's a complicated question. Of course I worry about them. That's part of my job. We do our utmost to ensure the safety of our team, our community, and the environment. However, everything we do entails risk. It's the same in any industry. How does an auto manufacturer choose between one side panel and another? It's actuarial. There is a value for every human life, between six and nine million, depending on the industry."

Bernt whistled. "In Iraq we only paid out twenty-five hundred."

25

BERNT ASSURED LINDSTROM it was safe to book a room. He was fairly confident this was true, and he badly needed a shower.

Lindstrom lay in one of the beds, listening to the hiss of water behind the bathroom door. As he drifted toward sleep, he wondered who exactly had made the decision. He began with C-suite. It could have been any of them, most likely all of them. Decisions like these were how they earned those salaries. He could imagine just how it had happened, in a meeting to finalize the Chinese deal, someone raising the issue of the Waimea plume, probably Barrett, inoculating himself against his own culpability. They would have spoken euphemistically about a range of options, assigning probabilities. Nothing made a difficult decision easier than turning it into a formula. How often had Lindstrom discussed mortality rates and cost structures with the same detachment they must have talked about him?

It was time to call Char. He'd been ignoring her text messages.

"Michael?" She answered immediately but tentatively, as if half-expecting someone else to be calling from his phone.

"It's me. Sorry. I know I've been out of touch. We're in full crisis mode."

"Michael we've been frantic."

"I'm sorry."

"It's been three days."

"I'm sorry. I've been—It's bad."

"Bad."

"The project is over. I'm out of the loop. They reassigned Erin. They broke up my team."

"Have they fired you?"

"No. Not yet. They won't tell me anything."

"Michael, I know how important this work is to you. But I don't understand why you haven't called."

"It isn't just business it's—" He stopped himself.

"Yes?"

"It feels personal."

"Is there something you're not telling me?"

Always! he wanted to scream. "No," he said.

"I talked to Pastor Mark this morning. He'd like to see you when you get back."

Fuck Pastor Mark. "I'd like that."

Char was silent for a long time.

"You used to be an optimistic person," she finally said. "You were the only man I'd ever met who seemed smart *and* happy."

Lindstrom said nothing, not even to himself.

"But they changed you." She was crying.

They didn't change me, Lindstrom wanted to say. *I changed myself.*

But he was crying, too. Until this moment, he'd always thought that she, at least, must understand what he had done, and why.

Char pulled herself together first. Her professional training; he couldn't help admiring it. But when she spoke, her voice was raw and naked. "Listen to me, Michael. You were a wonderful, thoughtful, caring man when I met you, and you are still that man. I wish all the love and pride I feel for you, that the children feel for you, I wish you could feel that for yourself. For just one moment."

Then she hung up.

Sleep was a swift plunge into a black void. Lindstrom emerged into the afternoon light of the hotel room like a disoriented diver bobbing to the surface. His head felt clearer than it had in days. For the first time since Miyake's death, he considered his situation rationally and without emotion. But no matter how many times he reran the analysis, it kept telling him the most unlikely explanation was still the most logical. Someone had killed his entire team, and they might be trying to kill him.

So what next? If he shared this theory with anyone else, they'd accuse him of having a psychotic episode. And he couldn't rule that out. By definition, his own paranoid delusions would strike him as completely rational. He slid off the bed, felt the hotel carpet on his knees, let his elbows sink into the duvet. But no words came. So he laid his head on his outstretched arms, and, at some point, he ceased to feel alone.

He found Bernt on a chaise by the pool, scrolling through his phone.

"We need to see hard copies of Miyake's files," Lindstrom told him.

"Why?"

"The only things we don't have access to on our servers are invoices and work orders. Those are stored at the Waimea facility. And yesterday they wouldn't give me access."

"Are you saying we need to break in?"

"Not necessarily."

They arrived at the mall ninety minutes early. Lindstrom stood in an open-air concourse across from the restaurant while Bernt wandered among the outdoor tables and tapped the one he wanted Lindstrom to choose. Lindstrom spent an hour sitting on a bench, trying to read a newspaper. At 4:30, he walked in and asked the hostess to seat him at the table Bernt had indicated, resisting the urge to glance up at each person walking by.

Evans arrived early, too, deeply tanned and blandly handsome. He was happy here. He wanted nothing more than to keep exactly what he had. Lindstrom was sure Erin hadn't slept with him. Maybe she had blocked a transfer. A favor big enough to get Evans to this table, but not enough to guarantee his cooperation.

The shadow of a palm leaf moved across the tablecloth. Evans checked his phone, lifted the menu, set it down again, looked around for the server, all to no purpose, nervous energy.

"So how's life treating you?" Lindstrom asked, friendly as he knew how to be.

"Life's good," said Evans. "One kid off to college, another still at Island Prep."

"Still surfing?"

Evans nodded. "I switched to stand-up a few years ago. It's a life-saver for us old men."

Lindstrom nodded. "I never could get the hang of it."

The server arrived and they placed their orders. Silence settled when he left. Bernt and Lindstrom had debated how the conversation should go. Bernt had called for subterfuge, on the principle you never share operational information. But Lindstrom was the expert on office treachery. The goal was to obtain access to records he technically still had a claim to. There was no plausible reason for asking Evans to get them himself or give him access to the building. Lindstrom would have to offer the truth, or something that sounded plausibly like it.

"I asked you to meet so I could deliver some news," said Lindstrom.

Evans nodded, the wariness of someone who knows he is out of his depth.

"Golden Valley is still keeping it under wraps, but I'm sure you've been reading the tea leaves. There's been a struggle for direction. Erin and I did everything we could to protect our product, but when it became clear the company was moving in another direction, we went into triage mode with one priority: protecting our people, making sure you land on your feet. I won't name any names, but there is a lot of envy for our team's success. It may seem strange, but at a certain level, being the best at something becomes a liability. We threaten them."

Evans must have known he was being flattered, but he seemed to be enjoying it. It surely didn't happen often.

"There's a reason I'm having lunch with you in particular. Erin insisted we need to keep you here, on this island. I won't deny I tried to talk her out of it. I told her it was enough to make sure you kept your title and salary; it wasn't worth risking her career. But she persisted, and I'm afraid she crossed a line. Now they're trying to cut her down a notch, dig up dirt on her. And I'm no longer in a position to help, not officially. You've probably noticed some new faces. Those men are going through files at this minute trying to build a case against Erin. I tried to stop them yesterday, but I was shut out."

Now Evans' face was impossible to read. Maybe she *had* slept with him. He hoped so. Otherwise this story must sound wildly implausible. He hadn't meant to lay it on quite so thick.

"What exactly do you need?" Evans finally asked.

"I just need you to put in a few extra hours of work today."

The server arrived and set their plates in front of them.

"You mean wait in the office and let you in?"

"Yes."

"You don't have access?"

"I told you. They've cut me out."

"They'll know I let you in. They can see it on the cameras."

"That's all right. You can tell them you didn't know anything. There's no official reason I can't be in there."

Evans used two hands to raise an overstuffed taco to his mouth. He tilted his head. "I wish I could help you," he said, then took a large bite.

"I'll take the consequences," said Lindstrom.

"Tell me again why you don't have your own access card?"

"Because they're trying to wipe out the team and want to make sure I can't defend you."

"That's weird," said Evans, with something new in his eyes. Was it pleasure? "We all just received our reassignment notifications. I'm not going anywhere."

"Those are meaningless," said Lindstrom. "You know the Chinese are coming in soon. No one can guarantee you anything. Your only chance is to find an ally with influence."

"It was the Chinese who gave us the assignments. Mr. Chen signed all of them."

Lindstrom forced himself to swallow a chunk of raw ahi.

"I'm just trying to help Erin," he said. "I thought you might be interested in that."

"I've been wondering about something," said Evans.

Lindstrom waited.

"Do you remember the first performance review you ever gave me?"

"No," Lindstrom replied honestly.

"I was still an agronomist. You never said a critical thing all year. Then, in my review, you wrote that my work had been deficient. I didn't get a bonus. The next year it was fine."

Lindstrom nodded.

"Why did you do that?"

"Probably a budget thing. They cut the numbers and leave the managers to do the dirty work. You manage people now. You know it isn't personal."

"I've never given someone a review they didn't deserve."

"Times were tighter back then."

"I just wondered how you felt about it."

"If I'd felt anything," said Lindstrom, "I wouldn't have been doing my job."

After Lindstrom paid the check, he told Evans he was going to find the bathroom. He walked through the kitchen and out the back door into a loading alley. Bernt was waiting. Lindstrom climbed into the back seat and lay down in the footwell.

Was this rational or delusional, Lindstrom wondered, to be lying in the footwell of a Mercury Sable, fleeing surveillance by a global corporation? And which answer was worse?

"It didn't work," said Lindstrom.

"It worked perfectly," said Bernt.

Something landed on Lindstrom's thigh. A plastic card on a lanyard. Evans' ID.

"It was in his glove box."

"You broke into his car?"

"I didn't break anything."

"They taught you to do that in the Army?"

"Among other things."

26

I T WOULD HAVE been possible to approach the Benevoment facility on foot through the cornfields. Bernt considered this but decided the risk of being stranded miles from their vehicle was as great as the risk of being spotted and trapped if they drove up the road. Well, not nearly as great, if he were to be completely honest, but he was tired of crawling around in the bushes.

Lindstrom had been able to offer a detailed description of the site's security. He'd just received a report on the current arrangements: cameras in the usual places, a two-man team during business hours, and the standard alarms required by insurance. Maxwell had requested a permanent security presence, or at least the capacity to monitor a live feed from the cameras. Lindstrom had seen the cost estimate and told him to resubmit next fiscal year.

There was no gate or any sign of a camera at the intersection where the private drive met the highway. It was ten o'clock and dark outside. They'd been passed by only three cars since Hanapepe. When they left the highway, Bernt turned off his headlights. Corn grew thick on both sides of the road.

"I think we're almost there," Lindstrom whispered.

"You don't have to whisper," said Bernt. He stopped the car in the middle of the road. "Put on your mask." They'd made a trip to Walmart earlier in the day. Lindstrom pulled a black bandanna taut across the bridge of his nose and donned a trucker cap with an eagle descending from the American flag. Bernt had the same bandanna and a black cap that said ISLAND VIBES above an image of dancing stick figures.

"Get out and walk normally to the edge of the field," said Bernt. "Tell me how much farther we have to go."

The air was dry and cool. Lindstrom took one step, then another. He'd never wondered whether he was walking normally. It reminded him of the time he and Char had taken dance lessons. The instructor kept telling him he wasn't stepping, a criticism he couldn't understand. It had something to do with shifting his weight.

The corn was silver in the light of clouds. He began to worry he would walk right into the parking lot. It felt like he had been walking a long time. But when he looked back, there was the car. Then he could see the parking lot. He moved closer to the corn, so the leaves were brushing against his arm. He walked forward until he could see the entire lot and the building beyond. There were no cars, no lights. The walk back was much shorter than he'd expected.

"It's two hundred feet."

Bernt nodded. He'd left the car running. Now he pressed the gas and rolled forward, drifting wide to the right, almost into the corn, then slowly making a U. Lindstrom reminded himself they weren't robbing anyone or stealing anything. It just looked that way.

They'd decided to go in through the back door, since there would be fewer cameras. Four floodlights illuminated the glass front of the building, but it was easy enough to remain in the dark. Lindstrom followed Bernt's lead, walking quickly but not hurriedly across the short-trimmed grass, making a wide turn around the corner, keeping the covered picnic area between them and the building. A single light shone above the door. They stopped beside the picnic table. Bernt had asked Lindstrom to draw a map of the interior, as well as he could remember it. They only had one keycard, so there was no point splitting up.

Lindstrom had told Bernt what to look for. The records were classified by product and location. There would be a section for Efloxiflam and a cabinet for the Namahana field. They'd debated whether to empty the files straight into their packs or make photocopies. Both agreed on photocopies. Now, Lindstrom reconsidered this decision. It had made sense, to minimize their legal exposure. As far as he knew, he still had access to this building; he could bring in guests; he could review files on his projects. Anything they could do to avoid being charged with a felony would be beneficial. Taking the files seemed like a commitment to a line of reasoning Lindstrom still wasn't ready to believe.

But photocopies would take time. And now that he was about to enter the building, wearing a mask, creeping through the darkened hallways, it seemed to Lindstrom that maybe it would be better to get in and out as soon as possible. His body was telling him to do this faster than he had ever done anything before. It was telling him to run.

"What did I tell you?" said Bernt.

"Slow is smooth. Smooth is fast."

Bernt nodded.

"Maybe we just take the files and go," said Lindstrom.

"The plan is set."

Bernt hoisted the backpack and walked down the concrete path, stepped into the light, and pressed Evans' card to the reader. Its small light blinked green. He turned the handle, then looked back at Lindstrom, who grabbed the straps of his own backpack. Bernt nodded at the sill beside the door. Lindstrom remembered what they'd practiced with the bathroom door in their hotel room. He flattened himself against the wall. Bernt pulled the door open, keeping his body behind it. Lindstrom leaned into the doorway and looked down the hall, dark and empty, of course. He slipped inside, heard Bernt follow, heard the door swing shut and click. Bernt's face was illuminated by the red glow of the exit sign above the door. There was a similar sign at the T, fifteen feet away. They took a right. Another sign glowed in the distance, but after just a few feet, they were in darkness so total it was impossible to make out the doors. Bernt clicked on a pen light and played it over the walls. Their world narrowed to the small circle moving over doors, nameplates, finally settling on a sign, RECORDS. Now the light moved to the card reader, Bernt held it up and again the blinking green.

Lindstrom's hands were sweating in the nitrile gloves, but he was glad for them when he grasped the handle and turned it.

He groped for the light switches. It took a moment for the fluorescents to hum into full brightness. The room was the most nondescript space imaginable: gray walls and rows of beige file cabinets. Bernt tapped him on the shoulder, held up his watch. He'd started a timer the moment before he unlocked the outer door. Somehow, only two minutes had passed. Lindstrom would have guessed ten. It was quite likely they could spend all night in this room and drive away before dawn without being detected. Bernt had given them thirty minutes.

Lindstrom went left, Bernt right. They converged simultaneously on Efloxiflam. The section took up two walls. After five minutes yanking open drawers, Bernt tapped twice on the metal. He'd found Namahana. Each year had a divider, each month its own folder. They'd agreed to start with the most recent documents and work back as far as they could in the time they'd set. Bernt carried November through May to the copier beside the door. He set the first stack in the tray and hit COPY. The men developed a routine, with Bernt stacking the originals and retrieving the copies; Lindstrom refiling each month back into its folder, then returning them to the cabinet and bringing back a new batch. Fortunately, the copier was fast. Lindstrom had tried to rein in the budget for office equipment but had been told they were locked in a contract.

He and Bernt worked well together, despite the silence. This type of physical cooperation with another person was something Lindstrom hadn't had to do in a very long time, outside of executive team-building challenges. There was a soothing normalcy in the ritual of copying and refiling documents. Satisfying, too. It took sixteen minutes to go back two years. The Namahana project had only existed for three. Lindstrom began to hope they might get everything. There were just a few more folders to send through the machine.

Bernt tapped him on the shoulder and held up five fingers. It was their cutoff, nonnegotiable, they'd both agreed. Lindstrom looked at the two folders still un-copied. Bernt looked at them, too. He mouthed two words: *Fuck it*. He opened the second-to-last folder and set it on the printer tray. Suddenly Lindstrom felt very vulnerable, as if by violating their own arbitrary rule, they'd crossed a karmic line. A stack of folders slipped from his hand. Papers spilled across the carpet. Lindstrom dropped to his knees and began sliding them back in. Their edges stuck against one another. He lunged for one that had slid farther than the others. It was the feeling of a bad dream. He felt a hand on his shoulder, looked up into Bernt's face. Bernt widened his eyes, patted the air with two flat palms: *Slow down*.

Lindstrom slid the papers into the folder, carried it to the drawer and hung it by its tabs. Bernt was behind him with the last two folders. He shoved them into the gap. The copies were stacked in the order they'd come out of the printer. They were well over the thirty-minute mark. Lindstrom handed Bernt stacks of paper and Bernt carefully stowed them in one backpack, then the next. He knew it would be heavy but was still surprised by the weight when he hoisted it.

They walked toward the dim red sign at the far end of the hall, turned at the T, stopped in the red light below the exterior door. Lindstrom moved to the side, Bernt opened it, and Lindstrom stuck his head into the night. The air was fresh. The landscape bright. It was just as they had left it. The picnic table under the shelter. Silver ridges silhouetted against silver clouds.

He slipped outside. Bernt followed. They retraced their route around the building, back to the car, and drove with lights extinguished. The highway was clear. Bernt flipped the headlights and turned left. They reached the hotel before midnight, using a side door and taking the stairs. In their room, Bernt carefully unpacked the two bags, stacking papers on the desk. They stuffed their hats, bandannas, and clothing into the backpacks. The gloves were in a receptacle outside a gas station. Bernt left with the two packs and returned half an hour later, empty-handed.

27

LINDSTROM KNEW THIS work would be mind-numbing and might take days, but he was looking forward to it. Early the next morning, he cleared everything from the desk except the stacks of copier paper. He opened his laptop and started a new spreadsheet, with columns for man-hours, agricultural inputs, facility expenses. He needed to establish a baseline to get a feel for how things added up. He'd seen the financials for the last few months, but when he saw just how few hours had been logged, how few men there'd been to log them, he appreciated viscerally how decimated the team had been. Miyake had struck him as almost hysterical over the phone. Now Lindstrom realized that, if anything, he'd been understating the challenge.

When he reached the first Good Neighbor report to the Department of Agriculture, he started a new column for Restricted Use Pesticides. For the first time in days, he thought about the dead boys. It occurred to him that all his certainty about Benevoment's innocence rested on reports he'd received in Golden Valley. He had no idea of the facts on the ground.

Bernt took a mug of coffee out to the pool area and lay on a chaise. The first sips of caffeine spiked his headache, but after that it subsided to a low throb. He wondered if he could get away with smoking a cigarette.

His phone dinged.

Nalani had texted him two days earlier, when he was still in the woods. The message reminded him he'd been a college student just a few days before. It had seemed like a joke at the time, now it was a total delusion. She had texted him three times since. This was the fourth.

Hey just want to make sure everything's all right.

He slipped his phone into the pocket of his shorts, boosted himself from the chaise, and walked down to the beach. He shook out an American Spirit, lit it, and watched a man hurl a tennis ball into the waves for a graying black Labrador. When he finished the cigarette, he took out his phone and typed, *I'm fine.*

It dinged before he reached the hotel. *I want to see you.*

Fuck, thought Bernt. He wanted to see her, too.

Back in the room, he cleared one bed and spent the next hour carefully stacking papers under Lindstrom's direction, each stack neatly perpendicular to the other. Lindstrom barely looked up. He was in some sort of mathematical trance, scanning pages and typing on his laptop with a speed and focus Bernt associated with cleaning a firearm.

The two men worked in silence. Lindstrom got up and took a new stack from the ones Bernt had laid on the bed. Finally, Bernt squared the corners of the last three months and set them on the mattress. He'd had to pile all the pillows on the other bed.

"I found something," said Lindstrom.

Bernt walked over to the desk.

"It's the leasing payments. The Namahana project was on private land. We were making monthly payments. But they're not nearly what they should be. It's just a token amount."

"So who was responsible for negotiating the lease?"

"Normally that would be handled out of the main office. But

Namahana was a special case. We were looking for very particular growing conditions, and I sent Miyake to find the land and work it out. He developed the site personally."

"So who owns it?"

"The payments are going to an LLC. I haven't found the lease documents yet. It's one of the big landowners, if I remember right. From one of the old missionary families."

"Do you have any idea how Miyake would get a deal like that?"

"Personal connections, maybe. But in that case I think I would have known about it."

"Maybe he was paying them off some other way."

Lindstrom shrugged. "I'll keep looking."

Nalani already had a table at the Starbucks. Bernt ordered a Venti black and joined her.

"Dr. Higa misses you," she said.

"I doubt it."

"It's true," said Nalani. "He asked me why you dropped out."

"I didn't drop out."

"Oh really?"

"I just stopped going."

"Because of your investigation?"

"Among other things."

"But you're still trying to solve the big mystery?"

"Yeah, I guess. I've got a lot going on right now, to tell you the truth."

Bernt was not very comfortable with this conversation. But it felt good to hear her voice, to watch her raise her iced coffee and take a long sip.

"You hanging or what?"

"I haven't had a drink all week."

She forced a smile. "Now I'm worried."

"Maybe I'm coming down with something."

She still looked skeptical, but let it go. "You really think that man was murdered?"

"Which man?"

"Your uncle. The man you lived with."

"Clifton."

"I asked around. Everyone says he drowned."

"Maybe someone drowned him."

"You just seem like a very level-headed person."

"You don't know me that well."

"I don't think you want anyone to know you."

"There's a reason for that."

Nalani calmly met his eyes. "I know plenty guys who like to scrap," she said. "You're not like them."

"Only sick fucks enjoy killing," said Bernt. "But everyone enjoys combat."

"What's the difference?"

"Imagine conducting an orchestra, but instead of a little stick, you have a .50 cal."

"So you miss it?"

"Of course. Greatest weapon ever made."

"I mean combat."

"I miss how good a cigarette tastes when it's over."

"So why did you leave the military?"

"There was more to it than combat."

"And you're hoping your 'investigation' will end in a gunfight or what?"

"I hadn't thought that far ahead, to be honest with you."

Nalani said nothing.

"I didn't leave the Army because I didn't like it. I left because I liked it too much."

"Why do you keep trying to convince me you're a bad person?"

"I just want you to have an accurate assessment."

"Well my assessment is that you got caught up in some really fucked-up situations."

"Yeah, and I happen to be very good at operating in fucked-up situations."

"So now you go out and find them."

"They find me. It's my special gift."

"You didn't have to join the military. You didn't have to take on this detective thing."

"No, I could have stayed in Oakland and shot up stash houses. Or I could have shot myself in the head."

Nalani put her hand on Bernt's arm. Bernt wanted to pull it away, but didn't.

"To be perfectly honest with you, the only time I give a shit about being alive is when I think I'm about to die." He hated talking this way. He knew he was about to get very, very angry.

"I need a minute." He stood up, stepped into the sunlight, crossed the street into the shadow of the pet store, and lit a Spirit.

Nalani crossed a moment later, held out her hand. He tapped another out of the pack.

"You keep saying you're a stone killer, but you can't even sit still long enough to finish your coffee."

Bernt squinted at the bright façade of the shops across the parking lot.

"And I don't know why you keep telling me you're an asshole. Trust me, it's obvious."

Bernt kept staring impassively, but now something was twitching in his cheek.

"If you don't want me to like you, that's fine. But if you're going to keep texting me, you better quit being such a panty and get over yourself. 'Cause if you need to be somebody's rescue case I got plenty people way more fucked up than you to take care of first."

Bernt said nothing. The twitch had turned into a full-blown smile. She was master of her emotions; he'd lost control of his. But somehow it was all right.

They stood side by side, smoking their cigarettes in a narrow band of shade, the sunlight hammering the sidewalk just beyond their slippers. Sweat broke out on their shoulders, ran down and mingled on the hot skin where her arm pressed tight to his. He extended his fingers, and hers found their way into his.

He ground out the butt of his cigarette under his slipper. "I may be out of pocket for a few days. I've got to go check something on the property where Uncle Clifton used to work."

He'd turned and was about to kiss her, but the way she suddenly pulled her arms close made him stop. He watched the emotions pass across her face like cloud shadow over the hills: longing, confusion, foreboding.

All the same things he was feeling.

He looked at her as he climbed into his car, lifted his hand before turning the corner. She kept staring, her arms held tight, her face blank with the same inscrutable expression he'd seen a thousand times from tea stalls, goat trails, village lanes, and highway shoulders, the look of someone who hadn't decided—or didn't have the luxury of choosing—whether to wave at you or spit in your face. The same expression, he realized, that people saw when they looked at him.

Nalani Winthrop, Bernt thought to himself. Against all odds, he was beginning to think this might be something he wouldn't ruin.

28

LINDSTROM WAS KNEELING on the floor beside the bed when Bernt walked into the room, a grid of papers laid out in front of him.

"I found something else."

The papers formed a topo map of the entire island. It was possible to make out individual valleys, but only the rivers and the largest streams were labeled, along with a dozen red dots.

"I'd forgotten all about this," said Lindstrom, not looking up. "Some professor was going to test the water quality in streams all over the state. We never found out until DLNR had already approved it, and he had his meters set. Look at this one." He pointed to a mark in the northeast corner of the island. "That's downstream from Namahana."

Bernt knelt down beside Lindstrom and looked more closely.

"It turned into a huge headache. We tried going directly to DLNR, but they wouldn't withdraw the permits. So we drafted up a bill for one of our state senators to create an oversight panel on permits in sensitive areas. But that would take months to pass. So I set up a meeting with the university president and explained our concerns. They ended up finding an issue with the guy's institutional review process and called him up for a reprimand. He left for a position on the mainland. But I don't think he ever removed the meters. Our file contains the professor's IRB proposal, and it goes into detail about the technology. Apparently, they're a passive solar model that can collect data for years."

"Are you telling me you *were* dumping stuff into this stream?"

"Of course not. We don't 'dump' anything. The industry standards for applying and disposing of restricted use chemicals are extraordinarily high. Unnecessarily high, to be honest. You wouldn't believe the amount of time our people spend on regulations and requirements, federal, state, county. We adhere to the science on these subjects. That's the whole point. You have these activists calling themselves academic researchers who use federal money to advance political agendas. It didn't matter what those meters found. He was going to take whatever he got and find a way to spin the numbers so he could argue streams are being poisoned. Decades of research could show something is completely safe up to fifty parts per million. He'll find five ppm and the headline will be 'Deadly Chemical Found in Local Stream.'"

"So if there's nothing in the water, why are you telling me about the stream meters?"

"According to procedure there should be nothing in the stream. But I've gone back two years, and I can tell you there is a definite discrepancy between what Miyake was reporting to me and what is in these papers. So far, I've only found it in the financials. Eighteen months ago, our leasing payments fell a few thousand a month. He seems to have covered it up by ordering extra ag inputs to taper off the drop in budget. I can't find any items in the invoices that don't obviously belong. But I do have to wonder about the quantities. These chemicals are completely safe at normal usage levels, but of course excessive dosages can be harmful."

"So he lied to you about how he was reducing expenses?"

"He led me to believe he was instituting across-the-board cuts."

"Why would he do that?"

"He was under a great amount of pressure to reduce costs."

"From where?"

"From me."

"He must have been employee of the year."

"I told him it wasn't enough."

"So he made a deal to save his job."

"I wouldn't put it quite like that."

"And we don't know what the deal was."

"That's right."

"And all the people who might know are dead or disappeared."

Lindstrom gathered the papers that formed the map, then looked at the piles of paper all over the room. "Checkout's in an hour."

Momilani was with her niece at the fence line. The little girl was pressing papaya skins gingerly through the wire. The goats on the other side stretched their long necks forward to nibble the peels with their big square teeth.

Anuhea was absorbed in the task. Her aunt watched the two men come down the hillside. When they were fifty feet away, she rose from her haunches, her muumuu falling around her strong calves. She said something to her niece and walked slowly up the hill to meet them.

Spreading her arms, she gave Bernt a profound hug. After a once-over she gave Lindstrom a more restrained hug with a peck on the cheek.

"We got your flowers," she said. "They were very nice."

Lindstrom hadn't known about any flowers. He silently thanked Neeka.

"We made some progress," Bernt told her. They were on the lanai in the plastic chairs. Momilani had brought glasses of iced tea. "We need to visit the site, go up in the hills."

"So you think it had something to do with their work?"

"We don't know yet," said Lindstrom. "But something up there might tell us."

"On the mountain?"

Bernt nodded.

"You need to go see Uncle Joe."

Momilani poked at her phone, then put it to her ear. "Ho, Joe. This Momilani. How you stay? Yeah you! Shoots. Listen. I get two braddahs like try find something over mauka. 'As right. Namahana side. They t'ink might help 'em find da guys had make Uncle Clifton mahke. Shoots. Raja dat. I tell 'em then. Mahalo braddah."

She turned to Bernt. "He says you're very welcome to go see him. And he would be delighted to show you his maps."

Uncle Joe lived outside Kilauea. Bernt turned off the highway and drove the Sable past miles of manicured shrubbery and gated drives. The road turned to gravel as it approached the lowest slopes of Namahana. Here the houses were more dilapidated, with rot spreading up the plywood walls, vines growing over old farm equipment. But Uncle Joe's house, when they found it, was neatly tended, with a freshly mowed lawn and a stone lantern beside the flagstones leading to the front door.

"Come in, come in," said Uncle Joe. "I lay out my maps already."

Bernt remembered him from the search for Uncle Kimo. An old Japanese man, stooped, tan, and wiry. His strength was evident when he cupped each man's hands in his own. He spoke slowly and walked lightly.

The table was covered with topo maps at a scale that delineated every valley and knob. Black rectangles marked the locations of buildings. The maps were dated from the 1950s and they were covered with bright marker lines—yellow, red, green, orange, purple. Most followed streams or rivers downhill through the valleys. But some inexplicably crossed tall ridges, often following paths unnaturally straight, as if laid down by a ruler.

"You like my maps?"

"What is this?" Bernt asked, tapping a straight line running through a steep ridge.

"Irrigation tunnel. I used to oversee 'em for the plantation. You could walk those ditches in white socks and never need wash 'em. Now most of them stay forgotten. These maps may not be perfect, but they the best there is."

"Our fields are here." Lindstrom tapped one map.

Uncle Joe leaned over. "Winthrop land."

Bernt saw Nalani pulling away from him.

Lindstrom took his own maps from the bag. "We need to find something that was placed in a stream right here." He pointed to the red sticker.

Uncle Joe pointed to a place where three valleys came together. "This area very tricky. Drains south, not east, because of this ridge, called Kamoʻokoa. Some of these ditches very ancient. But there are modern ones too, and just as good. Tongans fit rock even better than the Menehune."

"We are looking for a scientific instrument placed in the stream a few years ago. Can you show us how to find it?"

"Yeah, but you cannot reach it from the road above. It's one slot canyon that. They used it as one reservoir. You have to walk in from below. Unless you get one chopper."

"We have to get there," said Bernt.

Uncle Joe looked at him. "Then I like go with you. This old man needs stretch his legs."

29

WALKING THROUGH THE door for the first time in days, Bernt saw his bedroom through a stranger's eyes: gear lined up in the corner, clothing stacked neatly on the floor, a few pans and a single bowl on the counter by the stove. He started making piles from a checklist in his head. The headaches from his fall were finally easing.

Uncle Joe had said it would take three days to walk into the valley, find the instrument, and come out. Bernt packed for five, beginning with the most important item: socks. He couldn't have Lindstrom stumbling around with soggy feet, developing blisters, foot rot, staph. He chose T-shirts, board shorts, pants, long underwear, a fleece jacket, then packed his bivy kit: tarp, 550 cord, the sleep system. He threw in a roll of one-hundred-mile-an-hour tape, Marriott toilet paper and bar soap, aluminum pots, a cookstove that screwed into a pressurized gas canister, a spoon.

He turned to more specialized equipment: lensatic compass, signal mirror, fire starter, two Bic lighters, bag of matches, iodine tablets, a long knife. From a cardboard box he removed ten MREs. From the shelf under his stove, five cans of lentil soup and five packets of dry gravy. From a box below his bed, lickies and chewies: two packs of cigarettes, three cans of dip, a bag of Australian licorice. He considered for a moment, then tossed in six packages of Kalamansi Pancit Canton.

Finally, he double-checked his med kit: Band-Aids, alcohol wipes, gauze rolls and pads, waterproof tape, QuikClot, a folded SAM splint, burn dressing, tourniquet, wound irrigator, and a plastic tube that could be inserted down someone's nose to maintain an open airway.

Pondering the remaining nonessentials, he estimated his pack would weigh about sixty pounds, light by military standards. He packed his woobie, a lightweight poncho liner. They might make camp at higher altitudes, and it could save a life if someone fell into a stream.

The last thing he put into the bag was Miyake's Glock.

*

At home, Lindstrom had a garage full of ultralight, windproof, breathable, ripstop, ventilated, hydration-reservoir compatible, dual-layer laminated, high-visibility, telescoping, ergonomic, puncture-resistant, shock-absorbing, seam-taped, microporous, breathable, waterproof camping gear he used once or twice a year on trips up north. But he was taking a minimalist approach to this expedition. Momilani was donating a few of her husband's warm layers. Bernt and Uncle Joe said they'd make sure he had something to sleep under if it started to rain.

Now he was in the kitchen helping Momilani make mac salad.

"Your boy and girl," she said. "They must be in high school now."

He nodded. "Both playing hockey, if you can believe it."

Momi laughed. "I remember Saturdays at Salt Pond, two blond heads and brown from forehead to toe."

"It wasn't easy on them, moving. But they adjusted. I won't be surprised if they end up back in the islands. It's too late for them to be great skaters, that's for sure. They try to make up for it with stick-work, but—"

Momi laughed. "Don't talk to me about ice hockey. Nothing could get those two out of the water."

Lindstrom smiled. "Except Clifton's smoke meat."

Both fell silent.

"And how about you," Momilani said. "How do you like it in the big office?"

"I adjusted too, I guess."

Momilani turned to him. "What do you think happened to Clifton, to all them?"

Before Lindstrom could answer, Bernt walked in. He was in an excellent mood.

"Eat a hot meal and get a good night's sleep," he told Lindstrom cheerfully. "It may be a while before you get one again."

Later, Bernt and Momilani sat on the lanai, the hills dark voids against the constellations.

"What do you think of that man?" she asked.

"Hard to say. He reminds me of certain colonels. They could be assholes, but they were the ones you wanted to be serving under when things went to shit."

"I never knew him well. His keiki and his wife were always friendly. He was more standoffish. Maybe that was how he was with everybody."

"Did he care, about Clifton and the other men?"

Momilani shook her head. "He cared about his work, I know. He always wanted to do things well. Sometimes that drove Clifton crazy, but I think he took pride in it, too."

"We're going to find out what happened."

"I know you will."

"And if they're responsible, we'll shut them down."

"The company?"

"That's right."

"You cannot."

"I think we can. If we find the evidence we're looking for."

"My cousins in Waimea, they still work there. Plenty people do."

"You're saying you don't want to hold Benevoment accountable?"

"I'm saying those are good jobs, especially for that side. If you shut them down, you punish everyone."

"You asked me to do this. Now you sound just like them."

Momilani was silent in the darkness.

PART III

PART III

30

SUNRISE WAS STILL forty-five minutes off when they parked beside the vintage pickup idling at the Shell station. Uncle Joe wore a red and black plaid jacket over a hooded sweatshirt. To Lindstrom, he seemed much older than he had the day before. A tiny, bowlegged man, bundled up against the tropical morning.

"Chilly da air," Uncle Joe said happily. "Good day for get some exercise!"

Bernt stretched and nodded. There seemed to be an inverse correlation between Lindstrom's comfort level and Bernt's mood.

He followed the other men into the gas station, where they bought coffee and plastic-wrapped Spam musubi. Uncle Joe had told them the road was no good, so they left the Sable across the street from the gas station and sat three across in the truck. Lindstrom ate his musubi and tried to keep his knees clear of the shifter. Childhood again. Hunting season. Driving dark state highways with fried egg sandwiches wrapped in tinfoil. The mystery of the journey slowly lifting as darkness gave way to dawn's half-light: pastures and aspen stands, then the long, unbroken boreal pine forest. The musubi was delicious: greasy salted meat and warm white rice. In all the years he'd lived on the island, Lindstrom had never tried one.

Uncle Joe hit the Toyota's blinker. Lindstrom watched their headlights sweep the tall grass by the road, revealing a padlocked cattle fence. Uncle Joe got out and fiddled with the lock in the glare of the headlights. When it sprung open, he pulled back the chain and pushed the gate open. Bernt hopped out to pull it shut behind them. "Be sure and lock," Uncle Joe told him.

They drove for twenty minutes on the rutted track, heads bouncing occasionally into the sagging upholstery on the ceiling. Then the road grew wider and ended abruptly at a line of rocks.

Lindstrom asked to carry his share of gear, but when Bernt handed him the pack, it was suspiciously light. He watched Bernt grunt as he hoisted his own, twice as large, from his knee onto his back. A few feet away, Uncle Joe was sliding another large pack off the open tailgate. It was the kind Lindstrom had owned in college, state-of-the-art in 1978, with aluminum stays and space to attach a rolled sleeping bag and tent. Uncle Joe adjusted the straps, ignoring the waist belt, then slid a padded case out of the truck bed, reached into the unzipped top, and hoisted out a hunting rifle, which he slung over one shoulder.

He spread a map across the tailgate and pointed to a squiggle in a mass of squiggles. "We stay right here. Da kine stay somewhere up here." He pointed to another squiggle. "He set it high, da buggah. Probably use one helicopter. The company fields stay here, across this ridge. They get two tunnels, one upstream, one down, so they can divert water to this valley when they like store for later. They control it with one dam. The meter stay between the lower tunnel and the dam."

"Show me that peak on the map," said Bernt, pointing toward a gray summit.

Uncle Joe put his finger on a nest of concentric lines.

"And this one." He pointed at a different spot.

"If we get separated," said Lindstrom, "what do I do?"

"Find the tallest mango tree and climb 'em," said Uncle Joe. "When you see the ocean, try remember which side it stay. If you find a stream, see where it go."

"And if I get turned around?"

The old man shrugged. "Shout, I guess. Don't worry, we come look for you."

He slammed the tailgate and fixed two latches that held it to the frame. "We go."

Hitching his shoulder to slip the rifle strap higher, he turned his back and walked toward a gap in the boulders, his hand cupped under the butt of his rifle. Bernt followed. Lindstrom swung into place behind them.

The three men walked through a humid tunnel of tangled grass. The trail was a washed-out rut with mud in the deepest places. Half an hour after the sun rose, Lindstrom was sweating through his shirt. Young grass bent into the trail and swished lightly against his legs, eventually raising red welts. Every few minutes, a rooster screamed.

Eventually the ground became steeper until the grass ended at a forest. They passed between two rotten fenceposts, held up by rusted wire emerging from the bark of nearby trees. The forest was cooler, the floor covered in dead leaves and brush. Sometimes they passed under a gnarled mango and walked across a spongy layer of fallen fruit and dried pits, a humming mist of flies lifting with each step.

Uncle Joe stopped when they reached a stream, little more than a trickle beneath tumbled boulders. Leaning his rifle against a tree, he unslung his pack, took out a bottle of spring water, and offered some to Lindstrom. "When I was one boy, we had catch prawns here. Big fackahs, long as your forearm."

"In this stream?" asked Lindstrom.

"Was bigger then. They weren't diverting so much water. Flowed clear too, no matter how hard da rain."

"Were they all like that?" asked Bernt. "The rivers?"

"They was all clear then, and never brought no mud into the bays, neither."

"What changed?"

"Monocultures," said Lindstrom. "You see how open this forest is beneath the canopy? It's all invasives: octopus tree, strawberry guava, java plum, mango. They kill the understory, and the bare soil can't hold the rain."

"The forest changed," agreed Uncle Joe. "But not all of it. You'll see."

He shouldered his pack, tightened straps, picked up his rifle by its stock, and wandered slowly into the trees.

The trail disappeared. Sometimes Lindstrom thought he saw it clearly, but Uncle Joe would walk right past, following a course only he could discern. Bernt walked with both arms hooked on the straps of his pack, staring at the ground a few feet ahead.

"What are you thinking about?" Lindstrom asked.

"Absolutely nothing."

They were making such good time through the forest, Lindstrom wondered how far the stream meter could be. Maybe packing for a night in the mountains had only been a precaution.

They reached the banks of a larger stream. Uncle Joe was already hopping across, but Bernt halted. "Can you do that?" he asked.

"Yes," Lindstrom answered.

Bernt looked unconvinced. He watched Uncle Joe sit and slide down the last boulder onto the opposite bank.

"It would be good to keep our feet dry," he said. "You go first."

Lindstrom stepped carefully onto the first rock. He felt cold water misting on the hairs around his ankle. He shifted his weight and aimed his foot for the next rock, a larger one. He found his rhythm and leapt from one rock to the next until his feet touched the mud on the other side. He turned in time to see Bernt step awkwardly and slip down the face of a slick rock, waist deep into the stream.

Bernt grimaced—then smiled—and waded the rest of the way. "Better way to go," he said. "No broken ankles."

Resting his pack against a root, he sat down beside it, unlaced his boots, and turned them upside down to drain the water. He folded the soles against themselves and squeezed as much as he could, then

peeled off each sock and wrung it out. His feet were white and puck-
ered, the skin already red in a few places. From one of the pockets
in his pack, he pulled a thickly balled pair of fresh black socks. He
tucked the wet socks under one of his pack straps.

Finished, he jumped to his feet, and shouldered his pack. "You
wouldn't believe how many missions fail because one guy doesn't
take care of his feet."

Uncle Joe laughed. "I seen more missions fail because everyone
got shot."

"I'd rather get shot with dry socks on."

The old man turned toward the forest. The leaves were denser
here, limbs crisscrossing in every direction. "No get stuck in da hau
bush," he said as he grabbed a horizontal branch, chest high, and
hoisted himself onto another branch, diagonal to the first. He used
one branch as a rail and walked step-by-step across the other, balanced several feet off the ground. He hoisted again and repeated the
same maneuver, six feet up now.

"You next," said Bernt.

It took the men three hours to cross the hau. It was easier to go
up than drop down, so it wasn't uncommon for Lindstrom to find
himself ten feet or more off the ground. When the hau thinned,
they had to clamber awkwardly down to the dirt, walk a few feet,
then climb again. Sometimes Lindstrom didn't like the old man's
path, so he would go left instead of right, or down instead of up,
forging his own three-dimensional route through the hau. Occasionally, he would look around and see them all spread out like
boys on a jungle gym. Sometimes, Bernt and Uncle Joe had to
remove their packs and pass them along to slip through a narrow
gap.

Once, Lindstrom looked up and couldn't see anyone. He turned
slowly, trying to recognize where he'd diverged. Backtracking, he
saw nothing familiar, and his heart rate climbed. It was early afternoon. He pictured how far they'd come and how many directions he
could choose that would be completely wrong. He looked for a tree to

climb, but there was only the hau. Too embarrassed to shout for help, he stood on a slick branch, gripping tight to another.

Then a whistle, quiet but piercing. Bernt, beckoning.

When they finally emerged from the hau, the forest was different, darker, with varied shades of green, layers of sunlight and flickering shadow.

"No more da kine," said Uncle Joe. "Octopus tree. This one Ōhiʻa forest now."

They stopped to eat in a clearing covered in green ferns. "They call these kupukupu," said the old man, plucking one and looking closely at its tight green blades. "And this elama." He reached beyond Lindstrom's ear and pulled a branch with small red and green leaves. "A very sacred plant."

They went on.

In the cool and quiet of the forest, Lindstrom heard the calls of small and unfamiliar birds. For decades, the success of his line had been the biggest priority in his life. It justified the weeks away from his family and all the negative externalities. He'd honed himself, disciplined his thoughts and desires in service to fragile chemical sequences that could not propagate, defend themselves, evolve. He'd lied to colleagues, fired scientists, influenced politicians, defunded university research, all because they threatened the product. And now, instead of fighting for his line until there was no hope left, he'd followed these men into the forest, to save himself.

The sunlight slanted in shafts through the overstory. The shadows thickened. Uncle Joe stopped to take a bearing on his compass. It occurred to Lindstrom that he was walking through the middle of an extreme wilderness with an elderly man he'd met the day before. It was entirely possible they'd been walking circles ever since they left the stream, hours before.

He looked deeper into the forest. Leaves tossed in an invisible breeze. He carried with him the city-dweller's assumption that his surroundings were directional and purposeful. But this was simply there. Growing over and burying itself as it had for millions of years, since pioneer seedlings pushed their way through cracks in wind-swept lava flows. For a moment, Lindstrom saw vast deserts of black rock, lifeless as the surface of Mars. Some landscapes advertised their inhospitableness. Others beckoned you deep into their verdant valleys; by the time you realized they were just as deadly, you had already gone too far.

Lindstrom said a prayer. This was what set him apart from most of his colleagues, who cheerfully told themselves there was nothing terrifying about their materialist explanations of the universe. All of them were in denial. It was impossible to contemplate infinity honestly without being undone by the prospect of not existing. To point out the logical fallacies, the hubris, of claiming God was a two-thousand-year-old man in the fertile crescent, the absurdity and cruelty of all the traditions and rules created in His name, was to miss the point. We understood Him through our words and concepts, but His existence did not depend on those. The way Efloxiflam could have been invented by a different scientist, patented by a different corporation, branded with a different name, yet its fundamental nature, its chemical formula, existed independent and immutable, written into the physical laws of the universe even if no one ever discovered it at all.

Now he remembered why he'd quit hiking. It gave him too much time to think.

He could hear the stream again. In a few minutes, they emerged into a clearing with a ring of blackened rocks enclosing some charred sticks and one crushed aluminum can, papery with ash.

"We pau for today," said Uncle Joe. "Tomorrow we find the meter."

Lindstrom drank the last half liter from his bottle. The water was warm; the plastic crinkled in his fingers. The old man was stringing a tarp between two trees. Bernt was doing the same. Lindstrom wondered whether he had a tarp in his pack.

"I'm setting this for both of us" said Bernt. "I hope you like being the little spoon."

31

MOMILANI WAS HELPING her granddaughter with her homework when she heard the sound of a truck at the bottom of the hill.

There was a familiar pattern to the approach of any visitor: first the distant engine, then silence as the vehicle climbed the hill, then the engine louder, the crunch of tires on gravel. She thought it must be her daughter, who had been dropping by more often recently.

"Tutu what's this?" Anuhea pointed at a word. Momilani forgot about the truck and didn't notice it never came up from the bottom of the hill.

A man in camouflage kicked in the door. He wore an orange balaclava with round holes for his eyes and mouth.

Anuhea screamed.

Momilani pushed her granddaughter into the cushions, nearly concealing the girl's small body behind her muumuu.

"Where he stay?" The man stood in the doorway to the living room.

Anuhea stopped screaming and Momilani put her arms around the girl. She had gone silent, shrunk even more tightly into herself than usual. Momilani felt herself coming undone.

"Where he stay?" the man asked again. He ripped a koa canoe paddle off the wall, took it in both hands, and walked toward Momilani and Anuhea.

Clifton should be here. He kept an aluminum fish bat under the bed.

"Where he stay?" the man said.

Momilani understood what he wanted to know. But when she tried to tell him, her mouth did not open. She frantically tried to recall how she had done it, moved her body with her mind, but she needed more time, she couldn't remember the trick.

He didn't ask again. In one motion, he stepped within range and swung the flat of the blade at Momilani's head, veering upward at the final moment so it shattered against the wall. The little girl flinched when pieces of the paddle fell onto her shoulders, but she did not scream.

The man stood over them, sweat pouring from his head and running past his red-veined eyes. It soaked his shirt and traced the veins on his forearms.

"Where he stay?"

Momilani knew him. She had seen him many times, driving his truck around the village, lurking at the beach park or the Anahola Clubhouse. Once, she had seen him with her daughter.

The man in the orange ski mask punched her in the face.

She'd been about to speak, but the sudden pain stopped her. This was the last person Clifton ever saw, she realized. This was what it had been like. She leaned over and covered her granddaughter's body with her own.

The man in the ski mask hit her in the jaw. Then he hit her as hard as he could in the side of the head. She slumped heavily into the couch, her weight sliding off the girl.

"He stay with Uncle Joe guys," said Anuhea, as calmly as if she were answering a question from her teacher. "Mauka side Namahana. They packed to go camping with one haole."

The man studied her, then left the room. The girl listened as he moved through the house. When she heard him open the back door, she got up and watched through the kitchen window as the light went on in Uncle Micah's room. A few seconds later, the man emerged, holding what looked like a pair of underwear, and disappeared into the darkness.

Anuhea walked into the living room and sat down on the couch beside her tutu. She waited for the truck to start and thought about what to do next. She didn't like the way Tutu was sitting, with her feet on the floor but her body laid across the cushions. So she lifted one of her legs onto the couch, then the other. She put a pillow under Tutu's head, careful to avoid the dark bruises rising around her eyes.

Tutu would need the bag of frozen peas, Anuhea knew, and three of the orange pills. But she didn't know if Tutu had frozen peas or orange pills.

She was only halfway through her homework. She decided she would finish it while Tutu slept. That way, no one would be mad at her in the morning.

32

THE SUN HAD set, but the sky was still bright above the trees. Uncle Joe followed a green butterfly into the bushes and emerged with a fistful of leaves. He set them aside in an aluminum bowl. Bernt took four packages of pancit noodles from his pack and settled on his haunches over the small gas stove, while the others left to collect firewood. "You follow the stream that way," Uncle Joe told Lindstrom. "Then turn and follow it back. No wander off."

It did not take Lindstrom long to gather an armload. But darkness had come as he searched for the pale branches in the gloom of the forest floor. The river rushed so loudly it was hard to pinpoint its direction. He stood still, listened, looked. Individual trees emerged from the dark mass of the forest. The river was to his right.

After they'd eaten, the old man built the smallest sticks into a loose tower, then placed a handful of brown fibers at its base and lit them with a tarnished Zippo. Once the twigs ignited, he added larger branches. The men sat in silence. When the fuel had burned to bright embers, Uncle Joe laid two thick branches and set a blackened kettle across them.

It had been a long time since Lindstrom had stared into a fire, the small purple flames licking the edges of the wood, bright orange leaping higher, hazy yellow coronas waving back and forth. An exothermic chemical reaction, unique to this moment, yet identical to every fire, all the way back in time. What had Uncle Joe kindled it with? Coconut fibers, ripped from the husk. Something Homo sapiens had learned to do before everything else. Before they had anything, they had this: a circle of light, surrounded by darkness.

They'd been watching the kettle on the logs so long, it seemed momentous when Uncle Joe leaned forward and plucked it off, the steam from its spout becoming visible as soon as it reached the fresh air beyond the smoke.

"Too hot the water," he said, setting the kettle on the ground beside him.

A minute later, he used the cuff of his shirt to lift the lid, scooped the leaves from the aluminum bowl, and dropped them into the kettle. He took one leaf and handed it to Lindstrom.

"You know mamaki?"

Lindstrom held the leaf to the firelight. It was heart-shaped and slightly gritty, dark green on the upper side and lighter green beneath with bright pink veins.

"A nettle?" he asked.

The old man nodded. "Good medicine. Cure one sore throat. But us old men take it for energy!" He startled Lindstrom by leaping up and striding quickly back to his tent. He returned with three tin mugs hooked on his fingers. "Now maybe we never wake up sore in the morning."

"I've got medicine, too," said Bernt. He set a liter of Seagrams 7 in the firelight beside the three mugs.

"Shoots," said Uncle Joe. "For after."

Uncle Joe took the kettle and poured out the tea in three precise streams. He picked up a cup by its rim and handed it to Bernt, rotating it so he could grab the handle. He did the same for Lindstrom. The metal handle was warm, and he could feel the heat radiating from the thin metal. The old man raised his mug and the two others followed suit.

"To one last adventure."

"My last, maybe," said Bernt. "But not yours."

"I lucky for get even this one," said Uncle Joe. "I soon turn ninety."

Bernt and Lindstrom glanced at each other. "Jesus," Bernt muttered, under his breath.

The tea was hot, green and bitter, but it cooled quickly in the tin mug.

Uncle Joe leaned into the firelight and lifted the bottle of whiskey. He twisted off the cap and poured a few ounces into his mug. Bernt reached out and the old man did the same for him. Lindstrom took the last lukewarm sip of tea and held out the empty cup.

"Now," said Uncle Joe, "tell me about this meter."

"Something strange is going on in our Namahana field."

The old man laughed. "No shit."

"I mean the books don't add up."

"Must have been one bad math error, make three boys go mahke."

Bernt leaned into the firelight and refilled his mug. He set the bottle back half empty. "It's simple," he said. "As long as it was local kids getting poisoned and local workers disappearing, everything was situation normal. But as soon as it looked like it might cost the bosses real money, they booked this guy on the first flight over."

"We still don't know what killed those boys."

"Don't get me wrong," said Bernt. "I'm not judging you for what you did. We all take orders from someone."

"I've spent my career developing crops to feed the world."

"And I spent my career spreading freedom and democracy."

"Thank you for your service," said Lindstrom.

"I'd accept your appreciation if you had any idea what the fuck you were talking about."

"Maybe you don't know what he's talking about either," said Uncle Joe. "Not if you never worked on one real farm."

"They're not a farm, they're a chemical company. This isn't like plantation days."

"Eh, before times we had spray choke chemicals. Things stay mo' better these days guarantee."

"Like I said, I'm not judging. I just want him to drop the corporate bullshit for a second and tell us what he really believes."

"He believe in his mission," said Uncle Joe, "just like all of us."

"It was different for you," said Bernt. "You were fighting Hitler."

The old man reached into the firelight for the bottle, then settled back into the darkness.

"December 1941," he said, "I seen the Japanee planes. We was living in Niumila then, Camp Nine. When they form the Island Volunteers, my father guys all try for join but get turned down. Found out was because they was forming the Volunteers for watch us Japanee. One day, one FBI agent come to our house. Said we was hiding one Japanee flag. My dad had kept 'em in one drawer. They put him in jail one week. We never know what going happen with him. One haole got him out. Amos Winthrop. My father was his field manager and da buggah went down there an' said this Japanee was one loyal American and one good worker. So my father come home. And he never take it personal. Everyone knew one Japanee family on Ni'ihau had try for help one Japanee pilot who crash land there. But they was just rural people. They never knew no better. When we heard they was recruiting Japanee for U.S. Army, my dad said go join 'em. I had just turn eighteen, so I go."

"I'm sorry you were treated like that," said Lindstrom.

"Was nothing compared to mainland Japanee. My wife guys in California got locked up in one horse stable. Then they put 'em all on one train for Arkansas. I served with boys came from that camp. We called 'em katonks an' they call us Buddhahead. They said German POWs next door get treated better than American Japanee."

"You were a grunt?"

"Hoi, you think they was gonna let us be officers? Sent us straight Italy."

"Mountain combat."

"I never knew what one real mountain was until I had go Italy. Never need see another neither. We was the ones broke through at Anzio, but they never let us march in Rome with all the rest. Sent us France instead. Made us go rescue one haole battalion had got surrounded five miles deep in the forest. Took us six days for find 'em, fighting karang karang the whole time. Then they sent those haoles to the rear and tell us go capture the rest of the forest, too. Took nine more days for do that. We call ourselves 'Go for Broke,' but was U.S. Army try for break us."

"You should thank *this* fucker for his service," said Bernt.

"Shoots. Choke people stay thanking me now. Most guys mahke already, so us old farts get all da medals. They like fly me Washington, D.C. I say, Hoi, easier ship one medal here than send one old uncle all da way mainland. I never deserve those medals anyway. Da fackahs just feel guilty is all. They give you any medals?"

Bernt shook his head.

"No worry, you going get plenty once you my age."

"I don't think so. I know what I did. And so do they."

"You gotta let that go. No can blame yourself for what had happen in battle."

Bernt was silent.

"I'll answer your question," said Lindstrom.

"What question?" Bernt asked.

"You wanted to know if I believe in the mission."

"I was just being an asshole."

Lindstrom reached into the firelight. The bottle was a quarter full.

"I could go online right now and find someone claiming that anything I put in my body, keep in my house, spray in my fields, is going to make me sick. And some of them aren't wrong. But how do you know which ones? You have to run randomized experiments, double-blind placebo trials. And even for the tiny fraction that get those tests, maybe the benefits still outweigh the harm. The problem is, ninety-nine percent of questions don't have easy answers, and ninety-nine percent of people can't tolerate that uncertainty."

"So?" said Bernt.

"So I'm in the one percent. If you tell me a product might poison a thousand kids, I tell you a million kids will be malnourished if farmers in India can't control the bollworm."

"So you're saying you don't care if your products poison people?"

"I'm saying it's my job to make hard decisions."

"You didn't answer the question."

"If I was going to produce millions of gallons of chemicals that can be highly toxic at certain dosages, I had to accept fatalities as a statistical inevitability."

Lindstrom knew he sounded angry. But he was tired of being judged, tired of being misunderstood. He was doing some of the most advanced science on the planet to feed billions of people, but he'd never win a Nobel Prize. No one had ever thanked him for *his* service.

"Look, the world is full of people who stay clean, stand on principle, and carry nothing on their conscience. I call that selfish. Who knows what they could accomplish if they had the courage to admit the world is complicated."

Bernt reached into the firelight and emptied the bottle.

"The more I look back at it, the less complicated it seems."

Uncle Joe spoke up. "You did what you had to. No can change that now. You got to learn to live with it."

"And the night terrors?"

"For those you talk to one psychologist."

"I'm not allowed to talk about it."

"Well I'll be dead soon, and if this fackah stay as full of bullshit as you say, no one going believe him anyway."

The men sat in silence. Golden embers glowed between the logs.

"On my last tour, we were stationed at a shithole called Scania on a six-lane highway through the desert. Our mission was to wait on standby to escort VIPs—contractors, oil executives, that type of person. One night we repelled an attack on the way to BIAP, nothing out of the ordinary, except we ended up detaining a few combatants, and the VIPs turned out to be civilian Intelligence. I told them I'd do anything to get out of that dump, and a week later I was reassigned to a SMU—a Special Missions Unit—eight SEALS and a CIA who thought she was hot shit. My new mission was information-collection, which meant kicking our way into somebody's compound, detaining combat-age males and taking the poor fucks into an empty shed or whatever and making them give up our next door to kick."

Lindstrom and Uncle Joe stared into the fire.

"It turned out that out of everyone, I was the best at developing rapport, probably because the SEALS were all scary as fuck and the CIA was batshit. It didn't hurt that I'd been arrested a few times myself. So when it was me who lit their pubes on fire, they usually talked."

The gold pulsed gray as the fire settled deeper into the coals.

"I did more than light their pubes on fire."

"Shoots," said Uncle Joe. "At Castellina we took so much casualty was no one for guard even one prisoner. When the lieutenant told Ishida for light 'em all with his flame thrower, I never said nothing."

"I left a plume of carcinogens leaching into an aquifer under an elementary school."

Bernt raised an empty cup in the darkness.

"Cheers," he said, "to the ones with courage."

33

LINDSTROM WOKE WITH an ache in his side, just in time to feel the hard earth pull the last flicker of warmth from his body. He shifted his head, brushing the tarp, and raining cold beads of dew onto his face. He and Bernt had moved closer in the night. The weight and warmth of the other man's body pressed into his back. He'd been sure he would have a hangover, but his head was clear and painless. Jungle cocks crowed in the forest. It was completely dark.

"Go back to sleep," mumbled Bernt.

Lindstrom let his head fall back onto his pack. Bernt's weight shifted onto him, the warmth between them rising.

When Lindstrom woke again, he was shivering. It was almost dawn and Bernt was gone. He rolled off his aching side onto his back, stretched his arms and legs. Then the hangover hit. Rolling out from under the tarp, he found Bernt and Uncle Joe by the camp stove. A column of steam rose from the kettle. It was a foggy morning in the mountains. Lindstrom wanted to call his wife. He wanted to hold his kids, feel the hairs on the crowns of their heads tickle his nose.

"You look like shit," said Bernt.

"Mamaki tea, very powerful," said Uncle Joe. He held out a bag. "Dried aku. Eat."

The fish was tough and salty, but a few strips left him feeling energized and slightly better. They broke camp quickly. The forest high on the mountain grew so thick it was faster to walk in the streambed. The water flowed quickly, pouring into still pools and spilling heavily between stones and boulders. The sound was soothing. The pitted lava rock was solid beneath Lindstrom's hands. But the going was slow. Lindstrom hopped from rock to rock, keeping his shoes dry, while the old man and Bernt walked in the water.

"I can splint you up," Bernt said, as Lindstrom balanced on a pointed boulder. "But it will probably take three days to get you out. And it will be painful."

Lindstrom sat on the boulder, then slid into the cold water.

"Plenty low, the stream," said Uncle Joe, "even though we get choke rain."

"Is it being diverted?" asked Lindstrom.

"Could be," said the old man. "The dam not far ahead."

"Is this the place where the boys—"

"No. Cannot walk there from here. One slot canyon stay ahead. They use 'em, as one reservoir. The tunnel where the boys go mahke take water away from Namahana Mountain. They store it behind this dam and send it back to Namahana stream through the tunnel we about to see. Very complicated, the ditches. Had carve 'em right into da cliff. Make one big waterfall. Plenty guys go mahke building this."

Above the noise of rushing water, Lindstrom heard a faint sound, far down the valley.

"You hear that?" said Bernt.

"Hounds," said Uncle Joe.

Bernt scanned the trees below.

"Is that normal?"

The old man shrugged.

Up ahead, Lindstrom saw sky where the slope flattened. It seemed only a few hundred feet away, but it was half an hour before they stood at the base of a wide concrete spillway. The valley walls rose tall and narrow. A cold wind came down from the peaks. Tattered gray clouds filled the canyon. When Lindstrom looked back, he saw a dark blanket of treetops, acid green fields, the ocean. He was surprised at how much elevation they'd gained.

"We go," said Uncle Joe.

Lindstrom turned and saw Bernt disappear over the lip of the spillway. On the other side was a narrow path along the top of a concrete barrier. To the left, the streambed, with the same lazy flow of water between boulders. To the right, a deep chute blasted into the rock, black water flowing smooth along the cliffs. Only the bright yellow leaves spinning down the ditch revealed the speed of the current before it disappeared into a rough tunnel, blown into the base of the cliff.

A black plastic box sat on a pole. A small solar panel was mounted above it. Wires ran from the box into the stream. By the time Lindstrom reached the meter, Bernt had already flipped back the clasp and exposed the device inside.

"This is the data logger," said Lindstrom. "YSI. Pretty standard stuff. I don't know what we're going to be able to pull from it, but it seems to be recording, so that's good news." He reached into the case and began shifting around the different instruments until he found what he was looking for, the Signal Output Adapter. Setting his pack on the ground, he pulled out his laptop, wrapped in one of Momilani's rubbish bags, and set it on the ground. Retrieving a USB stick from a pocket in the laptop case, he plugged it into the SOA.

A small green light began to blink.

Uncle Joe had removed his boots and was sitting on the edge of the ditch, bathing his bare feet in the cold water. Bernt dug in his own pack, pulling out cans of lentil soup. The clouds above the valley were growing darker. Twisted wisps of fog drifted down the canyon walls.

When the light on the thumb drive went from blinking to a steady green, Lindstrom pulled it out and plugged it into his laptop. There were a dozen or so files he didn't have the software to open, but also spreadsheets labeled *Turb, pH, DO, NH4, Temp, ORP,* and *NO3*. He clicked on *NO3*, Nitrates. The logger was programmed to keep hourly readings, along with daily maximums, minimums, and averages. As he scrolled, he saw the hourlies had been saved ninety days, but the daily stats went back years. He highlighted the columns he wanted and created a chart showing the meter's history. The levels were high, not unexpected, but there was nothing he hadn't seen in fields around the world, the dots from August right in line with all the rest.

He made a graph for *pH* next. The numbers were higher, extremely high, before dropping off significantly in the last few weeks. This too, was no surprise, based on the amount of lime Miyake had been inputting. After decades of farming cane, the soil had been heavily acidified, and the steep slopes and frequent rain made it almost impossible to prevent the lime from sliding. It was what it was. High alkalinity wasn't ideal but shouldn't be fatal to large vertebrates.

Lindstrom glanced up, saw Bernt and the old man looking down the valley toward the spillway and the drop beyond. Then he heard it, too. The baying of dogs. Closer now.

Lifting his feet from the water, Uncle Joe scrambled with a few agile steps to his pack and the rifle that leaned against it. He removed a box of rounds and fed them one by one into the magazine. "Maybe one big boar on its way."

Bernt watched him load. "Is that a Remington 700?" he asked.

"Thirty ought-six with five-round magazine. One good rifle."

"Accurate," said Bernt.

Lindstrom whistled in surprise. Bernt looked over his shoulder at a vertical line rising ten times higher than anything else on the graph. "What is that?"

"NO4."

"What's that?"

"Ammonia."

Bernt scowled. "Those fuckers."

"Who?" asked Lindstrom.

"Watch out!" called the old man.

A pack of mud-splattered dogs was streaming across the concrete spillway. The leaders were already jostling one another as they ran full speed onto the path between the stream and the ditch. They wore transmitters around their necks, the thick antennae bobbing as the dogs bayed and barked in a frenzy, teeth bared.

"Where's the hog?" Bernt shouted, instinctively lunging for his pack and Miyake's gun.

"I never see 'em." Uncle Joe held the Remington uncertainly, ready to raise it and draw a bead, the barrel still aimed at the ground. He dropped to one knee and scanned the dry streambed for the object of the hunt.

Bernt made himself narrow on the concrete lip of the ditch, keeping his eyes on the lead dog, a few dozen feet away and closing, his finger resting lightly on the trigger guard.

Lindstrom slapped the laptop shut and cradled it against his chest, resting one knee on the cement edge, the current cold below him. The dogs didn't seem to be tracking anything in the stream, but something on the path. The lead dog passed Uncle Joe, who kept his rifle pointed down. It lunged at Bernt's leg and latched onto his thigh, quickly followed by a second dog, then a third. Bernt discharged the pistol and fell backward into the dark water.

Rising to his feet, Lindstrom watched the surface of the ditch. Finally, Bernt's head appeared, much farther down. The dogs were swimming for the sides of the chute, scrabbling their paws against the steep concrete and dipping underwater as their bodies went vertical. The rest of the pack gathered at the spot where Bernt had fallen, trying to pick up the scent, whining, confused and excited.

Lindstrom set his laptop gently in the center of the path and jumped into the ditch. He felt the cold shock, as he sank beneath the water's surface, the current whipping him around with unexpected force. Opening his eyes, he saw only darkness, and then a vague, shimmering brightness far below his feet. As he milled his arms, the light was beside him, then above him. He was rising toward it, everything growing brighter by the moment. The emptiness in his lungs grew hungrier. He fought the panic prying open his clenched lips.

The light was no longer a vague presence but a thin, unstable barrier above his head. Then he broke the surface and was on the right side of the world again. The dark concrete walls loomed above, moving rapidly. A dog in the water tried scrambling up and kept falling back. Uncle Joe was running toward him down the path, then stopped abruptly and turned his back.

Lindstrom grabbed at the concrete, but it tore his nails and offered nothing. He managed to grasp a root. The current slammed him against the wall. He held for a second, then another, the time it took for the water to work a tiny part of itself into the gap between his fingertips and the living root and effortlessly pry them apart. His head went under. When he raised it, he heard an echoing roar, a barking dog. Then he was whipped around a corner and slung into a rough rock wall. Desperately swimming against the current, he watched as the gray sky shrank to a circle that grew smaller and brighter as it carried him deeper into the tunnel.

34

UNCLE JOE STOPPED running when he saw Bernt disappear into the tunnel, stroking smoothly and calmly against the current. For a moment, he had that lousy feeling, the thing that tried to send him back to bed in the middle of the morning; the feeling that everything had already happened and there was nothing left to do but rest and wait. He met Lindstrom's eyes, less than fifty feet away but separated by the immeasurable distance between the dying and the living. The dogs were trotting up and down the trail, whining and uncertain. One brushed the length of its mottled coat against his thigh, leaning against him before moving on.

An idea came to him. He turned and ran with short, hopping steps along the narrow path. It seemed only a short time ago he'd run like this under a seventy-pound pack. He thought of the men who'd run beside him, the way they'd looked at one another, eyes wide, when they finally dropped behind the cover of a stone wall or a ditch. The familiar crackling whirr of a bullet ricocheting off a boulder seemed part of his reverie until a moment later he heard the flat report echoing off the rocks. To his left was a pool where large smooth boulders had piled up. He could slide down and take cover, find the shooter and engage him. But the mission was to reach the dam, and he had very little time, so he kept running on the exposed trail.

Another shot, the bullet pinging off the concrete near his feet. He resisted the urge to look back, just a few hundred feet to the dam. There were three iron steps and a rusted catwalk over a narrow gap where the water churned into the ditch. A steel sluice gate was suspended over the gap, connected to a flywheel on a platform nestled behind a narrow outcrop of rock, just wide enough, combined with a slight turning in the valley, to offer cover if he could reach it.

Someone punched him in the arm as he neared the first metal step, spinning him around.

He hadn't believed his friends who told him being shot didn't hurt. But they'd been right. He turned now, braced his rifle against his hip, and waited. Something moved behind a boulder. He fired off a wild shot, then wheeled around and ran up the steps, across the grate over the rushing water, and collapsed into the shelter of the rock.

The pain came in sets, each swell bigger than the next until a brief window when he could think almost clearly through the crackling alerts from his nervous system. His left arm was useless, the whole side slick and cool with blood. Leaning his rifle against the rock, he undid one button near his belly, then set his teeth before gripping his left forearm and guiding it through the gap in the shirt so it rested against his warm stomach. The arm still flopped when he pressed himself off the rock and walked toward the flywheel, but the pain was manageable, spiking then settling back into a rhythm that would allow him to carry on.

He worried the mechanism might be frozen with rust and corrosion, and when he gripped the wheel and leaned, it did not give. He scanned the wheel from bottom to top until he spotted the lever locking out the gears. Dropping to one knee, he braced himself against the pain, and yanked. It moved with little resistance, and when he tried the wheel again, it turned. He spun a half-turn at a time, resting his forearm across and pulling as far around as he could. Again and again he repeated this step, and as the sluice gate lurched lower, he felt the pressure of the water building against it. He thought Bernt must be through by now, somewhere on the opposite side of the ridge, headed toward the falls. He knew the shooter must be very close.

Uncle Joe's arm slipped out of his shirt, and he almost collapsed, but he stayed upright and kept turning the wheel. It didn't matter now, the pain. He felt sick to his stomach and wanted to take a nap. The sky was gray overhead, the walls of the valley dark. The water was pushing hard against the door.

It must be close.

The wheel stopped. The water went still beneath his feet.

Uncle Joe let go.

In the quiet of the rising water, he heard a footstep on the dam. Richard Winthrop came around the corner into the cold, damp shadow of the cliff. He had a rifle slung over his shoulder and held a .45 caliber pistol. The two old friends stared at each without expression. When Uncle Joe smiled, it was to himself. He'd lived much longer than he'd expected and had experiences reserved for men who lived much shorter lives. If he'd been entirely clear-headed, he might have felt afraid of what was about to happen. But in the moment, all he felt was tired and grateful. And his face reflected this as Winthrop raised the pistol and fired twice into his chest.

35

L INDSTROM WAS FACING upstream, toward the diminishing light. The current slammed him into the walls of the tunnel. Over and over he swallowed cold water, coughed it up, gasped in more before he could draw a proper breath.

Finally, he spun himself around to face the darkness, hacked the water from his lungs, drew a deep and unobstructed breath. For a few seconds, relief filled him with the most profound experience of peace he'd ever know. Then his head grazed the cold ceiling, and he realized any number of jutting rocks might lie ahead in the darkness. All he could do was lie back and make himself as flat as possible, his nose above the waterline, his arms loose at his sides, kicking gently with his heels to keep himself suspended on the surface.

As he surrendered to the helpless calm of the star float, the totality of the darkness, the tug of the current, the slap and echo of small waves, the smell of rock and taste of iron filled his mind until it seemed the universe was nothing but the endless sum of these sensations. It was a different kind of peace, pure and indifferent, not the resumption of life and hope, but the absence of fear and longing. It lasted until he remembered what Uncle Joe had said about the waterfall.

He thrashed at the walls. His fingers found a grip. He felt a tiny thrill of triumph until he considered the next step of this plan: to hold himself indefinitely in the dark below the mountain. He let go. He tried to pray, to think about his family, to get his final thoughts in order. But now, instead of lulling him into a state of suspended anxiety, the slap and taste of running water bore him ceaselessly back into the present.

The first, faint glow produced a feeling of dread. Between his outstretched feet, a distant point of light grew larger. He could not help but picture what lay ahead, the water pouring from the cliff-face and falling a thousand feet, one of the lovely white ribbons etched into the green mountains. He listened for the falls, heard nothing but the slopping echo of the tunnel. "Please God. Please God. Please God. Please God. Please God." He repeated the incantation as the tunnel mouth grew brighter. "PleaseGodPleaseGodPleaseGodPleaseGod."

Blue sky appeared. White clouds. It was like those dreams when he realized he could leap over houses, trees, higher and higher, thrilling and joyful, until he finally leaped too high, terror rising as he rose, his momentum slowing, a despairing moment of perfect equilibrium, then the long fall with the strange, cold, unbelievable knowledge he was about to die before slamming awake into his own dark bedroom beside his sleeping wife.

Again, he tried to grab the rocks. It was easier this time. He clung a few seconds before his hand slipped from the slick stone. A relief, to fight. He heard a difference in the sound, a vast openness swallowing the echo of water.

Finally, he caught a rock that was almost dry. His grip held. The water dragged at his shoes, stretching his body horizontally. But it seemed less urgent. In fact, the longer he held the rock, the easier it became. It seemed to him the level of the water was changing. His body was sinking. He lost his grip and was floating again. The current slipped over the ledge and brought him with it. He saw sky and mountain tilt and plunge.

He surfaced in a quiet pool. It funneled into a ditch that ran across a steep mountainside. A stunted tree grew overhead, and Lindstrom hooked its roots as he went by. The water tugged lazily at his legs. He looked back at the tunnel and saw only a trickle of water.

Lindstrom thanked God. He pictured his wife, his son, his daughter. He thought of Bernt somewhere below, alive or dead. He wondered if he should climb down to him or crawl back through the tunnel. He pictured himself on his hands and knees in the dark and realized the water could start again as quickly as it had stopped.

36

NALANI SENT A message to Bernt the day after she saw him at the mall. *How you doing?* The next day, she sent another. *Is every-thing all right?* Two hours after that, she tried to call. The phone went straight to voicemail. She sent him another text. *Check in when you can. I like know u r ok.* An hour later, she called her mother's cousin in Anahola. "Ho Auntie, where Momilani Moniz stay?"

She arrived at Momilani's late that afternoon. The shadow of the mountains had already crossed the house. There were two pickups in the yard and two men, cousins or brothers, sitting on each side of the door. Each held a rifle across his lap. They stared at her impassively as she shut the door of her truck and walked slowly toward them.

"This where Auntie Momilani stay?"

"Who like know?"

"I'm Nalani Winthrop," she said.

"Why you like see her then?"

"I'm a friend of Micah Bernt. I stay worried about him."

One of the men stood up, leaned his gun against the wall, and walked through the front door. He came out a minute later, opened the door wide. "She say for you to come inside."

Nalani walked up the steps, past the man in the chair, who never glanced at her, and past the man who held the door. He gripped his rifle casually by the barrel, and she couldn't help but cross its line of fire. She had grown up with guns, and the violation licked across her skin as she stepped past the muzzle.

"In da kitchen," the brother told her, nodding toward a doorway. Nalani came into a room with orange linoleum tile. A young woman was frying something over the stove, an older woman was seated at a small table. It took Nalani a moment to realize what she'd thought was a shadow was in fact a puffy black bruise covering the left side of Momilani's face, making her lip and eye socket swell grotesquely.

Momilani pushed herself up and took a few steps toward Nalani. "Aloha, I know your mother guys. I'm Momi, and this is my cousin Kahana. It's her brothers stay out front."

Momilani held out her arms and Nalani stepped in for an embrace and a peck on one cheek. It lasted longer than she expected. Momilani held her tight.

"I'm happy to meet you," said Momilani. "I never knew Micah had friends."

"We were in class together."

"He has one good heart. So I think that makes you good, too."

"Mahalo Auntie. We were actually just getting to know each other."

"And now you never hear from him."

"That's right."

"You stay worried?"

"I am."

"How much did he tell you?"

"He said he's been trying to find out who's responsible for your husband passing."

Momilani nodded.

"Do you know where he is?"

"He went mauka with Uncle Joe Hashimoto and another guy."

"They were looking for someone?"

Momilani shook her head. "For something, I think. For tell them what's been passing through the water."

"Will that take them long?"

"They brought supplies for three days. Today is the second day."

Nalani nodded. "You know where they went?"

"Somewhere Namahana side, up the valleys over there."

"I'm sorry to ask so many questions, but did something happen?" Nalani touched the side of her own face.

"A man attacked me," said Momilani.

"He came into your house?"

"That's right."

"For rob you?"

"For get information."

"What kine information?"

"Da same kine you come here for get."

"Did you know him?"

"Eh, I seen da buggah. One ice head. He wore one mask, but I knew him."

"You know his name then?"

"Eh, I never know. I just described him to the police. We'll see if they find him. My niece said he broke into Micah's room. But all he took was a pair of BVDs. That's what she said."

"And you're sure he was on ice?"

Momilani nodded.

Nalani was silent for a long time.

"Listen Auntie, Micah is in danger. If you know anyone who can help him, you need to call them. Now."

Nalani turned and left the house, ignoring the cousins. She drove down the hill and stopped at the highway. Then she turned north, toward Namahana.

37

LINDSTROM WALKED THROUGH ankle-deep water. Most of the ditch was chiseled from the rock face, but in places it was reinforced with cement blocks. To his left, the ridge rose steeply. To his right, the void. The valley floor lay hundreds of feet below. Namahana's twin peaks rose beyond.

He was in a strangely cheerful mood. Not since he was a boy had he ever imagined he would find himself following a narrow path on a perilous mission across the slopes of an extinct volcano. He did worry about his companions, but it seemed to him that if he had survived, Bernt and Uncle Joe must be alive as well.

Seeing the familiar mountain made him think he must be near the highway. He had no doubt he'd sleep in a bed that night. More important, the journey through the tunnel had cleared his head. So what if he lost his job? He and Char and the kids would be fine. It could be a blessing. He tried to put himself in the mindset he'd had just a few hours before, believing everything depended on finding a mysterious machine in the heart of the mountain. He couldn't.

Of course he'd heard of other people having nervous breakdowns. And of course it felt nothing like what he'd imagined. After pushing himself too hard for months, for years, he'd learned an old friend was dead, flown through four time zones, and discovered his career was over—all in less than twenty-four hours. By the time Cabral had dropped him at the company house, he'd been a grieving, exhausted, stressed-out wreck. He'd probably have gotten over it with one decent night of sleep. He could have signed the nondisclosures, taken his buyout, and been home with his kids by now. Instead, he'd panicked, then had the misfortune to fall in with a traumatized war veteran whose delusions reinforced his own. He'd been swept up in the momentum of someone else's nightmare, and he was going to have quite a bit of explaining to do, but he had *survived*—another word he'd finally come to understand—and he could finally think clearly.

The sun was descending. Treetops in the valley glowed in slanting light. Puddles in the ditch reflected golden clouds. The decline was gentle. Lindstrom's stride was free and effortless. Rounding each bend, he was sure he'd see Bernt walking toward him. The man had his faults, but he would never leave anyone behind.

He turned a corner and the ditch was gone. An enormous concrete halfpipe jutted over a dark crease of rock, slick with dripping water and hanging ferns. Drops of water whirled out of sight. White birds glided far below. He would have to find another way into the valley.

The land to his right seemed relatively gentle, covered in patches of tall grass and jewel-green mats of vegetation. By traversing a steeper incline, he could reach a ridge that seemed to offer a gentler grade. He could still be out by sunset. Without further thought, Lindstrom hoisted himself onto the edge of the ditch. As he let his butt slide off, he realized the slope was steeper than it looked. The friction of his body was not enough to stop his momentum. He was gaining speed. It happened so fast he was just getting truly frightened when his heel hit a firmly rooted tuft. It held, and he found himself flailing and grabbing for handfuls of grass with the same dark panic he'd been clawing at the tunnel walls with. He lay back against the slope, staring up into sky. He realized he was very thirsty.

Finally, Lindstrom looked between his legs at the forest canopy below. He didn't think he could go back. He shifted his weight to one leg, then stretched out the other and felt for another tuft, prodded the springy mass with his foot, slowly equalized his weight. In the middle of a very short prayer, he shifted his balance to the new hold. It held. He repeated the move, gaining confidence, sliding on his back through the grass as if lying on a bed. Finally, he reached the ridge leading down to the valley, where he could stand safely and walk.

He pressed downhill through waist-high bushes until he was in the forest. When he saw thick brush ahead, he ran forward eagerly, thinking it must be the stream. But beyond the bushes were more bushes. For the first time, he stopped to orient himself. He turned to look back and realized he had no idea which way he'd come. Since the moment he'd entered the forest, he'd been taking the path of least resistance, completely unconscious of the choices he'd been making, as if fixating on a goal was enough to bring him to it.

An unfamiliar feeling washed over him, of being very, very stupid.

He told himself to calm down. He turned in a circle, trying to spot something familiar among the gray trunks choked by broad green vines, the layers of dry and rotting leaves banked against moss-covered stones and branching, insatiable roots. The forest was quiet and cool in the twilight, majestically indifferent, utterly still, and yet, to Lindstrom's eye, a tropical maelstrom: organisms sprouting, propagating, dying, decomposing. Nothing could be more unlike the perfectly surveyed grids of genetically identical monocrops he'd spent his life cultivating.

He stood in the still eye of the storm, deeply and completely lost.

It seemed quite rational to run. There was no place worse than where he was, so no sense staying in one place. He found himself repeating his mantra from the tunnel. "PleaseGodPleaseGodPleaseGod," his only thought to fix things just as quickly as they'd gone wrong. When he was too winded to go on, he stopped and rested his hands on his knees. When he finally looked again at the forest, he knew whatever slim chance he'd had of retracing his steps was now irrevocably lost.

Lindstrom sank to his knees, then onto his side. With this final disappointment, his last reserves had been used up. He lay exposed and naked to the purity of his own emotions. Futility and regret washed over him like waves and left behind an incapacitating emptiness. Twigs and grasses poked him, but he didn't move. Gradually, things that lay in his field of vision—a fallen branch, a curling fern, a mango tree with green and yellow leaves—asserted themselves. How was his existence more important than theirs? Why shouldn't he remain here, too, allow life to complete its process, allow the universe to transform him into a perfect object. He was ready.

There were no shadows anymore, or rather, everything was shadow. Green leaves faded to gray. The yellow faded, too. Forest birds began to sing.

One of his arms had gone numb. Small sticks pressed into his legs and flank. Decaying leaves touched the sensitive hairs that covered his body. The light had left the sky. The temperature was dropping. The birds ceased singing.

He did not want to die.

He pushed himself to his feet. Again he surveyed the forest. And now it appeared to him plainly and directly, as if the emotions, assumptions, memories, and expertise that made him recognizably who he was were just layers of grime, accumulated year after year, suddenly scrubbed from his perception. He was no longer set apart from the forest, he was part of it, as oblivious and unconcerned about the future as any of the living things around him. A great weight lifted.

He had nothing to fear.

At that moment, he felt a tightening in his spine. Someone was watching him. He turned and stared into the dusk.

In the time it took him to be certain no one was there, all the familiar accretions of himself returned. He was a human being, lost. He crept as far as he could under the wide limbs of a Norfolk pine, rested his back against the trunk, wrapped his arms around his knees, rubbed the smooth metal bracelet with his wife's name, watched the forest fill with darkness.

During the long night, Lindstrom thought of many things. He thought of his children, advancing through life, good and perfect travelers to a future he would never see. He thought of his wife and relived several small moments of connection he'd always hoped he would recall again. He thought of God—whom he had worshiped industriously and dutifully—and realized some part of him had always expected, when everything was on the table, to examine the corner of his mind where he addressed the divine and find it empty. But as the darkness deepened, he found this little corner pulsing with a quiet, glowing mystery. It did not alleviate his fears, but it remained steadfast and did not abandon him, even as the dark and silence became absolute. Even when he brought his hand up to his face and could no longer see it.

It was in this darkness, in an unknown hour of the night, that the night marchers came. They walked in ones and twos and threes. They came as families and as solitary walkers. They filled the trees. He could not see them, but he knew them all. Farmers, field hands, fruit pickers. Shopkeepers, truck drivers, children holding coiled ropes for water buffalo. They walked with purpose and did not linger, yet the hours it took for them to pass seemed too long for a single night to hold.

Finally, the last walkers slipped between the trees, and soon the stars stopped whispering. Strange lights and pixelated patterns danced. Sometime before dawn, as the night was finally splitting into different shades of black, Uncle Joe stepped lightly past the branches of the pine.

When the leaves had faint silver edges, Lindstrom crept out, pain coursing through his joints. He looked up toward a peaceful point of light, the morning star. Half the sky glowed pink and orange. He kept it on his left. In half an hour, he reached the stream. He walked straight into the cold, stunning water, sank to his knees and lifted handfuls to his mouth. The cold burned as it went down. When he'd drunk enough, he lay on his back and let the water numb him.

Later, he stripped down to his underwear and followed the stream. It wasn't long before piles of water-tumbled rock marked the spot where two branches met. Lindstrom surveyed their banks. In the shadow of a boulder, Bernt was squatting on his haunches, boots laced tight to calves, looking back at him.

38

I T HAD TAKEN four men all afternoon to carry Uncle Joe out of the valley. They reached the ATVs at dusk. The old man was lighter than a boar, but his limbs were longer and they had to tie him in a fetal position before they could strap him to the cargo rack on one of the four-wheelers.

Winthrop opted to drive, out of respect. His friend's rounded back pressed against his own, leaning its weight against him on the down-hill grades, jostling as he bumped over the ruts. There were risks of course, in bringing the body onto family land, but Winthrop still felt something ease inside him when he passed the small ahu that marked the property line.

Growing up in the sugar fields, Winthrop had been expected to work just as hard as any of the laborers, and he'd spent decades ranching after he left the Army. He knew the feeling of heading home stiff and sore after a long day. It had always been one of his great plea-sures, the ease he felt at the end of a good, hard day of labor, with the assurance that he was doing his part, had not set himself above anyone, had outworked every other man. But it had been many years since he'd felt as bone-tired as he did this evening.

The yellow headlights of the ATV threw leaping shadows onto the trail. The potholes appeared bottomless. The branches pressed tight, and he made a mental note to come back with a chain saw. He drove slowly, deliberately, his men following obediently. The dogs trotting in a loose, long pack behind.

Finally, Winthrop turned on a muddy drive leading to a sagging Quonset hut. His lieutenant, Vierra, jumped off one ATV, the beam of his flashlight dancing across the ground. Winthrop left the engine running and went to find a tarp.

They'd collected anything from the body that could fall or be jarred off, and he dumped that onto the tarp, everything but the laptop they'd found in the center of the trail. Standing by the ATV, Winthrop gripped one handlebar, twisted the throttle, guided the vehicle forward then reversed it until the rear wheels were on the tarp. He unclipped the straps and gave the old man's body a push so it fell squarely. Shining the beam across the rear of the vehicle, he saw he would have to get a pig tomorrow and bloody things up. After guiding the ATV off the tarp, he threw one loose flap over the body, then the other.

"Ho," he shouted, "grab two blocks." He watched the others lug the cinderblocks over and thump them down.

That was enough for tonight.

It would be more direct to take the old trail, but it was no good, not at night. Fatigue had evolved from an almost pleasant numbing warmth to something locked and frozen. He wanted a hot shower and a glass of Scotch, to heat some leftover laulau and go to bed. It had taken more than an hour for the others to reach him at the dam. He'd sat with Uncle Joe in the cold valley for an uncomfortably long time.

When he first glimpsed the lighted windows through the forest, his adrenaline ticked up. He considered stopping the vehicle and walking slowly with his rifle, but whoever was there had heard the engine already. And this was not the night he would go creeping into his grandfather's house like a thief. Apprehension turned to a rare surge of happiness when he recognized the truck parked in the darkness. Nalani was still his favorite, despite all the trouble she'd caused, the only one remotely like him. She was young, but one day she would understand.

Parking the ATV beside her truck, he killed the engine and walked stiffly up the front steps into the light cascading from the windows, the old glass gently swirling the vision of his niece seated on the sofa, facing the door, her arms crossed. The defiant posture she'd adopted ever since she was a little girl, capable of throwing monstrous tantrums.

"Aloha Uncle," said Nalani.

"How you stay?" asked Winthrop.

"I stay worried about you."

"No need worry about me."

"Where were you?"

"Just hunting is all, tracking one big boar down the valley, but I nevah find the buggah."

Nalani nodded, saying nothing.

"You had supper yet?"

"Not yet."

"We get laulau in the fridge. Why don't you heat it up. I like go take shower."

Nalani didn't answer. She pulled her arms tighter around herself, then stood and walked toward the fireplace, ten feet of neat-swept, blackened stone.

"Don't do this Uncle. Not with me."

"What you mean?"

He knew he shouldn't be having this conversation, not in the state he was in now. He took a chipped tin mug from the cabinet and sloshed a generous pour from the bottle of Balvenie he kept under the sink. When he looked up, Nalani hadn't moved.

"What really happened to those men?"

Winthrop took a long burning sip. He walked to the sink and cut the rest with a few drops of water. "No worry about those men. They were thieves. One of them try blackmail me. Had tell Miyake he would go police if we no pay him off."

"So why you never pay him then? You pay plenty guys already."

"You cannot pay a man li'dat. He like one dog go killing chickens. Buggah never stop with one."

"And what about the others?"

"Look around," said her uncle. "You see how people living now? No more knowledge of culture. No more respect for 'oiwi or 'aumakua. They say we got to modernize this island. But it's not the new ways going save us. It's the old ways. And the old ways are cruel."

Nalani sat abruptly on the couch. She lowered her voice and didn't look at him. "You always have an explanation. And I always believe you. And bumbye I learn you've done something even worse. No lie you. What were you hunting today? Where have you been?"

Winthrop looked at his niece, trying to see what she knew, and how she knew it.

"I was searching for someone," he finally said. "Toward Nama-hana side. I heard men might be looking for me. But I never find 'em. So no need worry. I going to take one shower now. Never mind supper. There's beds made up in the bunkhouse. Tomorrow we take one ride."

39

"YOU DOVE IN after me," Bernt said matter-of-factly.

Lindstrom nodded. Bernt had given him two ripe avocados, and he was tearing out chunks of the yellow flesh.

Bernt pointed toward the trees on the opposite bank. "There should be a road along that ridge. I'll get you there and point you in the right direction."

"Where are you going?"

"To find the lab."

"What lab?"

"The meth lab."

"How do you know——"

"The spike in ammonia. The only people who get killed by ammonia are cooks and their girlfriends."

"It would take hundreds of gallons for it to register on the gauge like that."

"Obviously they had access to industrial quantities."

He stared pointedly at Lindstrom.

"We do order it." Lindstrom paused in thought. "But we'd have no reason to release it."

"Could it have been an accident?"

"If it were an accident, a blowout or a puncture in the tank, it would go airborne, not into the water."

"So someone bled a tank of anhydrous straight into the stream."

Lindstrom shook his head. "Not my guys. They know how dangerous an uncontrolled release would be. All they'd have to do is call the office and get it picked up."

"Okay, so they didn't dump it. But maybe they knew who did? What did you tell me earlier, about the budgets?"

"Miyake was getting a deal on the land he was leasing."

"This land."

"Yes."

"And you thought he was selling farm supplies."

"That's right."

"Was anhydrous in the budget?"

"It's an input on all our farms."

"We gotta get moving," said Bernt, "if you want to make it to the highway by sunset."

*

The forest was cool and rippling with birdsong. Fragile sunbeams angled through the leaves. Bernt strode confidently without pausing. More than once, Lindstrom wondered whether they were following the right course. A heaviness had settled over him, a shadow from the night before. He must have lost his job by now, with cause. What would he tell Char?

He remembered the hurt in her voice the last time they'd talked. He'd long ago accepted most people would never understand the strength of mind it took to do his job. But he'd always believed *she* appreciated just how hard he'd worked to transform himself, and why. Of course, he'd never asked her, not directly. Why not?

Abruptly, the shadows ceased, and he was bathed in sunlight. They were on the road.

It was bright and shadeless at midmorning, red dirt running straight in both directions. Bernt pointed. "Just walk that way until you hit the highway."

Lindstrom stared past the man's outstretched hand, down toward the plains and the sea. Then he looked back, toward the mountain. "I'll come with you."

Bernt frowned. "That won't work."

"I want to see this through."

"You don't understand what you're asking."

"Do you really want to do this alone?"

The answer, operationally, was yes. He would be a liability.

Bernt looked up the bright road toward the gray clouds gathering on the slopes of Namahana.

He shook his head, but said, "All right."

They walked a thick ribbon of hardened mud between deep ruts, listening for the distant sounds of dogs or vehicles. But the road was enveloped in an even deeper silence than the forest.

"Did you ever think you might die, when you were in the service?"

Bernt rolled his eyes. "There's no point thinking about that. You can't possibly prepare for what you're going to feel if things go to shit. Just focus on following orders."

"Okay. But did you ever write something, for your family, in case—"

"If I had something to tell anyone, I would have said it to them before I left. You can't be thinking about that kind of stuff in the middle of an operation."

"When I left I thought I was going to be delivering a PowerPoint in Minnetonka, not hiking up a mountain to find a meth lab."

"Every day, people get wiped out on their commute, or have a heart attack in the office. You should never walk out the door with shit left unsaid."

"Great advice. But, if something happens, will you tell my family I was thinking about them?"

Bernt sighed. "In what sense?"

"In the sense it sounds like!"

"Don't get touchy with me. You're asking me to deliver a very personal message."

"Tell them I was thinking about them at the end."

"But what if you're thinking about something completely different?"

"Never mind."

"You want me to lie to a grieving family?"

"Never mind."

"I don't know what I'll be thinking about when I buy it," said Bernt. "But I hope to hell it's not my family."

The burble of a stream broke the silence. They came to a spillway diverting water into a channel that flowed into the mountain through a narrow tunnel.

"This is where the boys went in," said Bernt.

Without warning, Lindstrom started running up the road. Bernt squatted by his pack, took a long drink of water, then stood and followed. He found Lindstrom a few hundred feet away, staring over a black plastic fence that rose to his knee.

"This is it."

There was not much to see. Overgrown bushes. Here and there a tattered orange ribbon, everything tinted a dull and sickly gray. "These were our all-stars." He stepped over the fence and walked into the field.

Bernt followed.

The bushes had small, round leaves. When Bernt reached out and rubbed one between his fingers, he felt a layer of ash slide off. He looked for berries but saw just a few dark and brittle clusters left to wither. He caught Lindstrom, who was reading a tag wired to a branch.

"One of these bushes could transform the coffee sector."

"Why are they covered in ash?"

"It's ag-lime. It raises the pH of the soil."

"Your pH must be off the charts," said Bernt.

"We were pushing the boundaries of where coffee can be grown.

Pushing aggressively. If we could make it work right, here, we could open millions of acres worldwide."

They followed a row back to the road. Their shoes slid in the loose dirt. The field was heavily scored by erosion. Long stretches of silt fence lay flattened and buried beneath red dirt and lime. A gray slurry stretched across the road, ending at the edge of the stream.

"Let's find the trail," said Bernt. "I want to finish this."

They walked back to the spillway. The clear water flowed into the dark mouth of the tunnel. Bernt plunged into the tall grass. When Lindstrom followed, he found himself on a narrow footpath, steep and slick. Soon their calves were red with mud. At the top of the ridge, they walked just a few feet before plunging down the opposite side.

Finally, they stepped out of the trees to the edge of a pool. To their right, the dark mouth of the tunnel. Straight ahead, the stream from the upper valley poured in a thin sheet over a rock ledge. A mango tree grew between the tunnel and the stream. From one long branch, a length of frayed line dangled. The water flowed out of the pool through a metal grate over a concrete dam.

"If the anhydrous didn't come from your field, it had to come from there." Bernt pointed up the stream. He walked into the pool, thigh-deep, then waist-deep, until he reached the other shore. Lindstrom followed, stepping carefully on the shifting rocks, steadying himself with the slippery black roots of the wild mango.

The two men walked up the canyon, past tall groves of green bamboo. Lindstrom looked at stones and leaves and logjams. He searched for signs of a path, or footprints, or drums of toxic chemicals, anything to suggest there was some significance in this minor tributary in a remote spur of an insignificant mountain on a small island surrounded by thousands of miles of open, restless, relentless ocean. Above them, green peaks staggered away, their slopes folded like a single sheet of fabric.

Bernt stopped, and Lindstrom noticed a dull flash of orange—a nylon ribbon tied to a bamboo stem. Looking closer, he saw a footpath, barely wider than a man's waist, wending up into the grove. He moved his eyes across the water to the left-hand shore, which was covered in bamboo except for one gap, about six feet wide, where a trail of dirt and half-buried rocks came down to the water's edge.

Bernt was already wading toward it. He beckoned Lindstrom. "I know where this leads."

40

DAWN WAS COMING late these days. Momilani sat in her kitchen, drinking coffee. When she could see the gray hills through the window, she rose from the table, walked through the house, past her nephews sleeping in the living room, one stretched out on the couch, the other leaning back in the easy chair, his big feet propped on the coffee table. They were good boys, more or less, but they weren't good for much. She pressed the button that unlocked her car and climbed into the driver's seat

She didn't have Jonah's number, but she knew where to find him. The Manokalanipos had been on their land a very long time. His dogs bayed when she parked at the foot of the cinderblock pillars. She sat in her car for ten or twenty seconds, long enough for whoever was at home to stop whatever they were doing and look through the window. Then she rose slowly from the vehicle and began to climb the steep staircase to the front door.

"Aloha Auntie," said Jonah, before she reached the first landing.

He stood in the doorway. A toddler with her short, black hair gathered into a topknot held his hand and stared at Momilani with serious brown eyes.

Momilani introduced herself.

"I know you, Auntie. I'm sorry for your loss."

"It's what I come for talk to you about," she said.

Jonah hoisted the young girl into the crook of one arm and stepped aside, gesturing for Momilani to enter. "Welcome, Auntie."

"I no like stay long," she said. "But this old lady needs to catch her breath."

She followed him in and sank onto the couch.

"I had one young man helping me," she said. "Was trying to find out more about my husband's passing."

"One hapa Filipino braddah? From mainland?"

"That's right. A young man named Micah Bernt."

"I know the guy."

"Three days ago, Micah had leave my house with one haole guy and Uncle Joe Hashimoto. They went up to Namahana, looking for something. I never know what. Then yesterday, one young wahine come to my house asking about him."

Jonah nodded. "How you like me help you, Auntie?"

"I thought maybe you know why Nalani Winthrop like know about those men."

"Winthrops own choke land that side," said Jonah. He was stern now. He set the girl down on the floor. "Go find your mother," he told her. Then he said nothing for a long time.

"And you never hear nothing from those guys?"

Momilani shook her head. "The Winthrop girl, she told me for send help, if can."

Jonah pulled out his phone. "I going call some of the boys together. And a few wahine, too."

41

NALANI HADN'T THOUGHT she would fall asleep. But the threadbare flannel sheets, tucked tight with her uncle's military precision, the musty smell of the bunkhouse, and the cold mountain air were instantly tranquilizing. When she woke, the day was already bright. Her horse, Emalani, stood saddled beside Kaimana, their reins looped around a rail on the main house.

Nalani let Emma nuzzle her palm, the horse's hot breath mingling with the cold morning air. She found her uncle in the kitchen with a mug of coffee. "We going ride the south pastures," he said. "Supposed to storm this afternoon."

Nalani said nothing. Pretense was not in her nature, nor her uncle's. Both of them looked grim. But she wanted to ride. And she wanted to see whether her uncle was really done hunting.

The south side of the property was Nalani's favorite place. They rode through tall grass across long, gentle hills that became the steep northern ridges, all part of twenty thousand acres her ancestor—the son of a Boston missionary—had purchased from one of Kamehameha's generals after the war of succession. Even if they had to sell off their land, she was determined to keep this. There had once been hundreds more cattle than the few dozen they kept today. Her uncle had spent his summers with the paniolos who'd roped them, branded them, cut off their balls, herded them into trucks for the slaughterhouse. Maybe it could be a working ranch again, under the right management.

It was strange, to think of the land without her uncle, not just to imagine it without his presence, but to dread something and long for it in equal measure.

They rode almost an hour, following the wheel ruts in the grass. The wind was from the north, dry and cool, even at midmorning. Nalani felt snug in her borrowed flannel shirt. Up ahead, her uncle was handsome in his canvas Carhartt jacket.

They reached the crest of a hill. In the pasture below, two dozen black cows grazed. Cars on the highway looked like toys as they zipped along. On the sea, a line of squalls—white clouds resting on graphite columns of rain.

"Are you ready to try it my way now?" she asked.

"What way is that?"

"I'm not sure yet. But it's going to be legal. And no one's going to get hurt."

"No one had to get hurt my way, either."

"No Uncle, we aren't arguing this again."

"No argument. Just facts. Dexedrine saved a lot of lives. Why you think they put it in our kits?"

"That was Vietnam. We're not at war. And we know better now."

"Helps plenty civilians, too. They had always hand out choke greenies during birthing season."

"You weren't manufacturing Dexedrine."

"You know how things is these days. Plenty people working two jobs just for pay rent. They need one boost for keep going. What we made was clean and safe. I cannot help if some people abuse. Is the clerk at Whaler's responsible if one customer abuse Bud Light?"

"I know what you're doing," said Nalani. "Just stop. You always have the best words for whatever you do. But you never say what they really mean. And I cannot ignore it."

"You ignore plenty! You and your mother, all your cousins, this whole family. You tell me you get plans. You going get one MBA then come back and do what your ancestors could not. What your uncle could not. What you going do for save this land? Build one organic holistic private resort? Make one solar field? You'll destroy what little we have left and call it saving."

"So you'll save the land by killing Kanaka Maoli?"

"What you think kapu was? For a thousand years our people had survive on one small island without nothing from the outside. Now we stay dependent, why? 'Cause we trust the men with MBAs. They say no more need make hard choices. Weak or strong, everyone can take and take and take the same. No one need give. No one need sacrifice."

"And who made you the one to decide how people give?"

"I took that kuleana for myself. No one else say strong enough for do it. Not the mayor, not the council, none of them who call themselves our leaders get the courage for make those kine choices."

"Uncle, you know how crazy you sound? You going go one county council meeting and say we cannot be self-sufficient unless we bring back kapu sacrifice?"

"The old ways worked for a thousand years."

"So what, that makes your ice lab one luakini heiau? And Vierra one kahuna?"

"Shut your mouth girl. No disrespect our culture li'dat."

"Don't lecture me about our culture. We get our name from missionaries and colonizers. And you're just like them."

"Colonizer just another name for conqueror." Winthrop swept his arm toward the ocean. "When the old kings needed mana that could speak beyond the islands, wasn't it our family they turned to for new blood?"

"Your words again," said Nalani. "Well I'll say it plainly. You were cooking ice and selling it. And now I think you've murdered people."

"No one was getting hurt," said her uncle, "until you stuck your nose in. Those boys brought all the attention. Got Jonah involved. Gave Miyake's guy one idea for blackmail us."

"I told you to shut it down!" Nalani shouted.

Emma rolled her eyes and threw her head back. Without thinking, Nalani yanked the reins in a sharp reprimand. Winthrop clucked to

Kaimana. The horse took one disdainful step away from the commotion.

Nalani rubbed Emma's neck and whispered an apology. "I never said to drain it in the stream," she said more softly. "Do you ever think about what you did to those families? And what you're doing to ours?"

"Our family all I think about! Just because this land been Winthrop for two hundred years, don't mean that's how it stay. There are levels on this island go beyond laws and politics. I'm trying to teach you, but you never like learn."

Kicking Kaimana into a trot, her uncle spun the horse and cantered back the way they'd come. Nalani nudged her own horse into a gallop down the hill, until the nearest steer lifted his eyes in placid surprise. She made a wide loop through the final pasture before climbing the hill and following the track back the way they'd come.

The wind had shifted, gusting from the east. A wall of cloud gathered over the ocean, and droplets of rain were already spitting cold against her exposed face and hands. Riding hard, she caught her uncle as he came into the yard. She couldn't avoid entering the stable with him. Quickly, she combed and brushed her horse, then brought a bucket of water and threw in a few forkfuls of hay. At the other end of the barn, she could hear her uncle tending Kaimana more thoroughly and without hurry.

She closed Emma in the stall, gave her a scratch in the soft whorl between her eyes, then hurried from the barn, gathered her things from the bunkhouse, and climbed into her truck.

The clouds had reached the island. It was only noon but felt much later. As Nalani's Tacoma bounced down the rutted road, she caught a glimpse of Vierra and the other men at work around the old Quonset hut, where the tractors and mowers and farm equipment were stored.

Growing up, it had been her uncle who told her she was special.

He'd always said no one else could understand his ideas. She'd built a world on this assumption. Somehow, she'd never once considered that his words could be hollow, his convoluted worldview just a self-serving delusion. Now she tried to reconcile the man she'd known her whole life with the one she'd seen that morning: frightening and pitiful. With a shiver she realized this was how she, too, must have sounded, obliviously parroting his ideas in class, taking others' disagreement as a sign of her own genius.

The road felt endless. The monotonous forest offered no distraction from her thoughts. Even after learning about the lab, after the boys, after those men started dying, she'd refused to see it. The more obvious it became, the harder she had looked away, protecting herself from the knowledge of her own self-delusion, and culpability. She thought of the one person in her life who might understand this.

Then he stepped out of the forest.

He had seen her, obviously. He was fifty feet ahead. Then thirty. Standing with his back perfectly straight, meeting her eyes. Fifteen feet. Covered in dirt. Empty-handed. Five feet.

He looked at her with an expression of absolute openness, hiding nothing. She saw wariness, resolve, suspicion, but also hope, something aching and bright. He never lifted his hands, and she never took hers from the wheel. He was waiting for her to stop.

And she wanted to. She could describe to Micah what had happened and where he was going. How dangerous it was. She knew where the guns were kept.

The car was still rolling. Now she couldn't see him without turning her head. But she could still feel his eyes.

Her uncle had been the only constant in her life. He had made her breakfast and packed her lunches. His stubborn insistence on her genius had allowed her to believe in herself. And the fearsome pressure of his love had compelled her to believe she was worthy of it, no matter what her mother said, no matter where her father was.

She could not betray him.

It was only after she could pick Bernt out in the rearview mirror, standing exactly as he had since stepping out of the forest, that she put her foot on the brake and brought the car to a halt. Their eyes met. The engine idled. Something passed between them, and when it became unbearable, she moved her foot back to the gas pedal.

42

LINDSTROM LAY ON the slick wet leaves of the forest floor. Bernt lay beside him. The noise of the engine grew louder.

When the truck came into view, Bernt watched for a moment longer, then stood and stepped out of the tree line, onto the road.

Lindstrom felt an unexpected thrill of relief. But the truck rolled by without stopping, and the feeling subsided. Then it did stop, and, like a camera clicking into focus, the faded tapestry of forest, sky, and rain popped into a state of perfect clarity. It was, he realized, how an animal must feel at every moment, eagerly reading the meaning of everything, a rapturous way of existing.

The engine shifted into gear and the truck moved on. Bernt turned. A glimpse of anguish, then he was as impassive as ever. Lindstrom wondered if he'd just imagined it.

As the sound of the engine faded to the silence of raindrops on leaves, he understood that, unlike Bernt, he was not prepared for whatever lay at the end of this road.

"We have to move," said Bernt.

"Who was that?"

"Someone I trust."

They walked close to the edge of the road. Branches brushed their shoulders, showering cold drops. After a few minutes, Bernt held up his arm at a ninety-degree angle, his fist clenched. Lindstrom stopped. Bernt lowered his arm as if patting something. *Down*. He flicked two fingers back and forth. *Come*. Lindstrom walked slowly, until Bernt pointed at a disruption in the trees.

"There's another road, smaller than this one. It leads to a clearing and a Quonset hut, a sort of storage area. There's a path we're going to take, but first I'm going to recon. I want you to walk fifteen feet into the woods and wait for me. If you hear anything, or if I don't come back, you sit tight, right there, no matter what you hear. Wait until midnight, then take this road to the highway and get the police."

"All right," agreed Lindstrom. "But what do I tell them?"

"You tell them to come back here. Tell them to look at the Winthrop family. Tell them everything you know. Then get the hell off this island."

Lindstrom walked into the woods, pushing past dripping trees. He counted thirty steps. There was a fallen log and he sat on it. At first, he listened. Listened as hard as he'd ever listened in his life. Then his mind wandered. He thought about his children, then said a prayer. It seemed insufficient, so he said it again. He looked up at the leaves against the sky. He listened to the rain.

Lindstrom checked his watch—two minutes had passed. He considered his possessions: sneakers, socks, nylon shorts, boxer briefs, quick-dry T-shirt. The watch. The ID bracelet. Seven items.

He shut his eyes and rubbed his wife's name with his thumb as he repeated the prayer. He took several long breaths and felt better. When he opened his eyes, Bernt was crouching a few feet away, staring intently into his face.

"How's your heart rate?"

"I don't know."

Bernt reached out and hesitated, as if to ask permission, then pressed two fingers into the soft notch between Lindstrom's windpipe and his jaw. The touch triggered something, the feeling of visiting his doctor, the relief of being in someone else's hands.

"Your pulse is good. You're not panicked. You're stronger than you think."

Lindstrom was confused by the way Bernt was looking at him, until he realized he was crying.

Bernt gripped his shoulder. "There are three people in that clearing. I recognize them. They are dangerous. But they aren't expecting us, and that makes us more dangerous. All right?"

Lindstrom nodded.

"We're mentally strong, we're in no hurry, and we have a plan. I can't tell you how many times I would have given anything to have those assets. We have two objectives: to disable their vehicle and to reach the path on the other side of the clearing. They're busy over by the Quonset hut. I need forty seconds for the vehicle, and I need you to keep watch while I'm under the hood. Then we're going to get behind the barn and make it to the trailhead."

They walked through the forest at an angle to the road until they reached the track that led to the clearing. At Bernt's signal, they crossed it and stepped into the forest. From there, Bernt walked patiently and carefully through the forest to the edge of the clearing. Bernt signaled Lindstrom to join him behind an abandoned tractor, its tall rubber tires collapsed and hardened, vines growing through the metal seat. Bernt crouched behind the small engine housing. "Take a look, slowly."

Lindstrom raised his head into a gap between the engine and cab. He saw a yard cluttered with empty chemical tanks, ones he'd expect to see on any small farm, the bestsellers. There were piles of yard waste, neglected machines, and a few plastic barrel-halves with roosters strutting back and forth in front of each one, rearing up and flapping.

Near the open doors of the Quonset hut, a bonfire released a thick plume of smoke, white against the wet forest. Two men were feeding the fire, tossing in items of clothing, then a rifle. A third was sitting in a plastic chair with his back to them, watching.

Lindstrom looked at Bernt.

"That was Uncle Joe's rifle," said Bernt, matter-of-factly. "They have two vehicles. The ATV we can't reach. But it can only carry two. If we take out the truck, it makes them less mobile. I need you to keep watch while I work. If anyone looks up, tap the hood twice. If they see us, we run. Head into the forest and try to make your way back to the spot where I left you."

Lindstrom nodded.

"Deep breath," said Bernt, before glancing for a moment beyond the tractor, then moving smoothly in a half-crouch across ten feet of open ground until he took a knee in front of the truck's grille. He crept around it, opened the driver's door, and reached in. Lindstrom heard the hood click. The men at the fire were absorbed in their work, poking the blaze with chunks of wood. The body of the truck lay between them and Bernt, who was now back in front of the grille, still crouching. He released the hood and raised it a few inches.

He glanced back at Lindstrom, then raised the hood high enough to lean into the engine compartment. If they turned, the men would easily see, but they had their heads down, intent on the fire. They were close enough that Lindstrom could see the rain dripping from the brims of their caps. One man turned as if he'd heard something, and Lindstrom rapped on the engine. The sound, he was sure, must have carried across the clearing. But the man only swept his eyes across them then turned back, saying something to the others that made them bob their heads, laughing. Bernt was crouched behind the grille. He locked eyes with Lindstrom.

Lindstrom glanced at the men and nodded. With the same easy strides, Bernt joined him behind the tractor.

He opened his hand and showed Lindstrom a gray plastic chip. "Main relay fuse." He slipped it into his pocket.

Lindstrom followed Bernt back into the woods. Soon the Quonset hut was between them and the fire. Then they reached the trail.

They followed the narrow path through the dripping forest.

"There's no hurry now," said Bernt. "It's about a mile, and I want us to be fresh."

"Fresh for what?"

"There's a house up ahead. An old man lives there, Richard Winthrop. This is his land. It was his name you found on all the leases. If he's not alone, we'll wait until he is."

"Wait to what?"

Bernt stopped in the trail. "Detain the subject and extract intelligence."

The trail was a dim red presence running before them. Now and then, a forest bird called. Sometimes the delicate whistles were answered in kind. More often, they melted into darkness.

After twenty minutes, Lindstrom saw sky ahead. Fear and adrenaline surged. But Bernt did not slow his gait. They passed a stone wall surrounding a massive area of piled rock. A single monkeypod tree grew at the center of the ruin, snaking its long gray limbs protectively above it. Bernt slowed only when he passed beneath a black log angled over the path. Lindstrom thought it was a fallen branch, slick and rotten, until he saw the carved mouth gaping with rows of pointed teeth, jagged and needle-like in decay.

He stopped a few paces beyond and whispered, "Micah."

Bernt went still, fading instantly into the shadows that surrounded him.

"If something happens, just tell them why I was here."

Bernt nodded and continued onward.

After ten more minutes, Lindstrom again saw brightness through the trees. This time it was a clearing with a cabin and a wooden stable, both well-maintained. Beyond them a low house with a broad tin roof and stone chimney, a thin line of smoke rising into the sky. And beyond the house, through a notch in the trees at the edge of the meadow, the dark line of the sea, some trick of perspective making it seem to rise even higher than the land where they stood.

A green Land Rover was parked in front of the main house. A tall man in a canvas coat with a rifle slung diagonally over one shoulder was loading something into the open trunk. Without a word, Bernt stepped from the cover of the forest and ran smoothly across the lawn with loping strides, like a long jumper approaching the pit. It was over two hundred feet to the Range Rover, and by the time Bernt had covered half the distance he was in full sprint, approaching from the man's right so that when he looked up and tried to shrug off the rifle, Bernt was already on him. He grabbed the sling of the rifle, jerking it up to raise the man's arm helplessly above his head, then brought the sling across the man's throat while pressing the rifle stock against the back of his neck. The man clawed the air with his free arm, grabbing at Bernt's fist. Eventually, he went rigid, then limp.

"Help me lift him," said Bernt, and Lindstrom realized he, too, had run across the yard and was now standing by the Land Rover. "We need to tie him before he wakes up."

43

THERE WERE THREE buildings: the main house, the stable, and the bunkhouse. Bernt chose the bunkhouse because it offered a view of the road and the forest where the path emerged. It was a single long room with four bunk beds lined against one wall and windows on three sides.

Bernt took a chair and placed it in the center of the room. They'd already bound Winthrop's arms and legs with a roll of silver tape from his trunk. Lifting him under the armpits, they set him in the chair. Bernt wrapped the tape around his chest and arms and did the same with each calf. He stationed Lindstrom by the window where he could see the forest and the road. Bernt had given him Winthrop's rifle—an antique Winchester bolt-action that held just three .30 caliber Magnum rounds—after a brief explanation of how to handle it.

Bernt had Winthrop's Smith & Wesson M1911, a gun he knew well. It was loaded with eight .45 caliber cartridges. They had eleven rounds between them. Bernt had decided the risk of delay outweighed the benefit of finding more ammunition. He'd briefly considered throwing Winthrop in the Land Rover, but his vision of the mission had been to keep it contained on the property, not kidnap Winthrop and create unforeseen complications.

With the .45 in one hand and Winthrop's iPhone in the other, he knelt and pressed the man's thumb to the small lock screen. When it blinked on, Bernt opened the camera and began recording a video, careful not to capture Lindstrom or himself before setting the phone lens-down under the chair. Then he slapped Winthrop hard in the face.

The old man opened his eyes wide. Then they went narrow. "I remember you."

Bernt said nothing.

"Special Warfare School. You're my niece's friend."

"Shut up," said Bernt. He was speaking on autopilot while he re-calculated the situation. It hadn't occurred to him until this moment that Winthrop may have been trained to resist interrogation. The 1911 should have tipped him. It was still standard-issue in Vietnam. If Winthrop had been a scout or Special Forces, this conversation would be a lot more challenging.

Winthrop turned his head suddenly toward Lindstrom. But Bernt had placed the chair so he was out of view.

"Who's that?"

"Just another soldier."

"It's that shit Mr. Lindstrom. I know who he is."

Bernt tilted his head to remind Lindstrom to look out the window and keep quiet.

"We know about the lab," said Bernt. "We know what you did the day those boys died."

"I don't know what you're talking about."

"I know you were trying to save this land. For your family. You never meant to hurt anyone."

"That shit won't work on me."

"It was your men who did it, right? You would have stopped them if you'd known they were going to bleed an entire tank of anhydrous into the stream."

"I don't know about any of that. But I do know anhydrous cannot poison one stream. Mixed with water it converts to ammonium. Safe enough for swimming."

"Interesting. And why exactly are you such an expert on the subject?"

"We work with plenty chemicals on the farm. I like to know my safety protocols."

Already, Bernt was tempted to escalate the interrogation. But he knew Winthrop would see it for exactly what it was, a sign of panic.

"Ammonia," said Winthrop, "*that* could kill someone, but would take one high pH to convert ammonium to ammonia. Nothing like you'd find in one mountain stream." Again Winthrop tried to turn and see Lindstrom. "You get one chemist right there. Ask him."

Bernt didn't follow Winthrop's gaze. "We know you dumped anhydrous the day those boys died. And we know you killed the men who supplied it."

"Are you talking about Uncle Clifton guys? If anyone had murder them, was probably those hippies protesting over there. Everyone thinks those dreadlocks mean peace and love, but those Rastafari worship one radical African revolutionary. Was right there in da kine's music, Marley. That's why CIA had take him out."

"It wasn't any hippies," said Bernt. "And it wasn't Bob Marley."

"So maybe was the father, Jonah, the one go blaming every kine person but himself. That family go way back. Plenty warriors in that bloodline."

"If he killed anyone, it would be the ones who killed his boy." Bernt wasn't even sure what he was arguing. The momentum of the conversation had shifted so badly, he was talking just to maintain a rhythm and prevent it from going completely off the rails.

"Exactly," said Winthrop. "And it was Clifton guys who dumped enough ag-lime on that field to turn the whole stream basic. So if one harmless chemical like ammonium did flow in, could turn dangerous. Your chemist never tell you that?"

*

Beside the window, Lindstrom pressed the barrel of his rifle to his cheek. The cold metal was soothing. He hadn't considered how the pH of the stream would affect the anhydrous, but as soon as Winthrop said it, he knew it made sense. For a moment, he existed in a world in which he was responsible for three boys' agonizing deaths. Then he saw through Winthrop's false equivalence. Miyake had let things slip a bit, but that wasn't the same as running a meth lab. His fields were subject to inspection. They had pulled the proper permits.

But it wasn't just Winthrop's words confusing him. Reality itself was suddenly fragile. His children would be out of school for the holiday. What had Char told them? Could he really be here, by this window, holding a rifle, waiting for men to come out of the woods? He heard a strange sound and glanced back at the room. Bernt's arm was raised. He slapped Winthrop in the stomach with the back of his hand and immediately leaned forward and pinched the man's cheeks, pulling the skin taut between his hands. "This is what you wanted?"

Winthrop was silent. *He's scared,* Lindstrom thought.

He turned his attention back to the window. Nothing had changed. The green lawn, the dark line of trees, the empty house and its empty windows, the gray sky. He was scared, too.

Since watching Bernt choke the man out, Lindstrom had been operating under the assumption that Winthrop would confess to everything, they would take the recording to the police, the murderers would go to prison, and he would go back to his family and start figuring out what came next. He now saw this had been magical thinking. The old man wasn't going to confess, and the police weren't going to show up and put those men at the barn in handcuffs.

He heard more sounds from the center of the room but didn't look, even after the clatter and thump of Winthrop hitting the floor. He stared out the window, stared so hard that by the time he realized what he was seeing, the two men who'd come out of the woods were halfway to the stable. And the four-wheeler that had come up the road—so fast its engine noise arrived just a split second before it crested the hill—was well on its way to reaching cover behind the house.

44

LINDSTROM FRANTICALLY KNOCKED on the windowsill three times, as an ATV whined in the distance. Winthrop's eyes flickered in that direction. Resisting the urge to sprint toward the window, Bernt pulled a rag from his pocket and whipped it around Winthrop's head, pulling until the stubborn man relented and the fabric slipped between his teeth.

"What do you see?" Bernt asked quietly as he tied the gag off with a reef knot.

"Three. All three!" Lindstrom was nearly shouting. "With rifles!"

"Positions?"

"Two came out of the forest and went behind the stable. One came on the ATV and went behind the house."

Bernt was beside him now. "Don't lean out. Keep to the side like I told you. I'm taking the rifle and giving you the pistol, all right?" He chambered the .45, released the safety. "There are eight rounds. The safety's off. Don't shoot at anything unless you're sure you can hit it."

Lindstrom looked at him, then his eyes flickered back to the window, his focus dancing with no purpose. Bernt considered keeping both weapons. "I need you to watch the house," he said. "That's it. You understand? Nowhere else. Your job is to watch the house. If you see anything you tell me what you see. If anyone tries to cross the yard, shoot him. That's your only job. If you do your job, I'll take care of the rest and we'll be fine. Understand?"

Lindstrom nodded.

"Take the pistol."

Lindstrom removed one hand from the rifle and gripped the pistol. Bernt held it for a moment, angled toward the floor, and when he released it, Lindstrom kept it there.

"Hand me the rifle."

Lindstrom reached it across the window. Bernt took it, then ran to the window facing the stable. He hoped the sky was bright enough, despite the overcast, for the glare to obscure him. He could see the full length of the stable, about fifty yards away. The yard between was a rutted mess of red dirt, softening to mud in the steady mist. Getting slippery.

"Micah, what's our plan?"

"We wait," said Bernt. "And when they come, we shoot them."

"How do you think they'll come?"

"Two will lay down fire and the third will make a dash at us."

"Do you have any, uh, tips on how to shoot them?"

"It's about twenty yards to the house. So you'll have about four seconds."

Lindstrom was unusually silent.

"Don't worry, that's a long time."

Lindstrom still didn't speak.

"Just remember. Speed is fine, but accuracy is final. Think about it. He's going to head for the corner between us, because that's the closest cover. So you know where he's going. Anticipate where he'll be and put a bullet there."

"What if he makes it?"

"Then I shoot him through the wall."

"What's to stop him from shooting us?"

"He knows his boss is here, but he doesn't know where. If he reaches the wall, drop to the floor and watch the windows."

"All right," said Lindstrom.

"Get ready," said Bernt. "They've had time to search the other buildings." He ran his hand up and down the rifle's stock and barrel, feeling the coolness, making sure he was loose. Squinting through the scope, he trained the crosshairs on the corner of the stable, bringing it into focus. "Take a deep breath. Let it out slowly."

For the next few moments, the room was silent other than their breathing.

A pane of glass shattered beside Bernt, followed by the *crack* of the shot, then its echo.

"Shit!" Lindstrom screamed.

A man stepped out from the behind the stable, directly into the center of Bernt's scope. He fired, but the man slipped and was already falling as Bernt pulled the trigger. The shot went overhead. He was lowering the barrel toward the fallen man when he heard the pistol firing behind him.

"I missed," said Lindstrom.

Shifting his rifle to cover the corner of the room, Bernt fired at the white plywood wall at waist height. Heard nothing. He was prone on the floor now, elbows propped, legs spread wide. He glanced at Lindstrom, who had dropped to his knee, holding the pistol with both hands, and called over for him to "Get—"

A hole opened in the center of the wall, with the *bang* of a shotgun. Lindstrom flopped over.

Fuck this, Bernt thought. It had been a shitty plan from the start. He rose to a crouch and ran across the room, eyes on the windows. Opening the door, he dropped back to one knee in the yard and brought his rifle up. No one. He hustled to the edge of the building, then turned the corner and charged with fear so wild it could have been joy, coming face-to-face with Sunny Vierra, Ice Man from Anahola, who was already wheeling the shotgun around but not before Bernt stepped inside its arc, pinned it against the wall with the side of his body, and slammed the butt of his rifle into Vierra's right arm. He felt the shotgun release and he wheeled the butt back toward Vierra's chin, but the man leaned back and it passed in front of his face.

Bernt stepped back, swinging the barrel down to release a shot into Vierra's chest, but now they were separated by several feet, enough for the men behind the stable to open fire. He fired a shot in their direction, his last, and ducked behind the corner of the bunkhouse.

He dropped to one knee and peeked out. Vierra was sprinting through the red muck to the stable. The others had found their range. A chunk of wood splintered from the corner of the building, just behind him.

Bernt ran back through the door.

Everything was as he left it. Winthrop was still on his side in the middle of the floor. Lindstrom lay on his back with his knees drawn up, hands clasped over his stomach, taking slow, deep breaths, staring at the ceiling and working something out inside his head, like someone looking up from a crossword puzzle, an expression Bernt had seen seven other times in his life.

When the man came around the side of the house, Lindstrom did exactly what he'd practiced in his mind, tracking him with the barrel of the pistol then squeezing the trigger. It operated more easily than he'd expected, a satisfying mechanical tension and release—*bang, bang, bang*—so uncannily similar to his most optimistic version of events that it took him longer than it should have to realize the shots had missed and the man was safe behind the wall of their very own building. He had remembered what Bernt had told him and dropped to a knee. Bernt fired at the wall, and afterward, as the room went oddly still, Lindstrom tried to remember if he was supposed to fire, too. He'd just made his decision, based on the principle that it was better to go down swinging than get called out looking, when something threw him to the floor.

As he lay there, collecting himself, he watched Bernt run out of the room. A childlike sense of abandonment surged through him. He felt wetness on his shirt and a terrifying complaint from places that had always been peaceful, dark, and anonymous. He patted his stomach and the right side of his body. Things were happening outside the walls. He could hear them, but they didn't concern him anymore.

Yes, here it was. He pressed tenderly against the hot, slick, ragged spot: mingled fabric, flesh, and blood. White pain poured down a long pipe.

He was on his back now, his knees drawn up in a comfortable, comforting way, his fingers interlaced over the wound. He tried out a prayer, *I will lift up my eyes to the hills.* Yes, this was better, solid to the ground, all his limbs looking after him while he looked after them, too. It pierced him then that this was himself, his only self, and he would be leaving it, going to wherever he had been before his birth. A place he would not leave again.

Lindstrom stared around the bunkhouse, its white plank walls and ceiling. Dark treetops through the window. Gray clouds. All moving, he realized, in the most intricate patterns. Strange how he hadn't noticed before, the spirals within spirals, so obvious now. The sea was out there, somewhere. He would see it, if he raised his head. But it was better, here on the floor, with just the treetops and the sky.

Bernt was with him now. A distracted, anxious presence. Lindstrom felt sorry for him. Sorry for all of them. What an awful thing, to be human; scared, confused. He felt Bernt gently lift his hands away to feel the wound. Pain down the pipe, the white fire. The sun cooling and swelling. Ashes and dust. He searched for his family, this final prayer, all his memories. He couldn't find them now, but he knew they were there, stored somewhere safely in his mind.

Not for long.

No.

No no no.

This was what happened to other people. Not to him.

He was on his knees in a dark place and the memories were spilling through his fingers, bright and slippery, disappearing down a black drain, a stone tunnel. He needed to slow down.

He summoned his family, Char and the kids. Mom and Dad. But it was the people from the forest who came slipping through the trees. And a black wind of despair that blew through him, sweeping into spaces vaster and emptier than he'd ever imagined.

He felt someone's fingers. They traced a delicate line down his jaw to the vulnerable skin only a few others—his mother, his doctor, his wife—had ever touched. He felt the pressure of his own warm, oblivious blood, still in its right place, building beneath his friend's cool fingertips, as if everything were still all right. Building and releasing. Ticking like a bedside clock. In and out like the tide. Something slipped free and now he made his final prayer: the faces of his family, each in turn and all together. A red star throbbing in the darkness, a heart filled up to bursting. But the sea was above the windowsill. Water pounded the glass. It pulsed against the place where someone's fingers met his skin. The pulse became a pattern, the pattern a rhythm, the rhythm a moment, a moment, a moment, a moment

45

ERNT STAYED WITH Lindstrom until his pulse stopped. He ran to the window, hoping there were six rounds left in the pistol, but could see nothing through the gray curtains of rain now beating the roof of the bunkhouse with a roar like silence. Releasing the magazine, he counted—five—then reloaded. A sound sent him whirling, almost releasing a shot into the wall before realizing it was Winthrop, dragging himself along the floor with his bound legs. Bernt leveled the pistol at his head. Winthrop met his eyes and held them for the long seconds it took to inch his way to a sheltered nook between two bunk beds. Bernt turned back to the window, felt for his own pulse. He didn't bother to count, just willed himself to calm down, slow down.

The rain stopped.

Bernt could see the stable. Still no sign of movement, but that would not last long. They would come from opposite sides, the third man in support offering well-aimed fire. With only the pistol he'd be hard-pressed to hit two runners at range, and if even one gained the bunkhouse, it would be impossible for him to protect his flanks. They'd shoot him through the window. For a moment, he considered joining Winthrop under the bunk.

He was fixating, he realized, and he was missing something. There were three buildings. And there were vehicles. He looked toward the house. If could reach it, he could take the ATV or the Land Rover.

He didn't know if Vierra had run back or joined his friends at the stable. If he was at the house, it would be almost impossible. But there was no better option.

As he crossed the room, the only question was whether to fire off a few rounds to keep their heads down or trust the element of surprise. He decided to save his ammunition and go straight to the ATV. It was slower and more exposed than the Land Rover, but the engine was warm and he knew it would start.

Creeping to the corner of the building, he didn't look around the edge, instead staring at the open yard. It was unnerving not to know what was happening at the stable. He walked back a few paces and dropped into a sprinter's crouch. At least he wasn't draped in M60 belts. Pushing off, he was at peak speed by the time he cleared the corner of the bunkhouse and entered the open yard. For a moment, he felt his boot soles slip on the wet grass, but he regained his footing and was almost halfway across when he heard an AR-15 firing to his right, from the stable. He was ten yards away when Vierra stepped clear of the house, dead ahead, rifle raised. Without aiming or slowing Bernt fired the pistol until the trigger clicked on an empty chamber.

He reached the corner of the house. Flattening against the shingled boards, he looked around for a weapon of opportunity and tried to come up with a plan, any plan. Reaching the vehicles was not an option. They could enfilade him on the open ground. He shifted his grip to the warm barrel of the pistol, clutching it like a hammer. With his left hand he unclipped his folding knife and pried the blade open until it locked. They would suspect he was out of ammunition but wouldn't be sure. So he had a little time.

Vierra would come through the house and wait while the other two flanked him. They'd be at the bunkhouse by now. Bernt dropped to his stomach, the wet grass chilling him. He was in front of the lanai, which was raised three feet off the ground, with latticed wood strips covering the crawlspace underneath. Bernt squirmed until he had an angle that allowed him to see through the lattice, both corners of the bunkhouse, the dark forest beyond. Cold water dripped from the eaves onto his neck. Of course he was going to die in the mud, in the mountains, who had he been kidding.

Instead of sadness, or regret, all he felt was irritation. Winthrop was going to get away with it. He should have put a bullet in him. It would have been a better use. They would take his body and Lindstrom's and dump them with Uncle Joe's, and that would be that. Vierra would be inside now, clearing rooms, and when he gave the signal, the other two would come. If he was lucky, he could take one of these assholes down with him.

Bernt's thoughts were interrupted when two men stepped into view from behind the bunkhouse. They were meth heads, but they had some discipline. Cocky now, each held a Bushmaster in a low carry, the barrel pointed at the ground. Vierra must be directing them from somewhere in the house above. They were walking forward, slow and deliberate, taking angles that would give them a view along the front and back of the house in just a few more seconds.

Bernt raised himself to one knee. He would go straight at the closer man, fling the pistol at his face, tackle, start stabbing if he got that far. He had three seconds, two.

He stepped into the open, running furiously.

Both men brought their rifles up aiming point blank.

Locking eyes with the nearest gunman, Bernt threw his pistol and braced for the blow of the bullets.

The man fell.

The pistol sailed through empty space.

Shots fired.

Bernt's momentum carried him past the fallen man. Still running, he turned to look over his shoulder.

Three Hawaiians stood at the edge of the old forest. Two more were kneeling, their faces obscured by rifle scopes. Jonah stood between the shooters, his arms folded over his chest.

A door slammed. Vierra, running toward the stable. The marksmen didn't have a shot.

Bernt changed direction without breaking stride. On the other side of the building, he saw Vierra heading for the tree line. His side ached and his lungs pumped pain as he sprinted through the wet grass. Vierra held a Bushmaster, but it was slowing him down. By the time he reached the forest, Bernt was only twenty feet behind.

The ground fell steeply.

Vierra had found a pig trail and was running and sliding down the slick red dirt, gaining distance for a moment, then slipping, his legs going out from under him as he landed hard on his ass. The rifle went flying. Vierra leapt to his feet, pausing almost imperceptibly as he looked back for the rifle. Then Bernt put a shoulder into him, so both men rolled down the hillside on the slick red mud. Finding their footing at the base of the hill, both spun, half-crouched in an identical fighting stance, staring at one another.

It took a moment, then Vierra recognized him. That listless grin, familiar now.

Bernt had held onto his knife and managed not to slice himself throughout the chase. Vierra unfolded a blade of his own. If Bernt had not just sprinted half a mile, he'd have bull-rushed already. But his heart rate was redlining. He knew his decision-making was affected, his reflexes untrustworthy. He could see Vierra panting, too. Neither had an advantage there. Both were moving, circling, triangulating with each step, never crossing their legs.

Vierra was moving to his left. Bernt glanced that way, saw a log bristling with broken limbs and wheeled right, forcing Vierra to circle away. Both men held their weapons right-handed, blade forward in loose hammer grip, thumb up on the spine. Neither had a true fighting knife. But Vierra was taller, and his wingspan looked even longer than his height.

Bernt needed to get a sense of his reach.

He feinted a few times. Vierra didn't react. They were almost in range, six feet from each other in a clearing of bright green ferns. Their footing was solid in the spongy soil. Their eyes met for the briefest moment. Their knives mirrored each other.

Bernt considered his options. Initiate with something basic and effective: a vertical slash or a combo culminating in a reverse thrust. Or try to catch Vierra off guard with a figure eight or a few redondas. He looked into Vierra's eyes, wary, almost unfocused, ready.

He didn't like the other man's advantages. If this fight was predictable, Bernt would die.

He made a decision and launched into a flurry of footwork he'd practiced thousands of times, flowing so naturally it took tremendous mental effort, when the moment came, to step falsely, cross his legs awkwardly, and launch himself so that instead of a textbook slashing attack at the limits of his reach he slammed his arm and shoulder into the other man.

Now it was no longer a Kali knife fight, it was a brawl, the two men rolling in the ferns, trying to free their knife hands and fending one another off with their live hands. Bernt's knife arm was trapped against the ground under Vierra's shoulder. Vierra tried to stab him between the ribs, but Bernt locked out his bicep and head-butted him in the face. Bernt's right arm came free, but before he could use his knife, Vierra hit him with a haymaker in the side of the head. He leaped back just as Vierra whipped a blade through the air where his torso had been.

There it was. Vierra's reach was even longer than he'd feared.

Bernt reengaged, swinging his left arm down so their forearms smashed painfully as Vierra tried to come back with a reversing slash. He thrust for Vierra's heart but was checked. For a moment their four arms interlaced. Then Vierra slashed open Bernt's thigh.

Without hesitating, Vierra slashed again. Bernt, acting on reflex, blocked with his right, then trapped the knife with his left.

Vierra punched him in the face.

Bernt threw Vierra's knife hand back and stepped away, feeling the flesh of his thigh sliding against itself. They were at range again; Bernt was vulnerable. Vierra knew this and attacked immediately. Bernt had to use both hands to trap the knife. He was getting fatigued now, making mistakes. He swung his head to avoid a punch that never came and was horrified to feel Vierra grab his right wrist and slam a forearm into Bernt's bicep, trapping him helplessly in a straight arm bar.

This was where the fight had always been heading, Bernt realized. Vierra wasn't just taller and stronger, he was more skilled. He'd been multiple steps ahead since they first squared off, setting him up for this fatal mistake.

The pain was building as he resisted the downward pressure. He tried to punch Vierra in the groin but the man easily stepped farther behind his back, cranking his arm even more. Something was about to give.

Bernt knew his limitations as a fighter. He had survived this long by sheer, stubborn aggressiveness. Most people instinctively risked death to avoid pain, and he'd assumed his luck would run out the day he met someone willing to endure more pain than him. It pissed him off, to die at the hands of someone with more skill and less courage.

There was just one option left. He gave up.

Abruptly buckling under the pressure of Vierra's hold, he dropped to one knee. For a moment, Vierra was off-balance, giving Bernt just enough time to transfer his knife from right to left. He managed a single blind slash toward Vierra's jeans before he felt his elbow pop.

As pain pulled down its curtain, he tucked and rolled, ready for the last thing he would ever feel: a cold blade between his ribs. It didn't come. Not that it mattered. Vierra's endgame was just beginning. He had no need to rush now.

With the futility of an outwitted animal, Bernt dropped his knife and tried to push himself back, driven by a primal instinct to move away from the source of danger, scrabbling his heels in the crushed and bloody ferns. He stared helplessly at Vierra, tried to clear his mind in readiness for the man who towered over him to step in and finish with a few quick strikes.

But Vierra just stared back. And after a moment, Bernt understood.

By the time Vierra followed Bernt's gaze down to his own leg, the dark spot near his groin had grown from a dime to a quarter. Soon it was a stripe down the inseam of his jeans. Vierra dropped his knife. He watched the dark column spread, then looked up at Bernt, his stare stubborn and defiant. Then his leg gave out, and he collapsed into the ferns.

Bernt sank back. He watched the tree limbs toss against the clouds. He used his left hand to examine the wound in his thigh, spreading the tear in his pants. It was in the meat of the muscle, already clotting. He felt very cold.

The forest was silent except for dripping water.

Some time passed before a spotted hound came into the clearing. It sniffed the bloody ferns, took a long sniff of the dead man, then noticed Bernt. It raised its ears, gave one languorous wag of its tail, placed its nose against his neck, and licked its long pink tongue from chin to cheek. Cupping its head, Bernt ran his fingers around the dog's ear, compressing the soft cartilage and feeling it spring back. The dog turned, trotted a few feet away, then stopped and looked back. Bernt pushed himself to his feet. Very carefully, he followed the dog up the hill and out of the forest.

46

B ERNT WALKED SLOWLY across the field. Two mud-splattered pickups were parked in the grass by the bunkhouse, bright green ti leaves knotted around their trailer hitches. Three people stood in the rain. Familiar faces. Doreen and one of the tattooed brothers had rifles slung over their shoulders. Mahea was the third.

They watched Bernt limp toward them through the high wet grass.

"Thanks," he said, with a slight bow of his head.

Doreen nodded. She looked him full in the eyes, but he could read nothing in hers. Whatever she was feeling, it was not for him to see.

Jonah came backward out of the bunkhouse, carrying Winthrop's bound arms hooked over his own. The other brother followed with Winthrop's feet. They carried the man around the pickup, dumped him onto the open tailgate, and shoved him into the steel cage in the bed.

The dog that had led Bernt out of the forest cocked its head.

"What you like us do with the haole?" Jonah asked.

Lindstrom was lying as Bernt had left him, his knees flopped to one side, his fingers interlaced over the wound in his stomach.

Bernt knelt by Lindstrom's head, used a corner of his shirt to wipe away the faint brown marks of blood under his jaw. His eyes were already closed. Bernt picked up the Winchester rifle and the iPhone, which had stopped recording. He paused in the doorway and took a final look around the stark, bright room. He tried and failed to connect the object on the floor to the man who'd stopped on the bright road just a few hours earlier and said he wanted to help make things right. He hadn't, of course, been any help in a firefight. But he'd been very frightened and still done exactly what Bernt asked. One more black day on the calendar.

The sun shone through a break in the clouds. A glint of metal. Bernt walked back to Lindstrom's body, knelt, and unclipped the ID bracelet strapped to his wrist.

He limped back into the yard. "What happens now?"

"We hide. Leave 'em like we found 'em."

They turned toward the vehicles. Bernt moved more slowly than the others. Jonah caught up to him. Said something too quietly for Bernt to hear.

"I'm sorry?"

Jonah looked back toward the forest. "What happened to the boys?"

Bernt looked at Winthrop in the cage. The old man breathing heavily.

"He was trading his lease with the seed company for anhydrous to cook meth. When they shut down the lab, they bled everything straight into the stream. It came down, mixed with runoff from the fields. It was a chemical reaction. It would have happened very quick."

Bernt forced himself to raise his eyes and look at the other man. Jonah was staring over the trees toward the dark flanks of the mountain.

🍃

Bernt felt an arm on his shoulder, guiding him toward a truck. The brothers helped him up into the back seat and held him between them as the truck bounced down the long road, the red lights of Jonah's vehicle shining through the mist. They drove down the steep forest ridges, then the gentle sloping pastures, until the land flattened and they reached the highway junction.

Bernt ducked his head to look back, but the mountain was a shadow veiled by rain.

Jonah's truck signaled and turned north. Their truck turned south.

"Auntie Momilani said we should bring you to her hale," said Doreen from the front seat. "You like go or what?"

The cab was silent, until one of the brothers spoke up from the back.

"Da buggah stay sleeping already."

Mahea shrugged and kept on speeding down the dark highway.

47

BERNT WAS DRAGGING his razor across the sensitive skin below his jaw when he heard tires grind over gravel and come to a halt. A familiar voice.

"You one difficult man for track down."

He wetted the razor and made a few more quick strokes, then lifted the mirror and surveyed his work. He tilted it again and framed Detective Carvalho, peering through the passenger window of a white Explorer.

"Good morning Detective."

Carvalho pulled in beside Bernt's battered green Sable.

"I know you seen me coming around these last few days. But you never like walk out of the woods and say hello. You make me get up early, just for you."

Bernt squeezed a dollop of product into his palm and stared across the parking lot toward the tents and the ocean. He'd known this would happen eventually. He'd been parking his car at the beach park and using the facilities in full view every morning.

"I saw you in the news," he told Carvalho.

"But you never called the number."

"Guess I didn't have any information to share."

"The lady just wanted to know what had happen to her husband."

"Seemed like you wanted to know a lot more than that."

"You don't think we going clear this case? We almost there. Just a few loose ends is all."

Bernt raised his eyebrows.

"When exactly did you meet this Michael Lindstrom?"

"Sorry," said Bernt. "What is this, exactly?"

"He had a room at the Marriott. People there tell me he wasn't alone."

A truck came down the pitted lot and pulled into a space fronting the beach. Two men got out dressed to fight giant trevally, high-definition cameras strapped to their chests, pole braces on their waists. They began unloading rods from the ski rack mounted on the roof.

"They come every morning," said Bernt. "Never catch shit."

The detective nodded. "I never understand these GT guys. Spend all that time to nail one ulua, then just throw 'em back."

"They like the fight."

Carvalho rolled his eyes. "These Marriott guys. They say Lindstrom had one local brother with him."

"I'm not local."

"We know you was up there, on Winthrop land, with Joe Hashimoto."

"Sure, me and sixty other people, searching for Uncle Kimo."

"That's right. Was you and Nalani Winthrop had search together."

Bernt said nothing.

"Nalani Winthrop. She never like talk at first. But she finally tell us everything."

Bernt's things were spread across the hood of his car. He began putting them back into his kit.

"We know her uncle was cooking up there on the mountain. We know they was getting supplies from Miyake guys. And they was the ones killed Clifton and Uncle Kimo. 'As what she say, anyway. She never like talk about you though, not at first."

Bernt turned and faced the detective.

"Everywhere you go," said Carvalho, "death follows. Clifton.

Miyake. Uncle Joe up there. And Vierra, the one you on probation for trying kill already. We had find him dead up in the forest. Slashed in the femoral artery."

"You never told me what this is."

"You think Nalani Winthrop much like her uncle?"

"I wouldn't know."

"I know him, little bit. One stubborn buggah. Ran things his way, up there on the mountain. Had his own ideas, too."

Bernt was silent, hating Carvalho for dragging this out.

"The niece. I see it, the family bloodline. I know her parents, too. I been the one to arrest 'em, more than once. She closer to her uncle than her own father. Plenty smart, that one. But you know that."

Bernt was only half-listening. He was seeing Nalani's eyes in the rearview mirror. She'd given him a chance to settle things the way her uncle had started them. But this was her future on the line. The family and its land. She must have gotten a lawyer. And the lawyer would tell her to cooperate. She was smart like her uncle, but she was different: from Winthrop, and from himself.

"She said you met outside of class."

"We had coffee a couple times."

"And you talked about what?"

"History, economics."

"History and economics. When was the last time you seen her?"

Suddenly, Bernt recognized what was happening.

"You aren't going to arrest me."

Carvalho's expression didn't change.

"I've seen the news. This guy Winthrop and those ice heads were selling meth and murdering who knows how many people. And this Lindstrom guy was dumping chemicals all over the place. I heard they're handing out bottled water in Waimea now."

Carvalho held up his hands. "Maybe you're right. Maybe these guys had get in over their heads. Some people seen something they shouldn't. Old man Winthrop trying tie up loose ends. Choke guys end up dead and he's on the run. But there was plenty trucks up there we ain't accounted for. And choke firepower. We get one missing person and plenty ammo we cannot match to any gun. I won't lie, this whole investigation hammajang. You know the FBI up there now, and in Waimea. EPA, too. They looking at everything."

"Sounds like you don't need me," said Bernt.

"Maybe we need each other."

"How's that?"

"No one knows I meeting you. And you no more one suspect. Not officially."

"All right."

"And your name never need come up, neither. All I'm saying is, I never like the AG and these federal guys be one step ahead of me on my own case."

Bernt stared at the detective, who stared right back.

"That story you just told," Bernt finally said, "it makes sense to me. Winthrop running a meth lab up there on his lands, accidentally poisoning some kids and deciding he needs to make sure no one could inform on him. But he's trying to cover up more and more murders, things get out of hand."

"That's the simple answer. But the scene don't tell no simple story."

Bernt chose his words very carefully. "In my opinion, it will never tell any other story."

"Maybe Winthrop tell a story, when we catch him."

There were no words careful enough for this. Bernt glanced around the parking lot. He shook his head.

Carvalho nodded. He checked the hatch of his Explorer for dust, then leaned back against it and crossed his arms. "So what you think, justice been done up there?"

"Maybe, more or less."

"'As the only way it ever comes," said Carvalho.

Bernt considered this.

"They got one tip," said Carvalho. "The EPA."

"Someone with a guilty conscience?"

"Plenty of those. People always was getting sick, Waimea side. Since way back. But they saying not just fines this time, going to be criminal charges. And lawsuits. Already one big deal had fall through.

Some Chinese guys never like buy 'em after all. But I hear they'll file bankruptcy before local people see any money."

"That's a lot of good jobs."

"My nephew get laid off already. And the town going have to find one new water supply. Only streams still clean that side stay up in the mountains. You know whose land that is?"

Bernt shook his head.

"Winthrop."

"Of course."

"Truth, is never going to be justice for all that's happened on this island."

"That's your job," said Bernt. "Not mine."

"You sell lawnmowers."

Bernt studied the beach. Families were stirring in their tents, children shouting under cold water showers. The school bus would be stopping soon.

"This weekend at the station, they offering one free prep course for the officer exam. I can put you on the list."

For the first time that morning, Bernt was caught completely off guard.

"You recruit every serial killer you interrogate?"

"Only the best ones, brah."

"I'm not a cop."

"We get plenty people like you in the force."

"Yeah, I've seen the videos."

"I'm talking about guys need to be part of something. I seen it many times. You're either all in or you're—" He glanced at the forest, didn't complete his thought.

"I'm good."

Carvalho held out his hand. Bernt took it.

"Maybe we never learn what happened on that mountain. Deep country got its own laws. But Uncle Joe never deserve what he got, shot in the chest li'dat. They say had eight hundred people at da buggah's funeral. An' I seen twice that many at the party after. And that wahine, the haole lady came out for get her husband, she loved that fackah whether he deserve it or not. Things stay hard for her, not knowing what had happen to her man."

Bernt said nothing.

"All right then. If you see me coming round again, you know there's one reason. And better to hear it from me first. So don't go hiding out. Maybe I never bother get up early next time."

"Okay," said Bernt. "Thanks."

That night, he walked through the moonlit forest to the cove with the silver water. He sat in the shadow of a boulder on the point. It had been tempting, for a moment, Carvalho's offer, to imagine his future could be solved with one exam. But he wasn't a cop. He was a grunt. Even if he wasn't.

Empty days yawned before him. The forest and the ocean were silent. The dead stayed dead.

He took out his phone. He could text her. It wasn't late.

She'd said she understood him. And she actually had. It was him who hadn't had the balls to believe he'd finally met someone who could see all the way into him and wasn't afraid of what she'd found.

Then, on the road in the forest, under the dripping leaves, she'd made something perfectly clear: the part of her that understood him perfectly was not the part she chose to be. Not any longer.

The screen went dark.

He slipped the phone back into his pocket and felt a smooth, silvery object: Lindstrom's ID. He rubbed his thumb on the engraved letters. Blood type. Emergency contact.

The stainless steel flashed in the moonlight when he brought it out. The ocean sighed. He heard the smooth stones clicking in the black waves below his boots. One underhand toss and there would be no trace.

EPILOGUE

FOR DAYS, A stifling stillness had settled over the island. But fresh trades had been building all morning. Anahola Bay was white-capping as people waded in. Surfers plunged straight into the steep waves and ducked under with their boards. Stand-up paddlers headed for the shoulders, gliding past the hissing lip. Children loaded onto plastic kayaks and charged as best they could, laughing when they were dumped in the whitewash. A few men and women waited for a lull to hoist themselves onto carbon-fiber canoes and surge rapidly through the red zone before the next set arrived.

Wave after wave of people waded into the ocean, timing their entry with the sets flopping onto the beach. Safely beyond the surf line, Momilani watched from her seat in the canoe. Ti leaves were duct-taped to its stern, flower leis draped over the bow. It was Clifton's birthday. His nephews had arranged the paddle out. A good excuse for a party, she thought, if nothing else.

The paddlers gathered in the center of the bay. They formed a loose circle around the canoe, a hundred people bobbing in the waves and foam. Momilani lifted the puakenikeni lei she'd made the day before, its fragrance out of place in the salt breeze. She laid it on the deep blue surface of the ocean, a gently writhing circle at the center of the circle. She looked into the blue beneath the flash and slide. She looked for Clifton's father and mother, his aunts and uncles, those she'd known. She looked deeper for the shadows of his grand-parents, great-grandparents, the long lines of his ancestors. She told them their son had no more home this side. She asked them to make a place for him.

When she lifted her head, she saw Hokualele and shark-finned Kalalea, their cascading green ridges encircling the bay. For a moment, the sunset cliffs of Polihale flashed before her mind.

Then one of her nephews shouted, "Chee!" and the paddlers beat the water, blurring the surface in an explosion of sparkling drops. Across the circle, she saw Jonah Manokalanipo kneeling on a board, exuberantly raising long, clear sheets.

"Pa'i pa'i," he shouted to the young kids around him. "Slap water."

Afterward, the nephews and their friends backed their trucks onto the beach and pitched pop-up tents. They lowered white marine coolers onto the sand and set up cutting boards and grills on their tailgates, placing chairs in the shade for the aunties and uncles. Someone had caught a pile of aholehole. Young boys used spoons to scrape their silver scales into the sand.

Momilani didn't mind the reggae everyone listened to now, but she was happy to see one of her nieces had brought an ukulele. She was playing a song from the days when Momi was a girl. Friends from her halau were laughing as they tried to make a hula to the lyrics.

It was just my imagination, running away with me.

Jonah was there, higher up the beach, outside the party. Momilani borrowed two bottles from her cousin's cooler, hitched her muu-muu in one hand, and walked up the loose sand. As she reached him, a shadow swept across the beach. Jonah held out his palm and caught a drop, then a cold gust carried a stinging sheet of rain across them.

"Never mind, Hawaiian," said Momilani. "It's just one blessing."

She handed Jonah a bottle. Raindrops sparkled in the sunlight.

"You know, me and your Auntie Ku'ulei grew up together in Mo-loaa."

"One spooky kine place that."

"Fo' real, I never like go out at night. But Ku'u no stay scared of any night marchers."

"She was one fierce lady."

"Yeah, a real tita that one." Momilani smiled to herself, remembering.

"What about the Filipino guy," asked Jonah, "Micah. I never see him today."

"He stayed with me a few weeks more, long as the wife was on the news, asking anybody for information. Then she brought her husband back mainland, and the next day, he left, too."

"Too bad she never know her husband was trying for help, in the end."

"Who say she never know?"

"What you mean?"

"Last time I heard from Micah, he gave me her phone number."

"For tell her what?"

"I never like say. But she knows her husband had try for make things right. And he did not die alone."

Jonah was silent a long time. Momilani stared into the mirrored lenses of his glasses.

"Eh, Hawaiian, where you stay right now?"

Jonah shook his head.

"No need say. I understand."

"My son—"

"No need say it—"

"—everyone try tell me it was quick. But I know it wasn't."

Momilani took the man into her arms. "Clifton, too," she said. "I knew I would outlive the buggah. And I thought I had imagined every way that he could die. But I was always with him in the end. I was always there to tell him, Hush now sweetie, it's all right."

"I see him in my dreams," said Jonah. "Always the same. I try tell him, It's all right boy. But how can I comfort my son, when he already passed on to something I never seen?"

Momilani held the man tight as he shook. "Those dreams," she said, "they're good. I know it. That's your boy saying you was with him, even if you never knew. He's trying tell you no more nothing you need do for him now. You have living family needs you."

Jonah was shaking his head. She pulled him even tighter, not sure whether she was holding him up or leaning on him.

"You cannot let this swallow you," she said, "or the evil that hurt those boys is going to keep hurting people never even born yet. How you think your ancestors felt, when the sickness took entire villages. Whole family lines wiped out, the rest just one or two surviving, all their people dead. Every one of us today—you and me, those young girls down there—we come from those survivors. Imagine if the only ones they'd cared about was those who'd passed, and not the ones had yet to come."

Jonah lifted his shades and stepped out of her embrace.

"Damn, Auntie."

Momilani laughed. "I never knew I had that in me."

"Maybe someone speaking to you, too."

"Just remember, you get one strong bloodline. I see how you carry your kuleana. Auntie Ku'u them would all be proud."

They stood in silence, the wind still rising. It chattered the palms and whistled across the mouths of their bottles. Her niece was singing a mele, but the wind snatched the words.

Momilani let her gaze travel from the line of trucks on the sand across the green sweep of the bay to the ocean beyond. "This reminds me of the old-time days," she said. "The hukilau. You can remember?"

"Those was my hanabata days," Jonah laughed. "But I remember."

The wind brought the smell of salt spray and fish frying in oil. The girls were dancing. Momilani could see it now, her niece's song. *The rain of Hanalei sweeping along the cliffs.*

She watched the women dance the verses.

And the sea murmurs as if to say, You and I should be together again.

AUTHOR'S NOTE

Liz and I moved to Kaua'i in 2014 with four duffels and our dog Matilda. We planned to stay just long enough for her to complete a one-year internship as a psychologist at Kapaa High School.

Growing up on the East Coast, I'd always envisioned Hawai'i as a vacationland of time-shares and resorts: Fort Myers or Boca Raton, but more remote. So I'll never forget going to the county fair, just a few days after arriving on island, and finding myself a distinct minority among thousands of brown-skinned local people speaking English in a dialect I'd never heard of and lining up for plates of Hawaiian, Japanese, Filipino, and Portuguese cuisine.

I'm embarrassed by my ignorance, but I recognize how typical it is, even for millions of people who have visited Hawai'i and many who live here. Although I'd served as a Peace Corps Volunteer in Kenya and lived with people still overcoming the consequences of colonialism, it had never occurred to me that America's fiftieth state is a colony from the same era, one that was never given back its sovereignty.

For my thirty-fourth birthday, Liz bought me a used outrigger canoe paddle and encouraged me to show up at the mouth of the Wailua River for an evening practice with Hui O Mana Ka Pu'uwai, the canoe club "with the power of heart." The racing season was just wrapping up, but a group of aunties kept meeting all winter to paddle the two-mile river. I was fortunate to start with such patient teachers. Eventually Liz joined the club, and in a few years we went from struggling with the basics of placing our blades at the proper angle and keeping time with other paddlers to using the rhythms of ocean waves to race across the blue-water channels that separate the Hawaiian islands.

Blending with six other people to surf ocean swells in a forty-foot canoe will always be one of the most profound experiences of my life. But we stayed on Kaua'i for seven years because of our experiences out of the canoe: gathered around someone's tailgate after practice, in the shade of a pop-up tent during a day-long regatta, at birthday parties, graduations, weddings, vow renewals, holidays, and all the other reasons Hawaiian people find to share a good time with people they love.

Hawaiian concepts like aloha and 'ohana have become clichés thanks to movies and tourism marketing. But they are real. It's been one of the greatest and most unexpected blessings of my life to experience them. The Hawaiian people have all the reason in the world to turn their backs on the outsiders who took their sovereignty and are still transforming their islands, largely for the worse. Yet they do the exact opposite, at least for those who take a step in their direction. It's a generosity of spirit that seems to come so naturally, I have to remind myself it is extraordinary.

I hope this book entertains, educates, and moves my readers, but most of all, I hope it honors that spirit.

ACKNOWLEDGMENTS

One of my goals for *Project Namahana* was to represent realities of daily life in Hawai'i that popular depictions often erase or push deep into the background. While I am confident in my ability to inhabit characters like Michael Lindstrom and explore the justifications and self-delusions of the privileged and powerful (and usually white and male), I am deeply humble about my ability to represent the perspectives, cultures, and languages of people whose ancestries and life experiences are distinctly different from my own.

I am grateful to the friends and experts who provided feedback and helped me make this novel as accurate as I could. In particular, I thank John P. Rosa and Mark McNally of the University of Hawai'i at Mānoa for their insights into the novel's treatment of Hawaiian and Japanese American culture; Genevieve Ke-hau'oliho'omaika'i Evslin for her close reading and commentary; and Sydney Yamase for her early encouragement and feedback.

I also thank the military veterans who befriended my family and helped us in innumerable ways: Chris, Teddy, and especially Jason, one of the most generous people I've ever met.

I thank Eloy Bleifuss at Janklow & Nesbit for plucking my manuscript off the slush pile, and my agent, Kirby Kim, for believing in its potential and helping me transform it into a much stronger (and shorter) work. I thank my editor, Robert Davis, for recognizing what this novel could become and pushing me to raise it to another level.

I can't express the thrill of seeing my words transformed into a thoughtfully crafted book, and I am grateful to Peter Lutjen, Jeff La-Sala, Jennifer McClelland-Smith, and Libby Collins at Forge Books for contributing so much of their care, attention, and talent.

I thank all my teachers, particularly Martin Lammon, Peter Selgin, and Karen Salyer McElmurray from Georgia College, and Alison Milbank, Debra Nystrom, and Charles Wright from the University of Virginia.

I thank my wife, Liz, for helping me, encouraging me, keeping me present, laughing with me, repairing things when we fight, and trying to see my side when we disagree. I thank my two boys, August and Max, for giving my life a purpose so much greater than becoming a published writer. I thank my brother George for being my best reader, and my parents, David and Jane, for the extraordinary gift of unconditional love.

I thank my children's godparents—Keone, Dana, Sharon, and Peter—for all the love and support they gave our family as it grew throughout our years on Kaua'i; our friends, coworkers, and neighbors on this island; and our paddling 'ohana in Hui O Mana Ka Pu'uwai and across Hawai'i. Kaua'i will always be home to our two boys, August and Max. The countless people who embraced us will always be our family.

You are the reason we made a life here.